PRAISE FOR A DI

'Both informative and dram
young readers'
Northampton International Acaucm,

'An **absorbing** final instalment to this wise and **exciting** trilogy'
Margaret McCulloch-Keeble, Library Assistant

I really enjoyed reading the themes explored in *A Demon's
Touch*. I felt that the story really embraces you and catches your
attention by making you want to read more. It was so **addictive!**
Emma, age 14

'The book has an incredibly strong message on what the
purpose of life is and the importance of not giving up easily.
It was **fascinating** to be taken back to another century which
differs from our own in so many ways. What I enjoyed the most
was the interplay of cultures, ideas, religion and ways of living.
So **captivating!**' Sofia, age 14

By the same author

Fiction:

A King's Armour

A Tudor Turk

Last of the Tasburai

Scream of the Tasburai

Non-Fiction:

Distracting Ourselves to Death

The Chronicles of Will Ryde and Awa Maryam al-Jameel

Book Three

A Demon's Touch

Rehan Khan

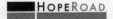

HopeRoad Publishing
PO Box 55544
Exhibition Road
London SW7 2DB

www.hoperoadpublishing.com

First published in Great Britain by HopeRoad 2022
Copyright © 2022 Rehan Khan

A CIP catalogue record for this book is available from the British Library.

ISBN: 978-1-913109-81-3

eISBN: 978-1-913109-15-8

Printed and bound by Clays Ltd Elcograf S.p.A

For Yusuf, who rekindled my love of stories, and Imaan, who taught me the importance of telling them.

CONTENTS

CAST OF CHARACTERS

Anver Jacob — Venetian affiliate of the Rüzgar unit

Atilla Berk — Commander in the Janissary guard

Awa Maryam al-Jameel — Songhai affiliate of the Rüzgar unit

Earl of Rothminster — Noble within the Elizabethan court

Fumu — Kikongo bodyguard to Princess Fatma Sultan

Gurkan — Turkish member of the Rüzgar unit within the Janissaries

Kadri — Captain within the Janissaries

Kanijeli Siyavuş Pasha — Grand Vizier to Sultan Murad III and betrothed to Princess Fatma Sultan

Lütfi Abdullah — Chief Miniaturist

Princess Fatma Sultan	Daughter of Sultan Murad III
Sardar Ferhad Pasha	Former Grand Vizier to Sultan Murad III
Sir Reginald Rathbone	Loyal to the Earl of Rothminster
Sultan Murad III	Ruler of the Ottoman Empire
Ulyana	Handmaiden to Princess Fatma Sultan
Will Ryde	English member of the Rüzgar unit within the Janissaries
Zawaba'a	An evil Jinn

1

BETRAYAL

JANUARY 1593

THE CELL DOOR SLAMMED SHUT. Will leant back against the cold stone wall. Exhausted, head in his hands, he slumped to the ground. Arrested an hour ago, the Rüzgar, what remained of them, were incarcerated, his own hopes of returning to England shattered. Not too long ago he had been fêted by Royalty whilst serving the gallant Commander Konjic, even courting friendship with Princess Fatma. Now, everything lay in tatters. In an isolated prison cell, deep underground, he solemnly recalled the voice in his head that had told him to go to England from Azerbaijan and meet up with Lord Burghley - he should have listened to it. The royal household of Queen Elizabeth would have taken him in, offered refuge: he was, after all, an Englishman conveying a prized holy item - a King's Armour.

He heard the sound of boots trudging towards his cell. Alarmed, he eyed the door. The steps moved on, the sound fading as they went on down the corridor. The Ottoman gaol was located on multiple levels, locations ominously below ground where neither light nor clean air penetrated. Once they'd descended two sets of spiral stairs, his gaolers had taken him along a narrow corridor, where a lone cresset was burning, its miserable light seeping into the space of his incarceration.

As Will shut his eyes, his thoughts turned to Captain Kadri, a good man. What had become of him? Commander Berk's accusation that Konjic and Kadri were in league with the Earl of Rothminster to assassinate the Sultan was utter nonsense. If anyone was suspect, it was Berk.

An aching hurt filled Will's heart as he considered the intricate trap they had fallen into, every one of them, from the late Konjic all the way to himself. Tears welled in his eyes, and his mind wandered, finding comfort in the memory of his dear friend Huja, a man of many talents, who was not present to experience such a calamitous return to Istanbul. Will knew he should have spoken to Konjic about Gurkan's apparent treachery before they left Istanbul. Instead, the reputation of the Rüzgar had been sullied in their absence. The one notable guardian the unit possessed, the stoic Grand Vizier Sardar Ferhad Pasha, had been deposed from his position in their absence. The Rüzgar had escaped the lair of the Lord of the Two Serpents, Azi Dahäg, back on the Karabakh Plateau, only to fall victim to an Ottoman viper, who without raising his own weapon had disarmed the entire unit. Will Ryde was a man of action. Political machinations were a dark art, one he loathed, but rotting in the cell as he was, he realised he should have paid more attention. Commander Konjic might be the fallen hero, but it was Commander Berk who had outmanoeuvred them all.

Boxed into this claustrophobic cell, furnished only with a filthy straw mattress and bucket in which to relieve himself, Will was powerless once more, a not unfamiliar feeling. He slammed the ground with the palm of his hand. What good were his aspirations for a better life for himself and his mother, whom he would never see again? He would be executed in the morning, and she wouldn't even know he had died or what he had had done since he left England. Apart from the clothes on his person, he was stripped of possessions, having been told to leave what few items he owned in the store at the prison entrance. So much had happened in the past two years, yet here he was, miserable and disheartened, as he used to be every bleak and weary day on board the *Al Qamar*, the Moroccan galley where he once laboured as a slave, fettered and chained.

Minutes ground out like hours. His mood darkened and dire, sinister thoughts washed over him. Fear threatened to paralyse him.

No! He was more than the man he had been two years ago. He recalled the words of Konjic, who once said, *You can be fearful of death, just don't be fearful of facing it.* Exhaling deeply, as though it was the first proper breath he had taken for hours, his thoughts turned to his comrades, Awa, Gurkan and Anver. They had been split up as they entered the penal complex, and he hadn't seen them since. They were all to be put to the sword in a few hours, but was a torturer waiting for them in the meantime, sharpening hooks and knives? Clenching his fists, he felt despondent for Anver, the young Venetian, who had travelled from his native city on Will's advice. The Venetian's incarceration was Will's direct responsibility, and he was saddened by this. Anver was a genius, and Will dreaded what effect the prison was going to have on him. Less than a third of a day remained till dawn, when the executioner would come calling. Once more, in a wave of emotions his eyes watered, as sorrowful regret for having left England to come and save the life of Sultan Murad III overwhelmed him.

The cell door opened.

Will hurriedly wiped his face with the backs of his hands, not wanting his tormentors to see his sorry state. He had to be strong, not give into their provocation.

Commander Berk entered. Two armed Janissaries beside him.

Will sat up, body tense. His instinct told him to reach for a weapon, yet he had none. He set his jaw, glowering at the Commander.

Berk turned to the two sentries. 'Wait for me outside.'

The men departed, shutting the door behind them. Berk must have noticed the wet patches around his eyes, for he sniggered at the sight. It made Will furious, wanting to go for the man. He almost did until he noticed Berk's hand firmly on the pommel of his sword, ready to strike Will down with a single killing blow should he have any rash notions of escape.

Rising on his haunches, Will straightened up. If Berk planned to slay him here, Will would rather go out swinging than be cut down whilst sitting timidly on the ground.

'I'm not here to kill you,' Berk said.

That was no surprise. His execution was in the morning, so what did Berk want with him now? 'What, then?' asked Will.

Berk surveyed the decrepit nature of the cell, turning his nose up at it. 'A most filthy place. The smell is quite odious, is it not? They never did quite get the sewage to flow away from the prison; it seems to swill around the complex instead, like foul water in an unsanitary *hammam*. Repulsive. But you won't be staying long enough for the odour to seep into your skin.'

Had Berk come fishing for information about their mission, having already interrogated the others? Did he want to check their story against Will's? Or was he going to let Will rot in this cell for longer, let him suffer its indignities, whilst preparing his ultimate demise? Will's panicked gaze darted around the cell, seeking a weapon he could use against Berk.

'How did Konjic die?' asked Berk.

'With courage.'

Berk sniffed at that. 'Yes, yes, we all die with courage, for without courage in the face of death a man would wet himself with fear. Tell me truthfully who killed him.'

'Azi Dahäg, the Lord of the Two Serpents.'

Berk seemed to take in the name for the first time, though Awa had already mentioned it less than an hour ago.

'Azerbaijan?'

'Yes, sir.'

'We will need to do something about that region.'

'Dahäg is dead. He was slain by Commander Konjic, moments before the Commander died of wounds sustained in their fight.'

'Quite an end.'

'As I said, sir, he died with courage, his sword swinging. In doing so he ended Dahäg's reign of terror over the people of the Karabakh Plateau.'

'Always the selfless hero,' snorted Berk. 'Valour is wasted in today's world, Ryde; the skill needed in politics, and collusion, is to know what ensures one's survival.'

'Nevertheless, he was a great man and will always be remembered so,' retorted Will.

Shaking his head, Berk replied. 'Mehmet Konjic may have been a good man, a generous mentor and heroic leader, but he was not a great man for our time. He will not be remembered by anyone beyond a small circle of those who came into contact with him. You need more than gallantry to thrive in the nest of deceit that is the Ottoman court. Master Huja knew this, and it is why his demeanour was so - forlorn, broken by the very people he served. No, Ryde, to prosper nowadays the world needs men like me and ...' Berk moved closer to Will, further from the ears of the soldiers outside the cell. '... the Earl of Rothminster.'

Will felt his jaw drop.

'Men who are unafraid of change, of upsetting the status quo, destroying the world as we know it and building a better one on its ashes.'

'The Earl ...' Will's voice trailed off.

Berk's wicked smile brightened his sullen features. 'Konjic suspected, but did not know how deep the collusion runs, for if it had been evident to him, he would have fled for the hills back to his native Bosnian village long ago.'

'Rothminster ...' Will remembered how Berk had slain the assassin on the night of the attempt on the life of the Sultan, when Thomas Dallam played his organ with great aplomb in the Hagia Sophia. The assassin was arrested, should have been interrogated to determine who his accomplices were, yet Berk had put him to the sword. The assassin might have implicated Berk and the rogue Commander knew it.

'Why?' asked Will, mind racing, incapable of comprehending the magnitude of what it meant to have a senior Janissary Commander in league with an English Earl, who was hell-bent on expanding eastwards and taking down the Ottomans in the process.

'For one such as you, Ryde, with such a feeble hold on this world, no higher than a worm in the soil ready to be trodden on, the *why* is not important. The *how* is.'

Will waited. The news weakened his legs. He supported himself against the wall, his strength having escaped him.

'I will spare your life, on one condition.'

Did he hear that right? He wasn't going to be killed? There was a chance of surviving the night. Will stood a little taller.

'You leave this very moment for England, carrying secret correspondence from me to the Earl of Rothminster. You do not tamper with this document or read its contents. You do not divert your course or attempt to notify anyone else. You will be accompanied by two of my loyal men, all the way to English shores. Should you speak to anyone, other than them, they have orders to end your existence at a stroke. If I do not hear from them within two weeks, your friends will immediately be executed. If my Janissaries return safely, I will spare the lives of your friends, and they can live out the rest of their miserable existence in these cells.'

Using his arms to support himself against the wall, Will managed to straighten his posture. Maybe he *was* going to see his mother again. Could it really be? He dared not hope beyond this night, for the world seemed to conspire against him whenever he felt things were finally falling into place for him. He wanted to be a man of his decisions, yet it seemed destiny would have him be a man of his circumstances.

'How can I be sure you won't execute them in the morning?'

'You can't.'

'And if I don't agree?'

'You will all be executed in the morning as planned,' Berk replied with a corrosive grin. 'It is in your hands, Will Ryde. Life or death. What will you choose?'

2

GRUDGE

S EWAGE REEKED FROM EVERY CREVICE, as though the foul waste of humanity swilled around the walls cocooning her cell. Hours passed. The bile steadily building up at the base of Awa's throat made her want to vomit. Eyes moist, she did not know whether physical confinement in such a rank place did this to her or she was tearful because her heart hurt after the events of the previous evening. Despite the odds and despite enduring tremendous adversity and personal loss the Rüzgar had completed their mission: recovering the Armour of David and bringing back the Staff of Moses. Yet what value did the rulers truly place in these objects, beyond seeing them as trophies and tokens of power? Objects, no matter how holy, were not worth human lives. The holy book taught: *Whoever saves a life, it shall be as though he had saved the lives of all mankind.* All souls were connected to each other and to the Creator, yet few truly felt this bond. At that moment, as much as she tried, she felt nothing, only a numb loss.

Currently, from her lowly vantage point, the world was a cruel place with crueller people. How she yearned to pass from what the mystics referred to as the horizontal realm, and ascend into the vertical realm, before ultimately finding solace in the realm of depth where only the souls of those who had moved on from this world resided.

It troubled Awa that the Rüzgar had placed their trust in the Janissary order, yet when they needed protection and safety most, it was not forthcoming. Who could you depend on in such an upside-down world? Recent events played back in her mind. Konjic and Kadri declared traitors, the Grand Vizier removed from office. Dear Huja, the scholar masquerading as a jester, murdered in the bowels of the earth at the hands of Zawaba'a, the Jinn caged by Solomon the Wise, whom they had inadvertently released. The Qareen of Sheikh Dawood had warned them about the perilous path they took, yet they went ahead anyway. Did she ever have a choice? After all, they were simply carrying out orders from Konjic, who was obeying his chain of command, right up to the Sultan.

The Rüzgar had sacrificed so much on their mission: in Aleppo they had tangled with the Knights of the Fire Cross, in Damascus they broke into the Umayyad Mosque, in Jerusalem they penetrated the bowels of the Tower of David, releasing Zawaba'a, at Mount Tabor they discovered then lost the Armour of David and finally in Azerbaijan they confronted the Lord of the Two Serpents, Azi Dahäg. The monstrous brute tormented the villages around his mountain fortress on the Karabach Plateau, forcefully removing children from their families and putting them to work in his mining operation. His freakish speed and strength made him a formidable opponent, and it was only by their combined efforts that they had brought about the ogre's death. What felt like a lifetime of adventure in a matter of months had left Awa exhausted, physically and mentally.

Worry for herself but also for her companions made her stomach ache. She thought about Gurkan, previously tortured at Leeds Castle. He would be terrified by what was in store for him. Yet he was a Turk, and perhaps they would go easy on him. Anver, on the other hand, was an innocent, the most recent member of their group, a curious inventor with a desire to help others. And what of Will, the first member of the unit she had encountered in Alexandria? He had come to her aid when she needed it most, and for that she was forever grateful to him. Yet over this past year they had grown distant. Will had succumbed to his lower nature, desiring the Armour, even making the outlandish suggestion that they take it to England. Was he going to survive till the morning, or would Berk's animosity towards the English see him put to the sword before dawn? Was she going to have an opportunity to say goodbye to her comrades in this world before they passed over into the next realm?

Reminded of their imminent demise, Awa considered it best to pray, to calm herself, to lessen the anxiety and tribulation hanging over her by devoting the last few hours of this life to the remembrance of the Creator. Considering everything that had befallen her since the Battle of Tondibi when the Songhai nation was annihilated, she in many ways longed for the passing of her soul into the next world, for there was very little left for her to hold on to in this one. Even her father's whereabouts was unknown. Was he even alive? She would never know until she died, which wouldn't be long now.

The remnants of her people, the Songhai, were scattered and slain, enslaved in foreign lands. Wrecked by civil war and hampered by poor leaders, the Songhai had seen their best days come and go. King Askia and his court had been counselled by men like her father that to wage a war they could not win, with out-of-date weapons suited to an era pre-mechanisation, was futile. Had the rulers listened to his sage advice and negotiated for peace, matters would have been quite different. She would be living in Timbuktu, her place of birth, occupying her days in learning and farming the land around her village. As would the other Songhai. Instead, she was never going to see her homeland again. In fact, she was never going to see her father again. A small piece of her had always believed a reunion with him in this world was possible, but now as the end approached she knew this to be a foolhardy notion. She wondered if the Angel of Death lingered nearby, ready to take her soul for its onward journey.

A beetle scurrying in the corner of her cell returned her focus to the present. When were they going to come for her? If they tried to torture her, she was going to fight back. She had suffered enough at the hands of others. If they waited till the morning and took her straight for execution, she was not going to fight; she resolved to die with dignity and as much serenity as she could muster. Awa cupped her hands together to pray.

She must have fallen asleep, for she was startled when the door to her cell was unlocked. Still on the floor, she pushed herself back against the wall. They had come for her, but was it already dawn? Time went so fast. This was it, the end.

Two Ottoman gaolers marched into the cell, placing a cresset in a holder on the wall beside the door. One man was exceedingly tall, stooping his head to enter, the other was squat with a noticeable limp.

Odo and Ja!

A gasp left her throat as she slid her way up the wall into a standing position, trembling arms out to defend herself. This must be a nightmare; she was surely still sleeping. She pinched herself and realised she was wide awake. How?

'What did I tell you?' Odo grinned, yellow teeth showing in his crooked mouth. 'I will find you, Awa. I will follow you to the ends of the earth, and I will find you!'

'No ...' whispered Awa.

'And here I am, along with Ja.' Odo stared up at the big man, who smiled, his white teeth shining like pearls.

11

He stepped closer. 'We went through a lot of pain because of you. Physically, financially ... even our reputation was ruined. People said if we couldn't handle a single girl, what hope did we have as slave traders? Our business dried up. All because of you,' he jabbed his finger at her.

'How did you ...?' Awa staggered, placing a hand on the wall to steady herself, mind shrieking, telling her to run, but where to? The way was blocked. Sweat ran down her anxious brow, leaving her light-headed, unstable on her feet.

'After the Citadel of Qait Bey we lost track of you. But we stuck around in Alexandria long enough, asked the right questions of the right people, greased a few palms and learnt of a motley troupe: Bosnian, Greek, Turkish, even an Englishman – though that was a new nationality to me – who had been seen travelling together. Apparently, they left town soon after you slipped away from us that evening. Didn't take much to figure out the only place where such a mixed bunch of people could come together was under Ottoman rule.'

'No,' said Awa.

'And so that led us here, to Istanbul,' said Odo.

Awa tried to put space between herself and the slave traders, but there wasn't anywhere left to manoeuvre in the tight cell. 'Not again.'

'Oh yes, and this time we're going to make it count.'

The slave trader always had a crooked grin on his face, and now under the light of the cressets it appeared even more warped. Her mind raced. She had to compose herself, slow her breathing, take control of the situation, stall for time.

'When did you arrive in Istanbul?' asked Awa, feet edging back.

Odo smiled. 'Last summer. Soon heard word in the markets and alleys around the palace about a ferocious Songhai warrior who was part of a secret Janissary force. Didn't take long to

12

figure out it was you. By the time we discovered where you were staying, some fancy fort on the other side of the river, we realised you weren't in town. We picked up a job in this establishment to pass the time till your return. Prisons are always looking for people who don't mind getting their hands bloody. Nice.'

The slaver rolled up his sleeves, flexing his shoulders. Ja closed the cell door.

'Thought we'd wait till you returned. And here you are. As fate would have it, the mighty Awa fallen low once again, down to our level; what a surprise when we came into work this evening to hear about a group of rogue Janissaries, incarcerated for treason. Couldn't believe our luck.'

Odo limped towards her. She noted the anguished look on his face.

'Oh yeah, it hurts every step I take. It's why you're always on my mind, Awa. I bore the pain because it had meaning, I knew I would get my revenge.'

'What are you going to do?' she croaked.

'You won't like it ... But I will.'

He advanced.

3

HEAVY HEART

REINFORCED IRON DOORS SWUNG OPEN, revealing the pathway leading to the street ahead, a flight of freedom from the prison to which Will had been hauled hours earlier. He never expected to leave other than for his execution, but the price of his miraculous reprieve was going to be high: by doing Commander Berk's bidding, he was going to deceive his friends. A soreness filled his chest when he glanced back to witness Berk grinning. The leather satchel containing the scrolls Berk had asked him to convey to the Earl of Rothminster weighed him down, as though he were transporting a lead weight.

Guarded by a tight group of six Janissaries, he left the prison. Two soldiers were to accompany him to England before returning. Maintaining a brisk marching speed they headed southwards down towards the shore. Quiet nocturnal streets meant slumbering residents, which suited the night patrol who were on duty tonight, as it left little for them to do other than chat and play cards. They joined a concourse leading towards the ruins of the Hippodrome. What seemed like an aeon ago, Will had visited it with Master Huja, who had informed him it was a venue where grand events and competitions were held by Byzantine rulers. Like the Roman Colosseum, the

Hippodrome entertained the masses, particularly in times of economic distress, when the public mood was made merry through performance, distracting their attention from what actually made them morose in the first place. The Romans, Huja said, called it *Bread and Circuses*.

The Obelisk of Theodosius, brought over from Egypt, another remnant of the city's past, loomed large before him as they strode straight towards it. It was then Will felt a prick on the back of his neck, as though he had been poked by a fine needle. His hand instinctively rubbed the spot, his head snapping up as he looked around.

'What is it?' growled the Janissary beside him.

Will wasn't sure. 'Nothing.'

'Keep your head down, prisoner,' the soldier ordered.

Will tightened his hold on the satchel and pulled its strap closer to his body. He was not armed and felt uneasy at being escorted by six fully equipped soldiers who could cut him down at a moment's notice. There was no knowing whether that was what Berk had actually asked them to do; the man was completely untrustworthy. The pommel of a trusty sword was always a comforting place on which to rest one's hand when feeling uncertain. Instead, he clenched his fists and continued to march on past the ancient obelisk.

Passing beneath the archway of a building complex, Will guessed it was a manufacturing site with timber workshops, built over two floors. Soon he found himself in the central courtyard, heading towards the southerly exit arch. Two feeble torches illuminated the surroundings. Their leather boots crunched over the ground, which was layered with fine pebbles.

Will kept his head down but had a feeling he was being watched. The sensation was unnerving. It was then at the corner of his vision he detected movement on their right.

'Stop!' the lead Janissary ordered the group, raising his right hand.

'What is it?' another asked, behind the leader.

The lead Janissary turned his head to the right. 'I thought I saw ...'

'What?' asked one of the others.

The man who had halted the group strode to the right. Will had also seen a shadow shift across the face of the building, lit by the torches.

Will swivelled left when he heard pebbles dropping to the ground. He couldn't see anyone. His heart pounded as an unnatural dread overwhelmed him. Hidden actions were happening around them, more than the eye could detect.

'Who threw that?' said one of the Janissaries as the group watched the last of the few pebbles hit the ground. The soldiers drew their weapons, scanning the courtyard.

Will peered into the dim surroundings, eyes scanning every inch of the place. The pebbles had fallen from a height above them. Who could have dropped pebbles from a such an angle and disappeared so quickly? All of the windows on the upper floor remained shut. Besides, the angle at which the pebbles hit the ground meant they could not have been thrown from a first-floor window without catapulting them high into the air first, which someone in their group would have noticed. Perhaps the pebbles were lobbed over the building by a person standing outside it. For a moment he thought it might be Anver, with one of his ingenious contraptions, and he was half expecting to see the Rüzgar show up and break him free from his captors. His heart sank as he remembered they were all incarcerated in the very prison he had just left.

The group spun right as pebbles fell to the ground, striking the earth directly as though dropped from the sky above. Once more they only witnessed the last few land. The soldiers looked up at the sky, clouded as it was. Surely it was not raining pebbles.

'Show yourself!' demanded the lead Janissary, an edge of fear in his voice.

As the company of soldiers swung their gazes left, Will felt something come up behind him. He twisted around. A blast of air pushed him hard, blowing him to the ground onto his backside. In fact, the freakish gust of wind knocked all of the Janissaries off their feet, before it rattled through the courtyard and then out of it, dissipating as it went.

'Breath of Satan!' said one Janissary.

'What was that?' asked another.

The band of Janissaries remained on the ground, heads turning from one side to the other, before Will was the first back on his feet. Seeing him stand, the others also got up. Will squinted into the dark recesses of the building about them, but the place was empty. Whatever phenomenon they had just encountered was gone.

'Let's get out of here,' said the lead Janissary.

Shoved in the back, Will was ordered to march on. Whatever had just happened was unusual to say the least, but then a lot of strange things had happened after their encounter with the Jinn in Jerusalem. The group headed towards the southern archway and left the building complex. Good riddance, thought Will. He didn't want to go back in there if it was haunted by an evil spirit.

Soon they bore around the Little Hagia Sophia, and from there exited the city walls through a fortified gate, which Will assumed was one used by the guardians of the city. A rowing boat waited for them, which they boarded, each of them gripping an oar as they pushed off. Dark waters lapped around the vessel as they headed away from the city, journeying towards the seaport from where Will was to travel with two of the Janissaries to

England. His thoughts went back to his friends. Would they see him as a traitor? Yet he was doing this to save them.

Will watched the city he had briefly called home ebb away from him as they caught the tide and headed out to sea. The magnificent skyline of Istanbul was a silhouette in the predawn hours. He doubted he would be back here any time soon, if at all. The future disturbed him, for he possessed neither the weapons nor the presence of mind in the present to prepare for what was coming.

4

FINISHING TOUCH

LEAPING FORWARD WITH HER HANDS stretched out like the talons of a bird of prey, Awa launched herself at Odo. He caught one wrist, but she managed to sink her fingers into his eye sockets with the other, causing him to cry out and back away. She followed up with a kick to his groin, sending him to one knee. She just needed to get to the cell door.

Slamming into the side of her with a long arm, Ja knocked her against the wall. She took the blow hard in the shoulder, pain flaring up. He followed up with a fist to her face, which she ducked under, kicking at the back of his knee which her sword had sliced through when they last fought in the Citadel in Alexandria. The wound was still tender, for he winced, backing off momentarily.

'Enough!' Odo growled, drawing his short sword. 'Let's just finish her.'

The slaver pounced, but his movements had slowed since the injuries Awa had inflicted on him, and she was able to dart out of the way of the blade but not the firm hand that grabbed her shoulder, then her neck, lifting then pinning her against the cell wall. Awa struggled for breath, writhing in the grip of the giant Ja. She remembered her friend Wassa and how she had been lifted by Ja when they were trying to escape from the Oasis.

'Like a swine, let's gut her down the middle,' threatened Odo.

Awa lashed out with her hands and feet. She had to land a blow on the giant. Despite her efforts, Ja held her in a vice-like grip, fury blazing in his eyes, his maniacal smile plastered across his face once more. She landed a sharp kick to his head, wiping the smile from it, leaving his lip bloodied. But he didn't drop her, such was the intensity of his resolve. Again she struck out with her legs. This time she managed to kick his windpipe, causing him to choke, lose his grip and release her. Awa hit the ground, landing awkwardly. Before she was able to take advantage of the moment, Odo kicked her hard in the stomach, leaving her winded. Awa supported herself with one arm, gasping for breath, then Ja hauled her up again, jamming her against the cell wall, her shoulders pinned back, his fingers jabbing into her joints.

Odo shook his head, a look of frustration on his face. 'You could have made me a lot of money. Such a shame to waste a good fighter, especially a woman. Crowds pay more to watch a woman fight a man,' he said.

Odo sheathed his sword and took out a hunting knife, eyeing its tip by the light of the cresset. Awa continued to struggle, but Ja's grip was firm.

'Yeah, this will do.'

Gripping the weapon like he meant to stab her with its point, he raised his arm up.

Awa prayed to the Creator.

'Yes, pray,' rasped Odo.

The cell door flew open. Odo whirled around. Meanwhile Ja kept her pinned.

A hulking African swept into the cell, followed by Gurkan and Anver.

'What!' Odo exclaimed, before Fumu, the personal bodyguard of Princess Fatma, landed a heavy punch on his cheek, sending him head first into the wall, his dagger spinning from his grip. Ja immediately threw Awa to one side and drew his dagger, aiming for Fumu's head. The bodyguard caught his arm.

'No, my brother, I am Kikongo,' said Fumu, forcing Ja's arm down. The taller man dropped his knife. Fumu rammed him up against the wall beside Awa. The two men locked arms; Fumu headbutted Ja in the face, leaving the slave trader with a bloody nose.

Anver was beside her. 'Awa, are you hurt?' The Venetian helped her up.

Awa's throat was too sore to speak. She concentrated on catching her breath.

Gurkan pounded Odo with his fists, then began kicking him whilst he was on the ground. The slave trader rolled up in a ball, recoiling at the onslaught.

Ja wilted under the superior strength of Fumu, his knees bending as the Kikongo warrior forced him to the ground. Ja might have been taller, but he was not stronger.

Awa spotted Odo's fallen dagger lying right in front of her. Moving past Anver in one swift movement, she picked up the dagger and whistled past Fumu, stabbing the knife straight into the heart of Ja, before whirling around, pushing Gurkan to one side and burying the blade in Odo's heart, holding the weapon there. Their eyes locked as his hand clasped hers over the hilt of the weapon.

'I made sure,' rasped Awa.

Odo blinked at her, a look of sheer disbelief on his face. Awa pulled the blade free, Odo gasped, then rolled to one side, dead. She had had the chance to kill him in Alexandria but spared his life. This time he left her no choice. With the deaths of these villains a part of her died, but it was a part she was willing to see perish.

Fumu stepped back from Ja, who crumpled to the ground, eyes wide open.

Awa dropped the knife, hand shaking.

Fumu placed a steady hand upon her shoulder, calming her. 'My sister, these were evil men. You had no choice.'

Awa nodded.

The bodyguard turned to leave the cell as Awa looked at Anver in confusion.

'This is a prison break,' said Anver, taking her by the elbow and guiding her into the corridor outside her cell.

She paused, turning back to look one last time at the slumped forms of Odo and Ja, praying she would never encounter the likes of such villains again. Then she accompanied her companions towards the door at the far end of the corridor.

'We can't find Will,' said Gurkan as she came up beside him. 'We checked the row of cells on our level plus this one. Nothing. We need to go down one more level.'

'What's going on?' Awa croaked.

'I don't know. He,' Gurkan pointed to the Kikongo warrior, 'appeared outside my cell along with Anver.'

Awa turned to the Venetian, who shrugged his shoulders. 'He let me out, I don't know why, but he had to take out the guards on our level. They'll be asleep for a while.'

Fumu led them down a spiral staircase, before they emerged into the dimmest section of the prison Awa had seen. The bodyguard reached for one of the cressets, turning back to Awa and the others.

'Wait here,' he instructed.

They watched Fumu march down the narrow corridor, shining the light of the cresset through the bars of each cell, causing some prisoners to shriek at the brightness. Fumu went down the line, shaking his head, and was returning when a voice called out to him. Awa noticed him halt, move towards one cell and engage in a brief conversation with a prisoner.

Had he found Will? Then the Kikongolese picked up speed, jogging back towards them.

'He is not here,' said Fumu. 'They took him a few hours ago.'

'Where?' asked Gurkan.

'I do not know,' said Fumu, a look of frustration creasing his face. 'Come, I must get you all out of here.'

The bodyguard led them to the surface, circling up three spiral staircases, to ground level. Awa observed the slumped, unconscious prison guards with small needles protruding from their necks. Sleep darts. She had not thought the giant Kikongo warrior could be so subtle. They stopped by a small storeroom where they had left their belongings – travel sacks, weapons and tools. The guards hadn't processed these, so everything remained as it was. The team slung their packs over their backs, fixed up their weapons. Anver appeared most pleased, reunited with his trusty sack, which seemed to contain the most obscure items ... things that came to their aid in just about every dangerous situation in which the team found themselves.

The companions burst out into the wintry early morning air. The cool wind was a welcome contrast to the muggy atmosphere within the lower levels of the prison.

'I have done what I can do,' said Fumu. 'You are now on your own.' He turned to leave.

'Why?' Awa croaked, her voice barely a whisper.

Fumu stopped. Turning back he said, 'Not everyone is pleased with the way things have turned out.' He bowed and left.

Awa turned to her companions, unsure what to do next. So much had happened in the last few hours.

'We have to leave the city now,' said Gurkan.

'Where do we go?' Anver asked.

Gurkan gave them one of his boyish grins. 'I think it's time I introduced you to our *Mevlânâ*.'

5

GUARDIAN

CLOUDS HUNG HEAVY AND LOW over the city ruled by her father and his father before him, going back through the generations to Mehmet the Conqueror. Fatma felt the bitter cold of the evening air despite the low cloud cover. Venturing out at such a late hour was not something she usually did. Planning it was difficult; accomplishing it, even harder. Without Fumu and his trusted band of men, it would not have been possible. A Princess should not be roaming the streets of Istanbul and never at such a time as this, or so she was told. Yet sometimes you just had to do what your heart felt was right.

In truth she wasn't so much roaming as sitting comfortably, albeit in a state of heightened anxiety, within an unmarked, ordinary-looking carriage used by the royal family to move around the city unnoticed. It might look average on the outside, but within it was furnished with all the comforts a royal traveller expected - embroidered cushions, fleeces, velvet covers.

News of the arrests of the Rüzgar had reached her soon after their return. The Janissaries who took them in could not help spreading the news. Apparently, the unit had recovered the Armour of David and returned with the Staff of Moses. Yet if

25

rumours were true, neither the chivalrous Commander Mehmet Konjic nor the wise Master Huja returned with the young unit. Dead, gossip said. Such news only deepened her sorrow. Why was it that good people died in such circumstances? Where was the justice in this? Surely this could not be the will of God? These thoughts led her to do something rash and unexpected: she deliberately went against the orders of her betrothed, the newly appointed Grand Vizier, Kanijeli Siyavuş Pasha, the man who had ordered the arrests of the Rüzgar on the advice of Commander Berk.

Ever since her father had informed her of her engagement to Kanijeli Siyavuş Pasha, she had been troubled. Not because it was unexpected, since all royal marriages for Princes and Princesses were arranged by the court in agreement with the Sultan. It was more to do with Kanijeli's reputation. He had been Grand Vizier before, and was considerably older than her, but it was the stories people told, not nice ones at that, of his appetite for power and his desire to use lawful and sometimes unlawful means to acquire and retain it.

Meeting him during an afternoon of introductions arranged by the court, her fears were confirmed and she took a fundamental dislike to the man. There was nothing he could do or say – no matter how flattering he tried to make his words – that convinced her to revise her first impressions. Fatma downright detested the fellow. Life, she believed, was simple, but her family made it complicated.

Yet it was her duty to marry him, and they were expected to produce offspring. She would do these things, but before that she planned to make matters as awkward as possible for him. Breaking the young Rüzgar out of prison was one such act of rebellion. She was after all a Princess and daughter of the ruler, so what was the worst they could do to her? Tell her not to marry Kanijeli? Well, that was fine by her.

'See anything?' asked Fatma.

Ulyana, her handmaiden, sat opposite, peering out through the window of the carriage. She had unfastened one of the slats and through the small opening this created was staring intently in the direction of the prison, fifty or so yards away on the other side of the square.

'Nothing, Your Highness,' replied Ulyana.

She always felt a little more emboldened when her Ukrainian handmaiden was accompanying her. Not because Ulyana held any rank at court, but simply because the Kiev-born woman was the one who had taught her swordplay. Being able to grip a weapon firmly in her hand added, in Fatma's estimation, a degree of confidence. The Princess fondly recalled practising with Will and Awa. The bashful Englishman and the intense Songhai woman. Both individuals she would love to have called friends were it not for the enormous gulf in their social status. Prior to sparring with the Rüzgar, she had only undertaken drills with Ulyana. The experience with the Rüzgar gave her a taste of their adventure-filled life that she savoured long after their departure from the palace. Covert practice sessions with Ulyana organised under the guise of painting tuition were difficult to schedule, and she was only able to do them once a month. Still, she would rather have some skill with the blade than none at all. Would she ever be able to use her newfound martial skills? She doubted it, but a part of her wanted to test herself in a real situation, not just safely organised drills.

Fatma rubbed her gloved hands together. It was bitterly cold, and sitting in one spot for so long wasn't helping. She unrolled the blanket beside her and covered her legs, tucking the fabric around them for extra warmth.

'You should take one, Ulyana, or you will freeze.'

'Thank you, Your Highness, but in my country ...'

'I know, Istanbul's winter is like our spring,' Fatma finished the sentence for her.

Her handmaiden smiled then went back to monitoring what was happening outside.

'Your Highness, take a look,' said Ulyana.

Fatma pushed herself to the edge of the seat and threw open the slat on her side to gain a better view of the square. The front gate to the prison was open, and the formidable presence of Fumu stood under the arches, looking left and right, before ushering others through.

The Rüzgar! Yes, he had got them. She could see Gurkan the Turk, Anver the Venetian, Awa of the Songhai and ...

'Where is Will Ryde?' asked Fatma.

They waited.

'I do not see the Englishman, Ulyana. Do you?'

'No, Your Highness. Maybe he is on his way.'

Fatma observed a short exchange, before the Rüzgar dashed off in one direction and Fumu started the march back towards her carriage.

'They did not find him,' whispered Fatma.

Ulyana leant across, grasping her gloved hand. 'There will be an explanation for this, Your Highness.'

'Yes, but I fear it will not be one that pleases me.' Fatma stared once more out of the opening as Fumu drew nearer. Behind him everything was silent. She waited till her bodyguard was finally by the carriage.

'What happened, Fumu?'

Keeping his gaze lowered in her presence he said, 'The young ones are safe but ...'

'Will Ryde, where is he?' asked Fatma.

Fumu peered to his side, before continuing. 'I was told he was taken some hours ago. Where and by whom, I do not know.'

'Is he still ... alive?'

'I cannot say, my Princess,' Fumu replied, lowering his gaze further.

What had happened to the young Englishman to whom she had felt attracted? Surely death would be too cruel a fate for one with so much promise and such a bright future ahead of him.

'Keep looking for him. If he is in Istanbul, I want to know. We need to get him out of whatever cell they have put him in,' said Fatma.

'I will, Your Highness. If he is here, we will find him, God willing.'

'Thank you,' said Fatma, closing the window. Maybe God had not willed it, but then what *was* the will of the Creator? Surely not more suffering.

Fumu motioned to the carriage driver, and the vehicle lurched forward as the horses broke into a trot.

6

ALLUREMENT

SEVEN HUNDRED AND SIXTY STEPS. After reaching this number by counting in his head, Anver let out a sigh of relief. His breathing eased, and he looked up and around. There had been seven hundred and sixty bricks in the walls of his cell. The correspondence between the number of bricks in the cell walls and the steps he marched offered him some relief that he was now safe and would not return to prison. Harmony was restored once more, and he could move on to counting other things he came across.

Fifteen torches lit this stretch of road. They needed to remain twelve feet to the right of them to ensure they passed along this thoroughfare in shadow. After all, he had no desire to go back to prison, where he had had to count the iron bars in the cells to keep himself occupied. Some cells had a wooden door and six vertical bars, others had eight. There was even one with twelve. Did it mean a more dangerous prisoner lodged in that one or had they just run out of wood? He was curious, but since the only way of finding out was to be incarcerated again, he would not let his inquisitiveness get the better of him when it came to this particular question.

'Stay right,' whispered Gurkan, leading them down an alley before they crossed a quiet thoroughfare, skipping across the street as silently as possible.

Anver had been down this road in the daytime; it was a street market with twenty-five fruit stalls and twenty vegetable ones. Anver once sat here the whole day, observing the number of customers who purchased from each of the stalls. He calculated four buyers per hour, which in a ten-hour day meant forty customers. If each purchaser spent half a dirham, the merchant earned the tidy sum of twenty dirhams for his day's efforts. In a city like Istanbul this would be enough to comfortably feed a family of four. However, he noted that some people owned more than one stall, and he deliberated whether they employed others or used family members to serve their customers. Next time he would ask them. Obtaining this information would help him calculate the potential earnings for a stallholder who had multiple outlets, after subtracting their costs. With this data, he could estimate the earnings of all of the stalls across the city. He wasn't sure how useful this information was, but his keenness in the matter required he perform the calculation.

'Anver,' said Awa, seeking his attention. He always listened to what she had to say, as she was the smartest of the group and could at least fathom his ideas and appreciate the books he liked to read.

'What?' he replied.

'When did they separate you and Gurkan from Will?'

'As soon as we entered the prison.'

In fact, it was ten paces after they entered the prison, but he didn't think she would be interested in such a response. Over the years he had come to realise that most people, in truth, everyone he ever met, did not see the world as he did – broken into numbers, forces and actions, one leading to another. So, with bitter experience, he had learnt to converse in a manner alien to him but comfortable for others.

'Were they planning to do that before you got there ...?' Awa spoke out loud without looking at him directly.

Anver wasn't sure she was asking him the question, so he remained silent. Instead, he followed her, staying in the shadows twelve feet from the torches, crouching low when the street lights illuminated the pavement around them.

They pressed on, heading west out of the city. Empty streets, but for a few cats on the prowl, their suspicious eyes observing the group. Anver's sack was firmly secured on his back, with a strap across his chest to keep it firmly in place. He carried all manner of oddities within it, but always found a use for the objects. Since joining the Rüzgar, he had taken to wearing a dagger in a leather sheath, which he kept hooked to his breeches, but always behind him, as he preferred not to be able to see this ferocious item. He was comfortable with tools, not weapons, on his person. Yet in their line of work, fighting was inevitable, and he had certainly poked the odd villain with the tip of the dagger on occasion.

The past year had been filled with skirmishes in all manner of places. He was never thrilled by the violence; he only enjoyed making contraptions that proved useful for the Rüzgar when they were in a tight spot. Unfortunately there were fewer of them now. It did pain his heart, even after so many weeks, to remember that Commander Konjic and Master Huja were no longer in this world. Both had showed him great kindness and listened keenly to his ideas. It wasn't his usual experience of how people reacted to him. In the past he had been seen as odd and peculiar. Not with the Rüzgar: here he was appreciated and he enjoyed every minute of it – though not the minutes spent in that cell.

Gurkan raised his hand, and they came to a stop. The Turk gazed up and down the thoroughfare, searching for movement.

Empty. On the Konyan's signal they crossed the street and entered a different neighbourhood with more tightly packed houses, its cobbled streets lined with small shops, occupied during the day by tailors, seamstresses and clothmakers. There was a well in an alcove beside a madrasa.

'Wait,' whispered Awa, pointing in the direction of the well.

At first, Gurkan didn't look happy to stop, but he soon realised it was a good idea to fill up their water canteens. Anver also removed his, and after Gurkan wearily hauled the bucket up, they began to fill their containers.

'Who was the big African?' asked Gurkan.

'Fumu is the personal bodyguard of Princess Fatma Sultan,' Awa replied.

'The same Princess you and Will duelled with?' Gurkan enquired.

'Yes,' said Awa.

'Why did he help us escape?' asked Gurkan.

'I don't know, but he wouldn't have come except at the Princess's instruction,' Awa replied.

'You must have made an impression on her,' replied Gurkan.

Awa shrugged her shoulders.

'What about Will?' asked Anver. He felt guilty at not having discovered where the Englishman was.

Awa and Gurkan shared a look.

'We cannot go back to that hell-hole,' said Gurkan.

'He is not there,' said Awa.

'Where is he then?' asked Anver. They could not just leave Will behind. They had been together like a family; they could not split up now.

'By God, I wish I knew, Anver! But in a city the size of Istanbul ...' Gurkan threw his arms up to indicate he could be anywhere.

33

Awa placed a hand on Anver's arm. 'We need to find him, but right now we are the most wanted people in all of Istanbul. We have to get out of the city tonight. Let the situation cool down. The Ottoman court, Master Huja taught us, is a fickle place and the political landscape is always shifting. Today's heroes become tomorrow's villains, and maybe it works the other way around, too.'

It didn't make sense to him. If someone was a villain, then how could they become a hero? Would Azi Dahäg, the cruel tyrannical villain of the Karabakh Plateau, have become a hero? If so, why did they kill him? He thought it best not to ask her.

'Come on, let's go.' Gurkan shut his canteen, placing it inside his satchel, as did Awa. The two moved on.

Anver was about to join his friends when he noticed a red glow emanating from one side of the alley branching off to his right. Looking more closely at the crimson apparition he saw a swirling mist. It seemed most odd, yet fascinating to look at. Recalling the hundreds of scientific books he hed read, he tried to identify this phenomenon, but could not explain what he was seeing. He screwed his eyes shut for a moment, then opened them again. The apparition remained. Oddly, despite the danger they were presently in he felt a need to explore, an urgent desire, in fact, to follow whatever it was. He had never felt like this before.

He saw some mice on the corner of the path, but for some strange reason he didn't count them. He wanted to, but the urge to follow the red mist was stronger, luring him into a comforting embrace. As he passed further into the alley away from the street, the red light moved ahead of him, skimming along the ground, maybe even under the ground. He couldn't tell. The only thing he knew was he had to follow. It was important, something inside him explained. It drew Anver closer, and closer, till his hand reached out to the red mist, almost within touching distance.

'Anver,' a voice called out.

He stopped. Was the mist addressing him?

Then Anver heard footsteps running up behind him, and he swivelled to see Gurkan at his side, shaking his arm. 'What are you doing? Come on.'

Anver wheeled back towards the red mist.

Noticing the confused look on Anver's face, Gurkan asked. 'What is it, what happened?'

'I ...' Anver said. 'I ... can't remember.'

Awa turned up. 'What's going on?'

'The Venetian got lost,' explained Gurkan. 'Istanbul is a big city, so it's not surprising for a little-city dweller from Venice. This way, let's go.'

Anver paused, staring at Awa.

'Anver?'

'I don't remember anything that happened in the last two minutes,' he said.

She looked concerned. 'We can talk about it once we get out of the city, but right now we need to keep moving,' Awa said.

She was right. He followed her back to the well. What had just happened? Nothing, it would seem. But there was a shadow of a memory and it had something to do with the colour red. Why? How was it significant? Removing the thought from his mind he raced to catch up with his friends. They had to get out of Istanbul and there wasn't a moment to lose.

7

WICKED DEAL

ONE MONTH LATER

ROPLETS OF RAIN TRICKLED DOWN from the entrance arch at Leeds Castle in Maidstone. Incessant drizzle had met Will upon his arrival in England, and he remembered this was what England was like most of the time: wet, damp and dark. But it was still home. Once they'd crossed the Channel he travelled across land on foot, gaining means of transport wherever they would accept his coin. He stopped off to see John the Moor and his English wife, Meg. Thankfully, despite having aided the Rüzgar on their previous adventure, they still lived safely on their farm and welcomed him into their home for a night's rest and meal before he set off again the following morning. They were only disappointed not to see Awa and Gurkan, and sad to hear of the demise of Commander Konjic, whose life John had previously saved. Konjic had spent many nights being nursed by the couple as he recuperated from his injuries sustained during a fight with Sir Reginald Rathbone's men at 'The Stag' in Canterbury. John unrolled his treasured Moroccan prayer rug and offered a *Dua*, a prayer, in Arabic for the deceased Commander. Meg also prayed for Konjic in her own way. The respite at their farm was something Will welcomed, but it was soon over, and he had to face what lay ahead.

The road to Leeds Castle was heavily fortified. Previously he, Awa and Gurkan had entered in the dead of night via rowing boat across the moat, scaling the tower, from where they broke into the main castle and retrieved the Staff of Moses. This time he would enter in plain sight. Will didn't know if the guards were the same as on his previous trip. Back then he had had the good fortune not to encounter anyone, so there was little risk of them recognising him. Had Awa been with him, then it would be a different matter. They let him pass through the outer barbican when he said he was a messenger with a scroll case from Istanbul that had to be personally presented to the Earl of Rothminster. He was told to leave his weapons in the barbican, which he did, before passing along the short dirt road. He felt naked walking into the nest of a venomous viper without the reassurance of a sword's hilt to hold on to.

From the inner barbican, he was accompanied by a guard wearing a long sword, which to Will's eye had not seen much use. Either it was very new or the man wore it ceremonially rather than for practical reasons. Will wasn't looking to get into a fight, but he doubted he would be leaving here without becoming embroiled in one. They went through the arch and crossed the moat. Focusing on the water sent a shudder down Will's back as he recalled the guilt he'd felt leaving his friends in the castle that evening. He bit his lower lip, considering how he had once more abandoned his friends, this time to rot in a prison cell back in Istanbul. He was here, out in the countryside, whereas they were decaying in a filthy jail. What type of friend was he? Never around when they needed him most. He always had something else to do, a place to go to, a person to see. He felt sick at the thought of Awa, Gurkan and Anver perishing in prison.

When they entered the outer bailey the guard directed him to a small room with a bench in one corner and a wooden table before him.

'Wait here,' said the guard, 'while I go and tell His Lordship he has a messenger from Istanbul. What's your name?'

He had thought long and hard about whether to give a false name. But if he did, they might not grant him access to the Earl himself. He might be fobbed off as a nobody. He could not risk that; Berk would want to be sure the message he sent was delivered into the hands of his disreputable ally. A part of the Englishman wanted to be fobbed off, but another part, the part trained by Mehmet Konjic, told him he needed to get closer to the Earl and his plans if he was to be of any use to his friends. It meant placing himself in danger, but when he considered it, every day since being in the galleys, bar a few, had been filled with near-death experiences. 'Will Ryde,' he replied.

'All right, wait here, Will Ryde, till I come back to get you. A boy will be along soon to give you a pail of water.'

'Thank you, sir,' said Will.

The wait was a long one. Midday came and went and it was early afternoon by the time he was summoned. In the interim the boy had come back and given him a piece of bread and butter to go with a glass of milk. Grateful for the refreshment, he consumed it with wolfish abandon, only considering whether it was poisoned after finishing the meal. However, he was in good health as he was led to the inner bailey. Truth be told, Will was on edge at the prospect of meeting Commander Konjic's nemesis, the Earl of Rothminster – and why shouldn't he be? After all, the fellow had tried to have him killed on more than one occasion.

Keeping the Ottoman scroll-case in plain view, to denote his significance as an overseas messenger, he fell in line behind the guard. The man led him inside the building and down a stone corridor panelled in oak along one wall till they reached the end and he could look out into a flower garden. It struck Will as odd that a merciless man such as Rothminster would bother with such niceties as cultivating fine flora, but then he reminded himself the Earl was cunning and devious. Keeping up pretences for the Royals was part of his game.

'Wait,' ordered the guard, before knocking on the wooden door.

'Yes?' said a voice from within. Will recognised the voice. How could he not? It sent a shiver up his spine and made his fingers and toes tingle.

The soldier poked his head around the corner of the door and announced, 'Will Ryde.'

'You may send him in,' said the familiar voice.

'Go on,' prompted the guard, opening the study door before ushering Will through and shutting it behind him.

Will realised he was holding the scroll-case out before him, as though it were a magical talisman to ward off the danger lurking in this room. He lowered it as he moved in to the study, gazing around the richly decorated interior lined with bookshelves and maps of the East on the walls. On a heavy timber table were two fine leather pen-cases, quills, ink pots, penknives, a compass and an astrolabe. Yet what drew his attention most, sending his heart racing, was the finely dressed English gentleman standing in the centre of the study, wearing a superior smile: Sir Reginald Rathbone. Seated at a table behind him, to the left, in a high-backed burgundy chair upholstered in Moroccan leather, was the Earl of Rothminster.

'You are full of surprises, Will Ryde,' Rathbone sneered. He removed the leather gloves from his hands, tucking them into his belt. 'But that is still no reason not to kill you.'

Will gulped. He noticed Rathbone's gaze flicker to his right. The Englishman had only turned his neck a fraction before he realised a dagger was at his windpipe. He hadn't even noticed the assailant approach. He must be losing his senses.

'Li moves like a cat. You won't hear him till it's too late,' Rathbone chided.

The Oriental! Rathbone's replacement for Stukeley, the man he had seen accompany the Earl in the bookshop in Aleppo. Will kept his gaze firmly trained ahead, his hands out. He felt his heart straining under the weight of the villainy around him.

'I have a message for the Earl of Rothminster,' Will nodded towards the seated Earl. 'From Commander Atilla Berk, of the Janissary Force in Istanbul.' He raised the scroll-case so they could see it clearly.

'I will read it,' said the Earl.

Rathbone took a few paces towards Will, swiping the scroll-case from him before inspecting it with a hawkish eye. 'Seal is intact,' he said, handing it over to the Earl.

Will kept as still as he could. Li was shorter than him, but Will remembered the physical prowess and presence of the man. The Oriental moved like a shadow. Will dared not make eye contact with Li and kept his gaze fixed on the Earl inspecting the seal once more, turning the scroll-case up and down, scrutinising it, before breaking the seal and removing its contents. He deliberately placed the empty case on his desk and unwound the paper scroll.

Minutes passed as the Earl read the letter, before handing it to Rathbone. The Earl rose up from his burgundy chair, taking a step behind it so that he could gaze out at the manicured green lawn, his hands clasped, like a statue, behind his back. Whereas the Earl kept his emotions guarded, Rathbone did not: it was clear to see the look of surprise followed by a sort of elation in his eyes. He placed the letter back on the desk. Will remained motionless, the tip of the dagger nipping his neck.

The Earl turned to look at Rathbone, who nodded.

'It seems we have need of you, Will Ryde,' said the Earl, sweeping back his well-groomed mop of dark black hair and placing his elbows on the back of his chair as he took Will in.

Rathbone motioned to Li, who pulled his dagger away before Will had even realised he was no longer standing beside him. How did he move so quietly?

'Yet there is a question of trust, is there not, Sir Reginald?' said the Earl.

'Indeed there is,' replied Rathbone.

The Earl continued. 'Allowing one who may have turned Turk into the inner workings of our operation presents a risk.'

'It does,' Rathbone agreed.

'How then, Sir Reginald, can we allay this threat?' asked the Earl.

'Collateral, I would suggest,' smirked Rathbone.

They both stared at Will.

'What do you have to offer, Ryde?' asked the Earl.

'I have only the possessions upon me, sir. I am a man of little means,' replied Will, his voice unsteady.

The arrangement he had made with Berk was to deliver the letter and wait for a message to return to the Commander confirming he had done so, whereupon Berk was to show leniency towards his friends and not execute them. Rothminster was now complicating the arrangement, and Will didn't like where this was headed.

Moving away from his chair, hands still clasped behind his back, Rothminster paced the room, circling Will before heading back towards his desk and sitting down on the edge of it.

'Collateral, Will Ryde, is given as a guarantee of fulfilling your obligation. You understand this?'

'I do,' replied Will.

'This letter obligates you to execute certain services for me,' said Rathbone. 'As to what these are, you will be told at the right time. However, we must be confident you will deliver your side of the agreement, otherwise you lose your collateral.'

'What could I possibly offer as collateral?'

'Something you hold dear, which you would rather die for than lose,' said the Earl.

There was only thing he would die for. He looked at Rothminster and realised where this was going.

Rothminster stood up and went back to stare out the window. 'How is your mother?'

'No!' said Will. 'Leave her out of it.'

'You are the one who brought her into it when you stole the Staff of Moses from the Earl,' scoffed Rathbone. 'From this very castle!'

'She has nothing to do with this arrangement. Let it be,' Will protested.

'You have anything else to offer?' the Earl asked.

'I ... I promise to serve you, in whatever way you would have me serve you.'

'You are going to do that anyway,' said the Earl.

'I ...' Will was at a loss for words.

He had nothing. What kind of son was he, placing his mother in mortal danger? All he wanted to do was make things simpler and better and now they had become a whole lot more complicated again.

'Very well, you will arrange for Mistress Ryde to be moved into one of my lodgings, close to Charterhouse in London, where she will remain under our watch and unharmed,' proclaimed the Earl as he stared at Will with dark penetrating eyes. 'However, should you break your side of the bargain, then we will do with her as we please.'

8
KONYA
TWO MONTHS LATER

PLACING THE COPPER BALL-BEARING into the
narrow steel tube left Anver with a satisfied grin upon
his face. He spun the ball on its axis, keenly observing
it whizz. Then it stopped. He spun it again, this time gently
nudging it, and the ball-bearing careered along the tube and
out onto a metal runner he had fastened to the wooden beams
in the ceiling. Anver went back down the ladder, listening to
the sound of the ball-bearing as it picked up speed, hurtling
around the sloping metal runners circling the outhouse. It
entered the first circular tube and emerged quieter, having been
bathed with oil. The oil-drenched ball-bearing disappeared into
a copper pipe. This was it: when it flew out the other end, it
would produce a magnificent exhibition of light and sound.
Then it emerged once more, still the same, softly rolling into
the padded cushions at the end of the runner.

'Oh,' Anver scratched his head. 'Something was meant to
happen.'

He knew exactly what should have taken place. The copper
ball-bearing was going to burst into flames as it was fired from
one side of the outhouse to the other. It's just that it didn't. The
more he read, the more certain he was that he knew nothing of
the mysteries of the world.

43

'Maybe I need a break,' Anver said, stretching his arms high into the air and cracking his back. 'Food. I need to eat.'

Leaving the outhouse he had converted into a laboratory, Anver stretched once more, taking in deep breaths of clean country air. Engrossed in the experiment since dawn, he had missed breakfast and his stomach grumbled, complaining at the neglect. Anver picked up the bowl of boiled barley, covered with a plate, set on a tray outside his outhouse. Awa would have visited earlier with the food. Noticing him engaged in work, she would have left the food so he could eat when hungry. Unlike everyone else he knew, she never distracted him when he was deep in thought, for that was when he would do his best work. He wolfed down the barley.

A quick scan around the Konyan village in Anatolia brought to mind some familiar sights for this time in the morning. Awa sat with her back against the oak tree, quill moving in majestic arcs as she penned her *risala*, her treatise, describing her journey since being forced from her home by the invading Moroccan army. She would always write before midday for one to two hours. She said it was the time of day she felt most energetic and focused and the words flowed with ease. Anver preferred the late evening time for his best work; in the dark and silence was his golden time. The day brought with it too many unwanted noises and interruptions by people and animals going about their business.

'Over here,' shouted Gurkan, his friend and also a local of the village. He was waving at some farmers tending an adjacent field.

There were six fields around the village to which its inhabitants could claim ownership. Five were farmed and one was kept fallow, on a rotating basis. The animals were alternated through the fields, keeping them fertilised. There were eighty villagers, in fifteen families. The food they grew was sufficient for the purposes of the village, and every Thursday, on market day, some of the men would travel into the city to sell their surplus to the inhabitants of Konya. The farmers considered the city folk to be lazy since they were used to buying their food as opposed to growing it themselves. It struck the farmers as strange that any person would want to be beholden to someone else for the supply of their meals. The idea seemed preposterous. If a man knew how to grow his own food, he and his family could survive no matter what happened. If you didn't, you were always at risk of starving. Anver, as a city dweller, had never really considered this notion before living amongst these farmers, but their reasoning made perfect sense to him now.

At times he missed Venice, the town of his birth, but not for long, when he took in the serenity of the village location. He had to admit it, this simple way of life had grown on him, and he could willingly remain here for quite some time. Based in his outhouse, where he chose to work and sleep, he pondered new ideas and most of all tried to work on his plan to find a source of energy which could self-replicate. As he saw it, the problem with anything that generated energy, such as wood or coal, was that the resource ran out. Sooner or later it was inevitable. After all, you couldn't cut down all the trees in a forest just because you needed the wood. Trees were living beings with their own communities, just like people. He had to find another way of fuelling his devices, without relying on a finite energy source. He often dreamt about it. A ball of red and orange energy, pulsating, like a miniature sun inside a jewel, resting on the palm of his hand. With it he could make people's lives easier, maybe do even more than that. Like the alchemists before him, he understood the theory of what he was attempting but could not fathom the practicality of how it could be done.

Finishing the bowl, he placed it back in precisely the same spot he had found it, swigged down a glass of water and decided to take a stroll, heading south along the path bordering the village. Members of Gurkan's village had welcomed him and Awa, after some initial consternation when their prodigal son who had gone to the big city returned with a Jew and an African as companions. However, these villagers had good hearts, and so pleased were they to see Gurkan, they soon forgot any reservations they might have about his companions. It didn't take long for Gurkan's smooth tongue to placate anyone else who was skittish about the new arrivals.

Anver knew very little about Konya, only having heard Gurkan speak fleetingly about his beloved city. It wasn't until Anver arrived that he realised how many libraries and centres of learning were there. The great poet Rumi was buried here, as were other notable saints. The whirling dervishes of the Mevlevi Sufi order were quite a sight when they performed. Anver tried to turn around on the spot in the same manner, hoping it might lead to a breakthrough in new ideas, but becoming dizzy he would fall in a heap on the ground. It wasn't for him.

The path swung around a clutch of aspen trees, which obscured the road ahead till Anver skirted them. It was then he noticed the approaching figure. Anver froze. The man looked strangely at odds with the surroundings. His clothes were too fine, his posture stiff and stern; he looked like a person used to giving orders. He walked beside his horse, reins in his hands, taking in the view across the fields. Anver thought of hiding, but the man spotted him and raised his hand to indicate he had seen him.

A sense of danger flared within his stomach, as it had whenever they were on a mission with the late Commander Konjic. The world had been robbed of a gentle soul when he was slain in Azerbaijan. The approaching figure was not like him. Even at this distance there was a haughty arrogance to his gait. Anver waited on the spot, since there wasn't anything else he could think to do. He did take a quick count of the thirty-two aspen trees he could see to his left, along with tracking the flight-paths of five butterflies circling close by in a merry dance. He took his hands out of his pockets and thought to clench them, as he had seen Will do many times. It seemed to relieve some of the tension he was feeling, as he knew whatever this man had come here for, it was related to Rüzgar business and things were about to change for the worse.

'Salaam,' the austere-looking man said as he got closer.

'Salaam,' Anver replied.

'I am looking for Gurkan, Awa and Anver,' he said.

'I am Anver.'

'Then I should say Shalom.'

Anver nodded, avoiding looking directly at the man's eyes, which had a penetrating intensity to them.

'My name is Sardar Ferhad Pasha.'

The name rang a bell in his memory. It had been used by Commander Konjic before they set off for their last mission.

'You are the Grand Vizier!'

Ferhad let out a small cough. 'Former.'

9

FALLEN PROTECTOR

THE ARRIVAL OF A DISTINGUISHED visitor to the village caused quite a stir. A goat was sacrificed, a meal made ready, the elders wished to know about matters in Istanbul. Awa simply observed Sardar Ferhad Pasha quietly at a distance, allowing the villagers their time with him, for it was not every day a guest from Istanbul passed through the hamlet. Ferhad asked the young companions not to disclose the purpose of his visit – not that he had told them anything – before being overwhelmed by the welcome and respect offered to any traveller passing through an Ottoman community. Midday prayers were said before the meal was served, followed by tea and an invitation to the guest to rest and sleep. However, against custom Ferhad declined this latter part and explained he needed to sit with Gurkan and his friends on a matter of some urgency, for he had to head back to the city of Konya before the afternoon was out. Despite their disappointment, the village elders relented, for Gurkan was everyone's favourite in the village and the visitor had come all this way to meet him.

The Rüzgar and the former Grand Vizier retired to the outhouse that was Anver's laboratory and accommodation. Tea was brought in by some of the local children, before the doors to the outhouse were shut tight and it was just the four of them.

'Quite a collection,' commented Ferhad, looking around the building.

Anver was about to say something when Awa cut him off. 'What do you want?' she asked, her words sounding more aggressive than she would have liked. Despite herself, she couldn't conceal the revulsion she felt for this man.

Ferhad was taken aback by her tone and sat up straighter in his chair, before taking in the mood of the companions. She had no affinity with this man, who had sent them on hazardous missions on behalf of his fickle ruler. And when they needed him most, he was not there. Konjic and Huja had died because of the needless mission they were asked to undertake. Why recover the Armour of David for the Sultan if he had little or no need for it?

'I know you are upset. You have reason to be. I would be, too,' Ferhad said.

He was trying to placate them by showing empathy. She didn't like it when politicians, and his was a true politician's nature, displayed false emotions to win trust.

'You know nothing!' snapped Awa.

Gurkan turned towards her and said in a soft tone, 'Let's hear him out, Awa, he's come a long way.'

She quelled the anger that had been bubbling up inside her since his arrival, nodded and sat back in her seat. Her father would not have been pleased with the approach she had taken with the former Grand Vizier, and she told herself to show more control.

'Commander Konjic, may God bless his soul, regularly wrote to me whenever possible. The letters would arrive weeks later, but they were and remain an important form of intelligence. The last letter he sent was from Tabriz, before you headed north into Azerbaijan. And before that from Jerusalem, following your encounter with the ... Jinn.' His eyes flicked between the three of them before he removed two envelopes from an inside pocket of his kaftan. Awa had been present when Zawaba'a was released, but there wasn't a day that went by when she didn't wonder if she had merely imagined the whole episode. She had not. Huja had died at the hands of the Jinn.

'I am not normally a man given to sentiment, but after reading these letters I was moved by your plight. The determination shown by the Rüzgar in the face of such formidable odds warrants respect from friend and foe alike,' he said, before tucking the letters away once more. Awa desperately wanted to read Konjic's letters, to hear the words of her dear Commander, to see his writing, but it would seem she was not going be given the opportunity.

'It got a lot worse when we arrived in Azerbaijan,' interrupted Gurkan. The story of what transpired in the mountains and the plight of the villagers remained an untold tale, known only to those who survived it. Even the three of them had barely spoken in the past two months of the events leading up to Konjic's tragic death.

'I would like to hear what happened. All of it,' said Ferhad.

Gurkan looked at her, then Anver. She didn't see what harm it could do to share the experiences of their journey with someone else outside the Rüzgar, so she nodded, as did Anver. 'All right,' said Gurkan, leaning back in his chair. The Konyan spent the next hour going over the events that had befallen them after they travelled north from Tabriz, ending with their incarceration and escape from Istanbul. Gurkan told the tale with great aplomb, and Awa noticed the normally placid Ferhad's astonished looks. He sat forward in his chair at times, gripped by the narrative as it unfolded, particularly at the part where the villagers of the Karabach region rebelled against Azi

Dahäg, and more so when Konjic showed consummate bravery in the face of death by taking on the younger and far more powerful Azi Dahäg.

When the Konyan ended his account, the former Grand Vizier leant back in his chair. All he could say was, 'Truly, a tale to pass down the generations.' He stood up, pacing the floor for some time, before returning and sitting once more.

'The fables of the Rüzgar have already passed into lore amongst your small but faithful band of supporters at the Ottoman court. When they hear of these as yet unknown events, then your tales will truly become legend in their eyes,' said Ferhad.

'Wait,' interrupted Gurkan. 'We have supporters within the Ottoman court?'

'How else do you explain your escape from prison?' replied Ferhad. 'Your advocates are also mine.'

'Who?' Gurkan enquired.

'Safiye Sultan, wife of the Sultan. And his daughter, Princess Fatma Sultan.'

'Why would they help us?' asked Gurkan.

'The Princess appears to have a soft spot for the Rüzgar. As for Safiye Sultan, she enjoys hearing about you from the Princess; besides, Safiye Sultan was never one to fall into line, she always likes to stir matters a little. Life at court is stifling. Your tales bring a freshness sorely missed.'

'And what is your connection to Safiye Sultan?' Awa enquired.

'Like her, I am also ethnically Albanian, and let's just say we have some common ancestral ties. As a result, she has retained me as a special adviser and thankfully restored some of my privileges, taken from me when I lost the title of Grand Vizier.'

'Even though her husband the Sultan was the one who removed you from your position,' Anver chimed in.

'The Ottoman court is a serpents' nest. To survive, you must give allegiance to the most powerful serpent who will tolerate you. And when that viper turns on you, for it will, you find another to attach yourself to before you are endangered once more. And so the cycle of alliances and associations is a never-ending game,' Ferhad commented.

'You still haven't told us what you want,' Awa demanded, her anger returning. 'And what happened to Will?' It was a question preying on all their minds. If anyone knew the Englishman's whereabouts, the former Grand Vizier should.

Ferhad sucked in air between his teeth. 'As for the Englishman, I do not know. His disappearance from prison the night you escaped remains a mystery. To the best of my knowledge, there has been no sighting of him anywhere within the city.'

'What do you think happened to him?' Anver asked.

'He is most likely dead,' Ferhad replied.

Her heart sank. Anver and Gurkan both slumped in their chairs.

'But, I might be wrong ...' Seeing their deflated reaction, Ferhad tried to make them feel better by adding, 'Really, I just don't know.'

No one spoke for a minute. Awa prayed for Will wherever he was, in this world or the next.

'What of Captain Kadri?' she asked.

'Thankfully, due to intense pressure from some within the court and certain senior members of the Bektashi Sufi order, he was not killed but is under a sort of house arrest where he must remain. His rank and title as a Janissary have been stripped from him.'

'Thank God he is alive,' said Awa.

They sat in silence for a minute, before the Konyan spoke up once more. 'You didn't come all this way to tell us you think Will might be dead.'

'No, I didn't,' said Ferhad. 'After you returned there were those amongst the Janissaries who felt Konjic was wronged when he was labelled a traitor, for all who knew him witnessed his integrity, kindness and goodness of character. They are working hard to see the charges dropped. I know Konjic himself is no longer in this world, but for the historical record, it is important his name is cleared. As for the Armour of David, this was presented to the Sultan, yet his ... unpredictable behaviour meant his attention had already moved on to other matters. As far as I know, the Armour remains in the Hall of Religious Relics within the palace grounds.'

Gurkan punched his left fist into the palm of his right hand. 'We sacrificed so much to return with the Armour. The Commander, dead, Master Huja, dead, because of the mission. And the Sultan has not even given it his attention! Does he know the losses incurred to bring it back to Istanbul?'

Ferhad offered a weak smile. 'The Sultan does not concern himself with such details. He has been told it belongs to him. Beyond that, when it takes his fancy, he may ask for it to be presented to him.'

Gurkan shook his head in disappointment. The Konyan had shown faith in the Ottoman ruler throughout the time she knew him. He was now hearing first-hand from one who personally served the Sultan what his true nature was, and it wasn't what Gurkan wanted to hear.

'What about his plans to go to war using the Armour?' Awa asked.

'Since the original mission to recover the Armour of David was conceived, the Sultan has had a change of heart. He no longer has designs to go to war with the Safavids in Persia, or the Moroccans, or even the Catholics of Europe,' Ferhad replied.

'What, then?' Awa pressed.

'The Sultan has announced the Empire will be holding the world's greatest trade fair in Istanbul in September this year,' proclaimed Ferhad, watching their faces for a moment, before continuing. 'It will be a sight to behold, bringing merchants, traders and artisans from all corners of the world. The Sultan seeks to present himself as a magnanimous ruler, above the politics of lesser men and their petty land disputes. The image he wishes to leave behind is of a man who ruled over east and west and did so by bringing all peacefully under his imperial banner.'

'That's quite a change,' Awa said.

'We all change, the important thing is whether we change for the better before we die,' said Ferhad.

She could not deny the truth of the former Grand Vizier's words. As to the true intentions of the Sultan, her doubts remained.

'Invitations have been sent out to allies and foes alike. Most have accepted and preparations are under way to receive the throng of expected visitors.'

'Have the Venetians accepted?' asked Anver.

'I believe they have,' replied Ferhad. The Venetian smiled.

'We are not merchants or traders, so what do you want of us?' asked Gurkan, echoing Awa's terse tone.

'Demons,' said Ferhad.

'What!' Gurkan exclaimed, rocking forward on his chair.

Awa felt a prickle of fear surge up her spine into her neck, before it set off a bolt of pain in her forehead. She tried to shrug it off, but her skull was beginning to throb.

'During the past three months, every community, in fact all faiths, have reported a surge in demonic possessions,' Ferhad said. He let the news sink in before continuing. 'Cases began as a trickle, so the imams, priests, rabbis and others did not take much notice, believing they were within the normal bounds of cases of demonic possession. These things have always happened and are dealt with in the way they are normally dealt with.' Ferhad waved his hands about, seeming unsure as to the specifics. 'However, over the past two months cases have surged. It seems every household knows of someone who has become possessed.'

'When you say "possessed", what exactly do you mean?' asked Anver.

Ferhad pursed his lips. 'At one end there is, let's call it *benign* possession, where the family of the one possessed or bewitched reports them standing silently for long periods looking at something, occasionally nodding their head, as though they were communicating with a person, but no one is there. Or at least the family member cannot see anyone present. The behaviour of such a person is odd, but is not threatening or dangerous. At the other end of the scale, the one possessed is foaming at the mouth, speaking in a language unintelligible to all, becomes violent and as a result is tied down in a room, for their own safety and that of others. They attack and bite anyone who comes close and bear all the hallmarks of an occult invasion. And there is everything in between.'

Awa did not want to ask the question, for she feared the answer, terrified in terms of what it meant and the gravity of their irresponsibility in Jerusalem. But she had to ask it. 'What does this have to do with us?'

Ferhad turned his head to survey the young companions before fixing his gaze on Awa. 'Along with the rise in possessions we have seen a group of zealots form a new sect in the city. These fanatics, adorned like holy priests, are stirring up trouble in people's minds. They call themselves the Zawaba'aians.'

'Zawaba'a!' Gurkan exclaimed. 'The Jinn from Jerusalem.'

Awa let out a long breath, shutting her eyes, recalling how she was overwhelmed by the ringing inside her head, calling her from a great depth, imploring her to speak its name. Zawaba'a!

Zawaba'a! Zawaba'a! It was sheer power and presence, unlike anything she could imagine. The shadow covered her mind, veiling her momentarily from reality.

'Awa,' Anver put a hand on her forearm.

She opened her eyes and looked up at Ferhad.

'It seems the Jinn you released in Jerusalem has taken up residence in Istanbul,' the former Grand Vizier said in a laconic tone.

'Why?' Gurkan asked.

'Why not? Beings such as this Zawaba'a are drawn to power, and Istanbul is at the height of its ascendancy. However, the Jinn brings with it a surge in possessions. It has attracted some human followers, these misguided Zawaba'aians. They are spreading rumours and dark whispers in the streets and alleys, planting suspicion, fear and doubt in the hearts of citizens. The authorities cannot find them, for they simply disappear by the time the Janissaries show up.'

'What do Zawaba'a or his followers want?' asked Gurkan, his expression perplexed.

'No one knows, but the number of possessions is getting out of hand. Even some ...' Ferhad paused, considering his next words carefully, '... senior officials have lost their minds. At the same time merchants are complaining of their warehouses and shops being broken into. Nothing is stolen, they are just ransacked. It was when these two factors – surging possessions and the impact on trade – combined that Safiye Sultan asked me to convene a covert meeting of religious leaders of all faiths. After this gathering they all came to the same conclusion.' Ferhad stared directly at Awa now.

Her throat dried and she felt a tingling sensation at the tips of her fingers.

'The one who released *this* Jinn, is the only one who can imprison it again.'

10

RUDE AWAKENING

THE PRACTICE QUAD WITHIN LEEDS Castle was surprisingly full when Will entered it for his morning drill. The castle in Maidstone had been his temporary home for the past two months. He had come to know it as sparsely populated, with only one battalion of soldiers, yet this morning something had changed. He stopped for a moment to take in the sight of all of the newcomers, who must have arrived recently, perhaps that very morning, as he had not heard them the previous evening. The faces were unfamiliar to him. Scanning them, he didn't recognise a single one. Probably a good thing, considering his history with the Earl and his men. Will decided to push forward and continued to where the grizzled quartermaster sat in his hovel.

'Morning, sir,' said Will. 'And how are we today?'

'Bah!' responded Allen the quartermaster. 'Too polite, you is. It'll be the death of you with this new lot.'

'Who are they?' asked Will, taking a glance over his shoulder.

'Real soldiers, that's what they call 'emselves. More like mercenaries for hire, if you ask me,' said Allen, spitting on the ground.

When Will had heard there was a resident quartermaster in the castle, he was pleased, offering to help the old fellow sharpen steel and fashion weapons. Allen was uncouth and vulgar, nothing like his kindly Moroccan quartermaster, Hakim Abdullah, in Marrakesh, who had been as sophisticated with his intellect as he was skilful with his hands. Yet Will still enjoyed spending time by the forge: it reminded him of safe and happy days in his early youth. And once you got to know Allen, considering his upbringing and the environment he laboured in, you'd think him all right.

'What are they doing here?' asked Will.

'Dunno, but the likes of 'em always bring trouble in their wake.'

Allen handed Will his practice blades, knowing the young Englishman always liked to warm up with his weapons before starting his day's work beside the forge.

Will thanked him, then circled around the groups of mercenaries in the centre of the quad, giving them as wide a berth as possible, hoping they wouldn't notice him. He estimated there were about twenty men, many wearing toughened leather, a few with chain mail across their arms and shoulders. They were loud and boisterous – safety in numbers bringing a sort of exuberance. Some eyed him as he took up a spot at the furthest end of the quad from them.

Will set to work with his warm-up routines. The cold morning air of England took some getting used to after the warmer climes in which he had spent most of his life. One week after arriving at Leeds Castle, having been given a tiny room that was more akin to a prison cell, he had contracted a terrible fever that he put down to a chill wind on his wet hair.

He sweated for days, hallucinating battles with the serpents of Azi Dahäg in Azerbaijan. He had been ill before, especially in his early days onboard the galleys, but this was different, for he was in the web of an enemy, where sympathy and assistance would not be forthcoming. Yet it did come and he had been asking himself why. Only after Li, Rathbone's Chinese bodyguard, visited him and administered a herbal drink did the fever break and he was able to get back on his feet. He never knew why Li had done that, whether he was told to do it or for another reason. However, by the time Will was well again, the man from Cathay had already departed with Rathbone, leaving Will unable to thank him.

'Oi, you.'

The voice was aggressive and gruff. Will hoped whoever spoke wasn't addressing him. He carried on. Then he noticed a rough-looking fellow and one other break away from the pack of mercenaries and head towards him. He looked up.

'You,' the man pointed his finger at Will.

This didn't look good. Will let the practice blade go loose in his hand in case he needed to use it to bludgeon this fellow, who was armed with a real sword.

'Yes,' Will said.

He noticed the other swords-for-hire turn their attention towards him to see what was about to happen.

'I know you,' the man snapped his fingers at him.

'Where'd you know him from, Ned?' asked the other fellow with him. Ned didn't look too bright and he was trying to express himself but having difficulty with it.

'"The Stag", Canterbury, 'bout two years ago,' said Ned.

Will had tried very hard to erase that day from his mind, for it had resulted in the deaths of Kostas, Mikael and Ismail and a terrible injury to Commander Konjic. He, Awa and Gurkan had only just managed to escape with their lives, before the place burnt down. It had been one of the most traumatic days of his life. The lifeless faces of his fellow Rüzgar who perished that day were still fresh in his mind.

'See,' Ned rolled down his collar to reveal a horrible burn mark on his neck. Will's face twitched at the sight of it. 'The witch, she burnt the place down, and you was with her, weren't yah?'

There was no denying it, Will had been there. This Ned fellow knew it. If he tried to refute it, or even defend Awa, it was only going to make matters worse.

'I was, mate,' said Will cautiously.

'Told yah,' Ned said, turning to the fellow beside him.

'The witch, she put a spell on me,' Will continued. 'Made me do terrible things, betray Englishmen, my brothers. It was horrible. Thank God Almighty, He freed me from her enchantment. I'm now employed by the Earl here.'

'Oh,' said Ned, who seemed not to know what else to say, having been caught off guard by this account.

'See, Ned, he's all right,' said the man with him.

'It hurts, though,' said Ned, rubbing his neck. 'Specially at night.'

'I'm so sorry,' said Will, forcing as much sympathy as he could muster.

The fellow with Ned nodded at Will, as if to acknowledge Ned wasn't the brightest spark around. The two men walked back to the group. Will let out a sigh of relief and continued his drill.

Later that morning, after he had completed his practice session and was returning his weapons to the quartermaster, he heard the sound of hooves on the gravel approaching the postern gate. Shortly thereafter Sir Reginald Rathbone strode pompously through the quad and towards the inner bailey. Will poked his head around the postern and could see Li taking the reins of their horses and leading them to the stables. Will decided to follow him. He needed to thank the Chinese bodyguard for helping to break his fever and wanted to do it before he missed him again.

The stables were down at the southern end of the castle. Will pursued the trail, hoofprints clearly marking the muddy ground. Li entered the enclosure that housed the stables and disappeared from view. Will followed through the gate of the enclosure and noticed four buildings, each of which had half a dozen box stalls with hay for the horses. Li took the two horses to the stall at the furthest end, having walked past another batch of new mercenaries, who must have arrived during the night. These six men lounged around a barrel, their clothing semi-military, their weapons confidently by their side. They seemed fascinated by Li, and Will spotted two of them sniggering at the diminutive Chinaman, who was wearing a pointed straw hat, which looked like a slightly flattened cone. Though it was odd in appearance, Will imagined it worked well keeping the rain off the wearer's face.

'You!' the tallest in the group shouted at Li, who was still holding the reins of the horses.

Li ignored them. He didn't even turn to look their way. Will slowed down, not wanting to get embroiled in whatever was going to happen.

'Speak English?' the tall man shouted at Li, who disappeared from view, going inside with the two horses.

'Must be deaf, Angus,' said a fellow with a brown hood.

Angus peeped back at his friend, then noticed Will standing by the gate. 'What do you want?' Angus asked Will. 'Clear off.'

Will held up his hands and decided to move towards the nearest stable to get out of Angus's line of sight. Will loitered by the door, as he wanted to speak to Li, but was also intrigued to see what these well-armed men were going to do.

Li emerged from the stables and headed back towards the castle as if nothing had happened, completely ignoring the mercenaries.

'No you don't,' Angus said, blocking his path. The other five fellows came to stand beside him, forming a line.

'Where you from, little man?' asked Angus, his thumbs hooked into his belt. He towered over the easterner, and Will had to shift his position in order to observe Li through the pack of soldiers surrounding him.

Li's expression was passive. He eyed the enclosure gate and noticed Will standing beside the first stable, doing a poor job of concealing himself.

Angus strode forward and shoved Li in the chest, but the smaller man barely moved. Angus followed up by taking a swipe at Li's pointed hat. The Chinaman simply squatted, and Angus arm swiped through thin air, causing the soldier to stumble forward. Li took a step back to avoid him and looked ahead once more.

'You what?' cried out one of the other fellows. 'What he do?'

Angus stood back up, rolling his shoulders. 'You trying to make me look stupid?' he said, as he drew a blade from the back of his waist. Will moved forward: he wanted to at least try to even up the fight. Li noticed Will's shift in position. Angus lunged at Li. The man from Cathay simply moved his body out of the way, so his chest was parallel to Angus's arm, before he grabbed the bigger man's wrist and with his thumb applied pressure to a nerve, causing Angus to release the blade and cry out. Li twisted the bigger man's arm, sending him spiralling full circle, landing in a heap on his back.

One of the other soldiers swung a cudgel at Li's head, but he ducked, before kicking the knee of the new assailant, causing his leg to buckle, then chopping the man around the ears, at which the fellow cried out in pain, falling to his knees. Two others hurled themselves at him. With what seemed like the slightest of efforts, Li launched himself into the air. A split kick saw his right foot connect with the face of one man and his left with the other. Both toppled over. As soon as Li landed, he went down on his haunches to avoid the attacks of the fifth and sixth men, then swivelled his legs around, knocking both men to the ground, before rising and chopping each one with his hand on the side of the neck. They also collapsed.

Li stood up straight. He adjusted his hat so it was centred once more and, without even looking behind him at the six figures sprawling injured in the mud, walked in Will's direction as if nothing had happened. Giving Will the briefest consideration, during which he must have noticed Will's mouth wide open, the man from Cathay passed through the enclosure gate. It was only after Li had walked back towards the castle, that Will remembered why he had followed the Chinaman to the stables. His gratitude would need to wait till the next time they met.

11

SIBLING MADNESS

CLANG WENT THE BLUNT SWORDS as they kissed and separated. Princess Fatma moved back with a deft skip as her handmaiden and first tutor in the art of the blade, Ulyana, advanced with speed. Fatma blocked the next thrust, before countering with a swipe to the left of her opponent, followed by one to the right. Ulyana avoided the last one by ducking low, then shifting out of the way and around Fatma, so she had a clear strike against Fatma's back. Despite the hours Fatma spent sparring with her handmaiden, she always seemed to fall foul of this particular manoeuvre. In a real fight it would be the end of her. It was fortunate then she was never going to be in a real fight, she often remarked to herself.

'Always miss that one,' said Fatma as Ulyana tapped her on the shoulder with her blade.

'Your Highness you must predict ...'

'I know, what the opponent will do next,' Fatma interjected.

'Exactly,' replied Ulyana.

Fatma was keen to practise her swordplay, but never sufficiently motivated to pay attention to every detail, since she would never have practical use for it. She was a Princess in the household of the most powerful family in the world, living in the most heavily protected city in the world, sheltered within the royal palace ringed with battalions of loyal Janissaries and regular soldiers. What threat could there ever be to her person? At the very most she might break her fingernail against a sword or twist her ankle landing from a jump. Yet, she still longed for the opportunity to test her skill in a real fight.

'Humph!' grumbled Fumu.

'Oh be quiet, Fumu,' jested Fatma.

Her personal bodyguard, appointed to her service when she was a child, was standing, back turned to her, staring out of a narrow window that offered a magnificent view over the Bosporus. They were in one of the outer rooms of the palace, used as a storage facility, but often covertly occupied for a practice session away from the prying eyes of the court and its officials. It was better to keep it that way, since a Princess was not expected nor encouraged to engage in such activities, normally the preserve of her brothers.

'I think we are done for the day, Ulyana,' said Fatma.

'Yes, Your Highness.'

Fatma rotated the sword around in her hand as she and Ulyana walked over to the table at one end of the storage chamber, where a tray of sherbet awaited them. Picking up a glass, she sipped the refreshing drink and offered one to her handmaiden.

'You can turn around, Fumu,' Fatma called out to him.

The Kikongo bodyguard looked back over his shoulder towards her and nodded. Though he never said it, she reckoned he actually supported her efforts with the blade, since in his tribe, both men and women were taught and encouraged in the martial ways. The decorum of the Ottoman court meant it was better he never saw her actually fight; should he ever be questioned about it under oath, he would not be lying. She would hate for him or any of those who served her to be placed in jeopardy for something she did. Too often she had seen her father remove an entire cohort to cover up a matter he wished to keep hidden, or to punish a group for the errors of one individual.

Had the moderating ways of Safiye Sultan not been present, there would have been a bloodbath in the household staff following the last assassination attempt on her father's life, on the night the Englishman, Thomas Dallam, played his organ. It had been an eerie evening, made unnerving and sinister by assassins coming from the ranks of the Janissaries. The presence of the gallant Rüzgar, and in particular another Englishman, Will Ryde, proved invaluable in safeguarding the life of her father, the Sultan. Young Ryde always seemed to be on the edge of her memory. What happened to him the night the other Rüzgar fled the city? He had not been seen since, nor was there any sign of him anywhere in the city.

Fumu approached, head bowed and waited a few feet away as she finished her sherbet.

'Still no news of Will Ryde?' asked Fatma.

'No, Your Highness,' replied Fumu.

It was more than four months since that fateful evening when she waited in her carriage, only to see Awa, Gurkan and Anver emerge, but not Will. How much longer would she continue to remember the gallant Englishman?

'I think ... oh, I really don't know what to think,' mumbled Fatma.

She was due to be married to the new Grand Vizier, Kanijeli Siyavuş Pasha, a man far senior in years than her. Like many royal weddings it was political in its nature, neither one desiring to wed the other. At least she knew she had no feelings whatsoever for Kanijeli and he also felt the same towards her. Their marriage would be purely transactional in nature; love was not in the equation.

'Any other interesting titbits of information you might have from the world outside the palace, Fumu?' asked Fatma.

'It is as it was,' replied Fumu.

'Something must have changed, or happened,' Fatma pushed back.

She could see his troubled brow and knew the topic he was avoiding mentioning was the very one she wanted to hear about. 'And what of the ... you know ...' Fatma fluttered her hand around the side of her head.

Fumu looked left and right before clearing his throat. 'There are more cases reported daily across the city.'

'So something has changed. It's got worse than before.'

'Yes, Your Highness.'

Fatma wiped her brow with a handkerchief before straightening her clothes and throwing on a loose-fitting robe, raising its hood over her head. Ulyana followed by donning her robe, and they both departed from the storehouse to which they had come under the pretence of doing some painting, with Fumu trailing behind. As they exited and joined the floral pathway leading back to the palace, Fumu made a clicking sound with his mouth, replicating the calling of a bird, which was a signal for two serving staff to rush in and tidy up the storehouse, removing all traces of the sword-practice.

The martial sessions with the blade always left her with abundant energy and as it was still early morning, when much of the household slept, Fatma planned to stay awake through her next class when her philosophy tutor arrived for instruction on comparative works and ideas from the pre-modern world. At times she wondered what the point of learning was, when she would have no reason to use it. Yet Safiye Sultan insisted Fatma sharpen her mind through study, as she would one day need guile and intellect to navigate the political world and the treachery of the Ottoman household. She reminded Fatma she would be sharing a pillow with the Grand Vizier, the right hand of the Sultan, which would in turn place her in a position of great influence. Suggestions she made could become policy and affect the lives of tens of thousands. It was not a trifling matter and Fatma knew it was a responsibility she ought to take more seriously, but spending hours in tedious talks about political alliances and administrative choices quite frankly seemed to her a dull prospect.

The path sloped up an incline, and as they crested it the palace proper came into view. 'Ulyana, were you able to fetch the obsidian stone from the souk?'

'No, Your Highness.'

'Why ever not?'

'They did not have it in the local bazaar.'

'Try the market over at Fatih: they are well stocked.'

'I did, Your Highness,' said Ulyana. 'They also had no stock, nor did the Grand Bazaar. Everywhere I went there seems to be a shortage of obsidian.'

'Whatever is going on, if even the Grand Bazaar has run out?' asked Fatma.

'It seems someone has been buying up all of the obsidian in the city.'

'What need has someone for a worthless volcanic rock?'

'You have a need for it, Your Highness.'

'Yes, but that is for jewellery. I can't imagine all of the obsidian in the city being used to make jewels. It would be absurd. What else can it be for?'

'I do not know, Your Highness.'

'Well, there will be new supplies soon. With the number of merchants and traders my father has invited to attend the Great Fair, Istanbul will be awash with plenty. It will quite something, unlike anything this city has seen before.'

'Yes, Your Highness.'

The pair continued to navigate the slope with Fumu some paces behind. Once through the palace gates and into the outer courtyard Fumu dropped back. Fatma and Ulyana strode on, passing the personal chambers of the Sultan where he would no doubt be resting at this time. The next corridor led on to the chambers of her brother, Mehmet, Crown Prince and heir to the throne. He was destined to become the most powerful man in the world after the death of her father.

Fatma came to a halt, as did Ulyana. She stared intently at the tightly shut oak doors to Mehmet's chamber, which had two guards posted outside, standing sideways, so they could at all times keep an eye on the door. It was an odd position, but then this was an odd situation for them to be in.

'Maybe he is sleeping, Your Highness,' Ulyana whispered.

'I hope so,' sighed Fatma, before continuing down the corridor. As she approached, one of the guards recognised her and he lowered his gaze. The other one followed his example.

It was then Fatma heard the ghoulish moan from within the chamber. She froze, as did Ulyana. The two guards tensed, gripping their spears. The sound was followed by feet running across the marble floor, before the thud of a body slamming against the other side of the door, sending a shocking vibration up and down it. Her brother's wailing voice grew louder; he was speaking in a tongue unfamiliar to her. The hairs on her neck stood up in fear every time she heard him utter such words.

'By God,' Ulyana whispered, gripping Fatma's hand.

Fatma didn't know if it was by God, but the Creator seemed absent from the palace. Great wickedness was perpetrated within these walls. It seemed to her there was no place for God within the Topkapi, other than in the Hall of Religious Relics.

'Come quickly, Ulyana,' Fatma said, tightly gripping the hand of her handmaiden as they hastily hurried past Prince Mehmet's chambers. She briskly marched on until she couldn't hear him. It was only after turning the corner at the end of the corridor that she slowed down. She had not prayed for longer than she cared to remember, but hearing her brother just now, made her reconsider. No, she steeled herself, she would not be driven by fear to turn to God. Faith was pointless if it depended on distress to bring its adherents to worship.

'The Crown Prince is ...' Ulyana was saying.

'Yes,' Fatma cut her off, placing her index finger to the lips of her handmaiden, so she did not utter what she knew.

There was no getting away from it: Mehmet, Crown Prince and heir to the Ottoman Empire, was, like many others in the city, possessed by some unknown force.

12

NICER PLACE

STEAMING BOILED MUTTON NESTLED ON a pewter platter for Will as he sat down at the table of his mother Anne's new home close to Charterhouse. He picked up a piece of bread, dipping it into the centre of the platter, salivating at the expected taste, before taking a mouthful. It was far too hot.

'Let it cool down, Will,' said Anne. 'You'll burn your tongue, my boy.'

Will madly waved his hand about before his mouth, trying to bring some relief, blowing out steam as he did.

'It's not running away from you, is it?'

Will continued to let heat evaporate from his mouth, eyes watering, before he was able to swallow the mouthful. 'No, Mother, it's not.'

'Well then, take your time and enjoy it.'

'Yes, Mother,' said Will.

His mother had been moved, courtesy of the Earl of Rothminster, to roomier accommodation on a street occupied by many tenants who were in some way connected to the Earl and his network. Anne had been mightily suspicious when Will turned up, informing her they were going to move into this new place, but there was no way he could let her know about the deal he had struck with the Earl of Rothminster. He intended to honour his promise to the Earl, no matter what happened. His mother's life depended on it.

Neither Rothminster nor Rathbone trusted him, believing he had turned Turk, but to guarantee his allegiance to them and not the Ottomans, he was to ensure his mother was housed in property owned by the Earl and surrounded by the English nobleman's cronies. *It's not as if she is in prison*, Will reminded himself. In fact, the living accommodation was far grander than anywhere she had lived before. His mother's friends from the marketplace even complimented her on the fact that Will was such a good lad, which these days was rare, that he'd chosen to invest his earnings in getting a better place for her rather than spending money on fancy clothes, which seemed all the rage these days in London. But the fact remained that in this place she was always under the watchful eye of someone loyal to the Earl – and this mightily troubled Will. Any suspicious move on his part placed her life in jeopardy. He couldn't allow that to happen, but at this moment his hands were tied; he was forced to play the Earl's game. He knew neither the rules nor the boundaries, and this left him anxious – always.

'Now,' Anne reached out across the table, squeezing his hand and speaking more quietly than before. 'Are you going to tell me what's really going on? How is it you can afford to move us here?'

There was no denying it was suspicious. He was neither an officer nor a gentleman of any standing, and the others occupying this row of houses were all of moderate worth.

'As I said before, Mother ...'

'I know what you said, my lad, but I don't believe it. One minute you're off gallivanting with them Turks in Istanbul, then you're back here in England living in a castle in Maidstone, and whenever you visit me in London, you're with that Chinese fellow out front, who is like a shadow, never too far away. What exactly do you do, Will?'

Will grimaced at the cross-examination. She knew about the Janissaries and how he was part of an elite guard, having met Commander Konjic, Awa and Gurkan when the rest of the unit had been in England. But trying to explain why he was posted to England, to Maidstone of all places, was difficult.

He turned his attention back to the present. 'It's a sort of exchange,' he mumbled, trying a slightly different tack.

'What?'

'We exchange information between the Turks and England and vice versa. As I am an Englishman employed by the Turkish Janissaries, I am a perfect candidate to act as a bridge.'

'Bridge?' enquired Anne.

'Like a liaison between two parties who want to trade information and maybe resources in the interests of a mutual alliance.'

Anne scrutinised him. Will turned away, not wanting to meet her gaze, and she was too maternally kind to push him further.

'All right, if you say so. But I'm not having it, all seems nonsense to me.'

'Politics is like that, Mother.'

'Now you're a politician. God in Heaven! You'll be telling me you're standing as a Member of Parliament next, all dressed up in finery and sitting in the Commons.'

There was no chance of that ever happening. Will took another spoonful of food so he didn't have to reply. Once more he took it from the centre of his platter and once more it was too hot.

'Anyway, I won't ask you again. Now tell me about the Chinaman. What's his name?'

'His name?'

73

'Yes. He does have one, doesn't he? Or are you going to tell me you don't know your own shadow's name!'

'I do, Mother. His name is Li.'

'Is that a first or a last name?'

Come to think of it, Will didn't know himself. 'I, umm ... must be a last name, I think.'

'So it's Master Li.'

'Yes, but why ...?' Will was saying when his mother got up from the table, made for the door and then disappeared out onto the street. Will sat in shocked silence for a moment, unsure what had just happened.

Then Anne reappeared, with Li beside her. Will tensed, seeing Rathbone's bodyguard standing next to his mother.

'Come on, Master Li. It was so rude of Will not to have invited you in before,' Anne was saying, as Will watched, gawping.

'Close your mouth, my boy, or a fly will go in,' Anne instructed.

Li paused at the door, surveying the room.

'No one will bite you, Master Li, come, sit, here,' Anne pointed at the chair between her and Will at a small table.

Will wanted to say something to warn his mother. He had seen Li fight. This was a dangerous man, perhaps deadlier than Stukely, Rathbone's previous bodyguard, but at present Will was lost for words.

Li hesitantly entered the home, taking his boots off at the door as he did. He came tentatively forward in stockinged feet on the creaky floorboards, looking at Will, before sitting in the chair next to him. The young Englishman was sweating, partly a result of eating the food when it was too hot and partly at the sight of a deadly killer at his dear mother's dinner table. Will's heart raced. Anne placed a platter before Li.

'Shall I serve you a portion?' Anne asked, motioning to the mutton.

Li looked from Anne to the mutton, then to Will.

'Ignore my son, Master Li, this is my home, and you are my guest. A home is a place of joy when all else is grim.'

Li nodded.

Anne loaded a generous portion onto Li's platter. 'There you go Master Li, now eat heartily.'

Li's hand went to the inside of his coat, Will froze, expecting the worst. Did he possess a blade or another deadly weapon? Li removed a narrow bundle wrapped in a fine silk handkerchief. He unwrapped the item: two narrow sticks appeared, each slightly thicker at one end. He held these items, which looked as long as the knife in Will's hand, before applying them to the pieces of mutton, which he then popped into his mouth.

'Forsooth, Master Li. What a curious implement!'

'Chopstick,' said Li, in a gentle voice. Will had never heard the Chinaman speak before, but now that he had, he felt a little more at ease.

'Stop gaping at our guest's eating utensils, Will. Apply yourself to your food or you'll be complaining that it got cold.'

'Yes, Mother,' Will replied.

They ate in silence. With fluid movements Li scooped the mutton into his mouth, all the while working from the outer edge into the centre, as though he was following a charted course across the plate. It made Will feel awkward and clumsy, as if he lacked good manners himself. He remembered feeling this way whenever he was with Awa, who came from a culture far more refined and advanced than his own.

'Now tell me, is it Master Li, or is it Master ... something ... Li?' Anne asked, with a smile.

Li sat a little straighter, returning the smile with a thin one of his one. Will had never seen him wear any other expression than emotionlessness or a scowl.

'Master Li.'

Anne turned to Will, nodding approvingly.

'Well then, Master Li, let me serve you some more.'

13

HIDDEN SCIENCES

DUSTY SHELVES FILLED WITH VOLUMES of academic works lined the walls of the *kitabevi*, the bookshop, which was a home from home for Awa. On her return to Istanbul two days previously with Gurkan and Anver, they had secretly taken up residence in the basement of the Society of Miniaturists, in the Fatih district of the city. They were sent there by the former Grand Vizier, Sardar Ferhad Pasha, who had visited them in Konya, to give them what during the time of Commander Konjic would have been called a mission, but as on this occasion they were operating outside any recognised boundaries, Awa wasn't entirely sure what to call it. This assignment was a plea for help from the city as the Rüzgar, were, after all, responsible for its current plight.

The unit could have refused the request, but collectively Awa knew they all felt answerable in some way for releasing Zawaba'a - though how they were going to banish the Jinn once more remained an absolute mystery to her. She needed to take her mind off such matters and so to relax she came to the *kitabevi* where she felt most at ease, because it reminded her of the libraries with tomes of scholarly works in her beloved home city of Timbuktu.

Draining the remnants of her *kahwe*, the Turkish coffee she had grown so fond of during her time in the city, she closed Muhyiddin Ibn Arabi's *al-Ittihad al-kawni: The Universal Tree and the Four Birds*, a book of poetry and prose. It was a book she had been looking forward to reading for some time, but surprisingly she had had trouble locating it in the libraries of Konya, though the librarian insisted they possessed a fine collection of works by Ibn Arabi and could match any volume found in Istanbul. Clearly not.

She scanned the bookshop, fairly empty this morning, and got up from the wooden stool on which she was sitting. She returned the manuscript to the bookshelf from which she had taken it earlier that morning, before tidying up her coffee glass and leaving it in the wicker basket on the counter to be washed later. As she left the *kitabevi*, she bade farewell to the owner who was pleased to see one of his regulars return after a considerable break. Their mission was covert in the city; they had to avoid detection by Commander Berk or any of his acolytes as well as steering clear of certain members of the royal family who might recognise them. However, the bookseller neither knew of her profession nor had any idea who she was so, as far as she could tell, visiting the *kitabevi* was not going to pose any sort of problem for their task or safety.

Awa raised the hood over her head and strode down the narrow cobblestone pathways of the Fatih district, its crammed buildings looming over large sections of the street, some threatening to keel over and knock into buildings on the other side. The area was normally busy at this time of the morning, but there was an eerie silence today. People were dotted about rather than packing the pathways, going about their daily business. Ordinarily the residents of this boisterous district were an enchanting group, always eager to engage her, a foreigner in their city, in conversation. Yet the inhabitants who had crossed her path these past two days were silent and sour, avoiding conversation and shuffling about as though deliberately avoiding human contact. Women hid their faces within the folds of their scarves, men did the same, pulling the material of their turbans across to cover their noses and mouths. There was no plague in the city as far as she knew, yet everyone was guarded, as though they might catch something from a passer-by. The mood in this part of the city had changed. People were afraid.

No one was able to explain to the populace why there was a spike in the number of citizens being possessed, whether in a benign or a violent manner. The authorities did not declare publicly what they knew secretly, nor did they reassure the people in any way. Rather, they let people muddle along, as the rumour mill got to work, and residents were left unsure as to when this situation would end. This uncertainty made fear a certainty – dread of one's neighbour and terror of the unknown. She spotted the stone building of the Society of Miniaturists and proceeded towards it. As she entered, a little bell over the door rang, and she was struck once more by the pungent smell of egg-white, a staple ingredient used by the artists.

'Salaam,' she said to the artist hunched over the table close to the entrance. He seemed a permanent fixture and, now that she thought of it, she had never actually seen his face.

He waved her through. Walking past easels holding drying paintings, Awa went down the corridor, emerging into the square vestibule with its images of mythical tales from Persia, Greece and further afield. She carried on, passing the room where over a year ago she had come across vivid, fantastical sketches emanating from deep in the Sultan's inner self, which were compiled in his *Kitabü'l-Menamat*, or *The Book of Dreams*. That had been when she first heard about the

Armour of David, though she didn't know what it was then, and there was mention of Zawaba'a, in the picture illustrating the manuscript of Haji Ataie. An inconceivable series of events had taken place since then, including the deaths of Commander Konjic and Master Huja. Possibly they could add Will to the same list, as no one had seen or heard of him since the fateful night they returned to Istanbul and were arrested by Commander Berk.

Further along the narrow corridor she came to stand beside a curtain. She parted it, opened the door behind it and proceeded down the tapering staircase into a basement, where she found Gurkan, Anver and Master Lütfi Abdullah, the Chief Miniaturist and confidant of their late Commander Konjic and, it would seem, of the former Grand Vizier Sardar Ferhad Pasha. They were seated on a set of *divans*, the couches placed on a fine silk-embroidered Persian carpet.

'Did you find a copy of *The Universal Tree and the Four Birds* by Ibn Arabi?' Anver asked.

'Yes, they had two copies at the *kitabevi*,' replied Awa.

'Unlike in Konya,' snorted Anver.

'No!' Gurkan interjected. 'We have copies. They were simply misplaced when you went to the library.'

'For two months,' said Anver.

'Overdue, kept no doubt by a book lover, much like our dear Awa here,' said Gurkan.

'I think not!' Anver replied.

'Are you, my Venetian friend, accusing the great Konyan city, the home of Maulana Rumi and Shams of Tabriz of being short of books?' asked Gurkan, rising to his feet in a playful manner.

'I am,' Anver replied without hesitation.

'Then we will duel for the honour of my great city!' Gurkan exclaimed, waving his finger about in the air.

'Now, now,' Lütfi interjected.

Gurkan searched around in his kaftan pocket for something. 'Where did I put it?'

Meanwhile, Anver went to his trusty sack and rummaged around inside it. A perplexed Lütfi looked from one to the other, then at Awa, who merely smiled. She had seen them go through this routine before.

'Aha!' Anver revolved on the spot, holding a hand-puppet, which he wore like a glove. It was colourfully designed in a patchwork of what appeared to be remnants of fabric from a tailor's shop. The puppet wore a turban and was clutching a pen.

'Wait ...' Gurkan was saying as he went to look in his bags.

'What is going on?' Lütfi asked Awa.

'A puppet duel, Master Lütfi,' Awa replied, grinning at the bemused miniaturist.

'I ... seem to have forgotten to bring my puppet,' said Gurkan looking up at Anver in disappointment.

'Then victory is declared to Ismail al-Jazari over Jalal ad-Din Rumi,' proclaimed Anver, jumping on the spot.

'Wait, you have hand-puppets of al-Jazari and Rumi?' asked Lütfi.

'Why, of course,' Anver replied. 'Engineering and science versus poetry and metaphysics. And the winner, engineering and science!'

Lütfi shook his head. 'Both of you have it wrong, it's not engineering and science versus poetry and metaphysics, it's all of them together. Our tradition is one in which different disciplines cooperate. We are not reductionists, breaking knowledge into separate baskets, for all knowledge is connected to the Creator. God encourages you to be both a scientist and a poet.'

Anver and Gurkan stood solemnly, heads lowered, before flashing one another a cheeky smile and breaking into a fit of laughter.

'What?' asked Lütfi.

'That's exactly what the imam told these two in Konya the last time they decided to have a puppet duel,' Awa said.

Lütfi cleared his throat, a smile curving his lips as he took in the strange humour of the young Rüzgar.

'All right, my young friends, we have plenty of work to do, so you now need to concentrate on the task at hand. Please draw up a chair and come and join me at the table.' The miniaturist stood up and walked over to a table laden with manuscripts.

Awa noticed the documents on the table were written in multiple languages, some of which she did not recognise.

'It is true I run the Society of Miniaturists and have the pleasure of illustrating a number of works. Yet I also wear another hat, for I am the Keeper of the Hidden Scrolls.'

'Hidden?' asked Gurkan.

'There is a *tafṣīl*, a section, within the palace library entitled *al-ʿulūm al-khafiyya*, the hidden sciences.'

'Why is it hidden?' Gurkan followed up.

'The knowledge contained within those books, scrolls and other documents, is not learning that can be shared with the masses, for it contains knowledge and know-how that can breed immense harm if harnessed by the wrong person.'

'Like what?' asked Gurkan.

'You will need to see it, for once I show you the catalogue of collections, it will become obvious.'

'Who else knows of its existence, Master Lütfi?' Awa asked.

'Only a few. You can count them on your fingers.'

'So why are you telling us about the library section of the hidden sciences?' enquired Awa.

'The Jinn Zawaba'a that was released in Jerusalem is from a previous time, when Solomon the Wise was King of Kings, and the Jinn were under his command. Some of the essential knowledge from that era is recorded in these books. The answer

82

to how to return the Jinn to its former state, by trapping it inside some sort of vessel, may reside within these collections.'

'Is there anything else you can tell us about the texts?'

'We who have been given this trust do not talk about the contents of the hidden section unless we are physically in its presence. This has been our custom since the first collection was compiled by the Ottoman librarian Khayr al-din 'Atufi. Should others learn of its existence, then protecting the knowledge will become problematic as agents with nefarious intentions may seek it out. Presently, it's simply under lock and key, deep within the palace library, in a room of its own. Even for the guards patrolling outside the library it is simply a room with a few more books. We would like to keep it that way.'

'Do you have any books written by al-Jazari?' Anver asked.

Lütfi smiled. 'More than you can imagine.'

'I have read all of his works,' Anver said.

'No, my young friend. You would not have read *these* works.'

14

UNEXPECTED RETURN

HAMMERING STEEL FELT RELAXING. FOR a start it kept him warm on a cold May day. Though Will waited eagerly for the arrival of kinder warmer weather, he was yet to experience such a thing in Maidstone. Most of the time it was cold, blustery and sodden with rain, or it was just cold. Quartermaster Allen's forge glowed red-hot, and Will found the familiar smells and heat of such a workshop were like a pair of well-worn shoes; he comfortably slipped back into the role of apprentice to a quartermaster, a role he had fulfilled as a young man in Marrakesh.

Over the past few weeks he had witnessed batches of new soldiers arriving, undergoing training and then departing, back to distant parts of England, most of which he hadn't heard of. But his sense of the geography of his native land had begun to improve after he found a map of the British Isles and started identifying where regiments of soldiers came from. Some arrived from Lincoln, others Dorset, a few from Durham. He tried to decipher from a few of them what they were doing, but most were gormless buffoons and had just been told they'd get a good meal and some shillings for their efforts. Each battalion was led by a Captain and they all steered clear of Will. It seemed to the young Englishman that the Earl of Rothminster was training up his own mercenary force, loyal to him, who would act at his beck and call. But what exactly were they planning on doing?

Whatever it was, Will warranted that Lord Burghley and the Elizabethan court weren't privy to it. In fact, it was most likely to be violating the goals of the Crown and its Government. Yet, what did he know, he would often remind himself. He had briefly met the rulers of England, but that was only because of being with Commander Konjic. Now his former officer was no more and Will found himself working for the very man they had opposed less than two years ago.

'Here's a new batch of knives needs sharpening, Will,' said the gruff quartermaster. He placed the clutch of metal on the stone table beside the hearth.

'Some of those look well gone,' replied Will.

'Bah!' Allen moaned. 'This lot wouldn't know a farmer's pitchfork from a knight's blade.' The quartermaster spat into the forge.

'Where'd they come from?'

'Arrived this morning from some hamlet in Wakefield. Lazy oafs, barking orders, when they haven't got nothing up 'ere,' he said, tapping his head.

Allen might be crabby and cranky, but as Will had learnt over the past three months, the old quartermaster kept his ears to the ground and knew a thing or two about the comings and goings around the castle. He rarely shared anything useful with Will; no doubt Rathbone had instructed him to keep his mouth shut when conversing with Will on anything that could be used by the young Englishman against the Earl.

'Just finishing this foil and I will get on to the knives straight after.'

'Good lad.'

The workshop was close to the stable lodge at the main entrance. This allowed visitors who needed work done on their weapons to drop them into the workshop and collect them as they departed. External tradesmen could also come in and leave their metal for Allen, when the quartermaster wasn't fully occupied with work for the Earl. They kept the windows open and the door ajar to let the cool air in. Will noticed a figure standing by the entrance. It was Li, with his pointed hat. He looked at Will and nodded his head once.

Allen also saw him. 'Looks like you're wanted by His Lordship.'

Will had not spoken with the Earl or Rathbone after the first day. He had seen both of them around the castle, but they had ignored him. Will imagined that in their estimation he was nothing more than a servant, only to be summoned when there was some need. Now there was a need and Will was eager to find out what it was.

'Can you continue with the foil, Allen, while it's hot?' asked Will.

'Suppose I can. Now off with yah.'

Will grabbed a cloth by the entrance, wiping the sweat off his face, before he donned a padded doublet and followed Li. They wound their way through the inner bailey, ending up in a spot Will had never visited before. Li swung open an iron gate, and they entered the garden Will had seen briefly on the day of his arrival. The lawn was neatly trimmed, with beds of cowslips running around the outer edges. A sole willow stood proudly in the centre of the garden and beside it some chairs and a table, at which sat the Earl of Rothminster and Sir Reginald Rathbone. Uncertain about their intentions, Will hesitated as he came forward, but he picked up the pace after he noticeably fell behind Li. Only when they were within a few yards of the pair did Li stop. They waited in silence.

It was Rathbone, seated opposite the Earl, who first looked up. 'Ryde, how are we doing?'

'Well, sir.' Will thought it best to use as few words as possible.

'And your mother?' Rathbone asked.

'She is well.' A sudden panic went through him. Had something happened to his mother? These two scoundrels would know before him.

'For her sake let us ensure you remember who you work for. Otherwise we'll send Li here one evening to make sure she doesn't wake up the next morning,' Rathbone passed his finger across his neck, a cruel smile upon his face.

Will glared at Li, who remained impassive. He had eaten a meal at his mother's table. Would he be so cold as to obey Rathbone's instructions and murder her in her sleep? Will didn't know Li well enough to say, but he couldn't risk his mother's life over such a matter.

'Let us turn our attention to more agreeable thoughts, Sir Reginald,' said the Earl, looking Will up and down.

'Indeed,' Rathbone added with a sardonic sneer.

'It seems, Will Ryde, that you will be returning to Istanbul,' said the Earl.

Will's mind raced at the statement. What were they going to get him to do? He wasn't exactly welcome back in the city. Berk had only released him to deliver a message, but if he were to go back what welcome was he going to get? Nevertheless, the opportunity would also enable him to find out where his friends were, or even if they were still alive. The thought was exhilarating yet depressing.

'The Ottoman Sultan Murad III has organised what his court claims will be the world's greatest trade fair in Istanbul this September. Invitations have been sent to all and sundry. The Sultan wishes to make peace and trade with all nations. Humph. Odd, is it not Rathbone?'

'Yes, Your Lordship, for a man who was hell-bent on making war with the Persians as well as the Moroccans only months ago, it is quite a turnaround,' replied Rathbone.

'Like Janus, the Ottomans present two faces to the world: trade with us or we will wage war. This is the result of power: those who have it, wield it with uncompromising force; those who aspire to it, play the game till it is time for them to take the lead. We are players for now, but England's time will come. The world is turning and the English are changing with it. We are incorporating joint-stockholding companies for merchant adventurers to go forth into the world and vigorously engage in commerce in new markets. The Queen, for all her faults, has at least listened to this advice and supported these ventures with military muscle,' the Earl stated.

Will remained silent.

'I have been asked by Her Majesty to represent this blessed nation in Istanbul, to present myself to the Sultan on behalf of the Queen, to forge an alliance with the Ottomans that will fill our Exchequer with riches from the East,' said the Earl.

Will still didn't understand why the Crown had assigned the Earl a charter to the East when they were presented to the Queen at Nonsuch Palace. Rothminster's hands were soiled by the theft of the Staff of Moses. Now he was possibly going to meet the Sultan himself, when Lord Burghley had tipped Will off that the Earl was the one who had sent assassins to kill the most powerful man in the world. He felt dizzy when considering the politics at play. Part of him wanted to run – to take his mother and flee from England. But where would they go? Istanbul was too dangerous for him to return to. Should he go back to Marrakesh? But there he held the status of a slave. The world was an immense place, his travels had shown this to be true, so maybe he should voyage further east. Since returning to England he had heard fantastical tales about the Mughal

Emperors of India and their Peacock Throne. Perchance he would be welcomed there with his mother.

'And you, as well as this Chinaman,' the Earl stared at Li, 'are to accompany us as part of the English delegation.'

'Your Lordship, I am truly honoured ...'

Rathbone cut him off. 'Don't flatter yourself, Ryde. The only reason the Earl is taking you is because he has a task for you.'

'Sir Reginald is quite correct, there is a mission that you and the Chinaman will undertake when in Istanbul. Fail me, and I will have no further use for you, and Rathbone can do with you and your mother as he pleases.'

Will clenched his fists, holding the rage inside him. He tried not to let the fury show on his face, but he was sure he was doing a poor job of hiding it.

'I may not be welcome back in Istanbul considering how I last left,' Will said. His thoughts immediately went back to his dear friends and the fear of what may have happened to them during this time. Were they still under lock and key in that terrible prison?

'Berk? No, I wouldn't worry about him. In fact, he asked about you in his recent correspondence,' the Earl replied.

'He did?'

'Umm, wanted to know whether we'd strung you up from the parapet by now,' said the Earl.

Rathbone chuckled to himself.

'You will be travelling as part of the English delegation and as such will have immunity against any action. That will be the least of your worries when in Istanbul. Completing the mission is all you will need to focus on,' the Earl said.

'And what is the mission, Your Lordship?' Will asked.

'Patience, Ryde,' urged Rathbone. 'You will be told when you need to know. Right now, you should return to servant duties. Be gone.' Sir Reginald waved him away as one would swat a fly and shifted his attention back to the Earl, engaging in hushed conversation.

For a moment Will stood there, but then Li grunted at him and he followed the man from Cathay back out of the gardens and towards the main keep.

'Do you know what they want us to do?' Will asked, uncertain what response he was going to get from the taciturn Oriental.

Li remained silent, marching him out, shutting the iron gate and motioning him away with his arm. Will looked into his face and thought he detected something a little different this time. Was it irritation at the way he had been addressed? Will trudged back to the castle proper. He was going to return to Istanbul, but what kind of second coming was it going to be?

15

LOCK AND KEY

THE EVENING AIR WAS WARM, balmier than in recent days. Despite the sun having set an hour ago, heat still radiated through the summer night as Anver trailed behind Awa and Gurkan. The three young Rüzgar followed the lead of Master Lütfi Abdullah, Chief Miniaturist and Keeper of the Hidden Scrolls, along the palace walls.

Anver's experience of the capital of the Ottoman Empire was limited. His previous stay had been in the fort occupied by Commander Konjic on the other side of the river. The young Venetian had set up an assortment of devices and contraptions for the Rüzgar to use in their line of work. As their current undertaking was not official Janissary business, he wasn't able to venture back to his workshop. He assumed that the items, which to others might have seemed like junk, would by now have been scrapped or sent for use elsewhere.

'Salaam, Master Lütfi,' the guard standing patrol at the outer wall said, when he saw the miniaturist.

'Salaam, Yasin, how is your family?' asked Lütfi.

'With God's grace they are well. You have some guests with you tonight?' Yasin motioned to the Rüzgar.

'Apprentices. Potential librarians who will look after these books when I am gone from this world.'

'You have many years left in you yet.' Yasin stared at the young companions before turning back to the miniaturist. 'They are not what I would expect,' he said with a smile.

'Were you expecting old men, half bent over with age, to look after these books? If we do not let the younger generation in, then they will not have a love for the wisdom in our libraries.'

'Wisely put, Master Lütfi.'

'They will be accompanying me to the library over the coming weeks and on occasion I may have to send them alone. I have complete trust in these three. They won't get into any trouble.' Lütfi stared at them.

Anver nodded his head. He just wanted to enter the library and find the collections written by Ismail al-Jazari. Yasin let them through. Only when they passed the outer wall did Anver notice four other guards seated just inside. They were enjoying some tea and playing a game of cards. Looking up, they waved at Lütfi, who returned the gesture. Anver also waved, not sure if it was the right thing to do or not.

Once inside the palace compound, Lütfi veered right, and they went up a slight incline, heading towards a solitary building set against the outer wall. Anver watched a peacock strut proudly past. He also thought he saw a large cat prowling in the shadows. He had heard about the Sultan's menageries, in which exotic creatures from far-flung places were assembled. He sped up, not wanting to be eaten by a cheetah or lion on the loose.

The library was a single-storey circular building with a set of double doors that Lütfi pushed open, lighting oil lamps as he went inside. Anver came in last and shut the doors, but not before he thought he saw a big cat amongst the trees on the other side of the lawn. The miniaturist walked around, lighting lamps in various places. They were on a raised floor, and in the centre of the hall, under a domed roof, was a circular space cut at a lower level, in which there were semicircular tables, some with chairs, others closer to the ground, beside which were padded cushions to sit on. Anver suspected this open space in the middle served as a sort of reading area for dignitaries who were permitted to use this library. To his left and right were shelves of books stacked up to double his height. Ladders were placed in a few spots for the use of readers wanting to reach the books on the higher shelves.

'Never, not even in Timbuktu, have I seen so many books in a single room,' Awa said.

'Quite a collection, is it not?' Lütfi spoke with a hint of pride in his voice.

'Does anyone actually read these books?' Gurkan asked.

'Amongst the Royals, there are a few who sometimes come here, but I suspect they frequent the library as a way of getting away from the politics of the court. The Grand Vizier and his staff are regular visitors, since subjects related to matters of state are archived here. Scholars under royal patronage are permitted entry, as are any visiting scholars from the Empire who may attend on the request of their local ruler.'

Anver passed along the shelves, his fingers tracing the books, periodically picking up a tome to gaze at it. He was grateful that apart from Hebrew, he could also read Arabic and Persian, for the first half-dozen volumes he scanned were written in those languages.

'How many books are there?' Anver asked.

'Oh, I have never actually counted. Perhaps we should do that one day,' Lütfi scratched his head, looking around the room. 'We do have ledgers where all the books are recorded, but even the ledgers run into several volumes. I will ask the head librarian when he is next in.'

Anver was calculating the number of books per shelf, by how many shelves, and the width. The problem was that the books were all of different sizes and shapes, so it was nearly impossible to make an accurate estimate. His brain whirled with the numbers he was calculating, so he decided it would be more prudent to check the ledgers himself when he found out where they were stored.

'Must be tens of thousands, if not more,' Gurkan mused.

'Come, my young friends, this way,' Lütfi beckoned them over.

Anver shadowed his companions around the raised level with the reading area to his left. They followed the outer curve of the building, arriving in the rear outside a room with a hefty padlock on its door. The Keeper of the Hidden Scrolls removed a brass key from within his kaftan and unlocked the door, before taking a lamp inside.

'Best to bring a lamp each. It gets rather dark in this part of the library,' Lütfi suggested.

The Rüzgar complied, following him into the sealed room. Once inside, Lütfi placed the lock upon a shelf and pocketed the key once more.

'The Library of Hidden Sciences,' said Lütfi with a flourish. 'It is said that the wise place their trust in ideas, not chance. This is a library of ideas.'

The shelves in this room were free-standing as opposed to built against the wall. Close to the entrance was a long wooden table with a set of chairs and a divan set into the corner of the chamber. The remainder of the library contained at least two dozen rows of bookshelves, each shelf running for ten yards, and packed with books from floor to upper shelf.

'God is great!' gasped Gurkan. 'There is a lot of knowledge that remains hidden.'

'Alas, yes, my young friend, but it must be kept hidden for good reason,' Lütfi replied, leading them to the first row of bookshelves. On the end of this row was a brass plate, engraved with some words that made Anver skip in excitement when he read them.

'This is the first collection,' Lütfi waved down a thirty-foot-long corridor of books. '*Ilm al-ta'bīr*, oneiromancy, or you may know it better as dream interpretation.'

'Dream interpretation,' said Gurkan. 'I might need to look at these books.'

Lütfi smiled before walking down to the next column of imposing books. '*Ilm al-kīmiyā*, alchemy.'

'The philosophers' stone,' Anver whispered.

'Yes, indeed, though it is yet to be truly discovered. The good news is that there have been some reports of ... no, let's save that story for another occasion.' Moving to the next column Lütfi announced, '*Ilm al-ahjar*, the occult properties of stones.'

'I would like to look at these. My people have many amulets that are made from stones,' Awa announced.

'*Ilm al-raml*, geomancy, a science I believe you will need to master to some degree in your mission.'

'Why is that?' Awa asked.

Lütfi hesitated before he said, 'For another time. Let us continue for now. *Al-fāl*, omens,' before he went to the next column. '*Al-ṭilsimāt*, magical talismans.'

He stopped to take in the next column of bookshelves, sighing deeply before announcing. '*Azā'im*, the adjuration of spirits. Another collection I fear you will need to delve deeply into.'

Anver was having trouble containing his excitement at all the hidden knowledge at their disposal within this room. There were ten lifetimes of reading just in this one place. How was he going to memorise it all?

'And, Anver, I'm sure in this one you will find your beloved Ismail al-Jazari, *sinā'at al-'ajā'ib*, *al-ḥiyal*, the manufacture of wondrous automata and related devices.'

Anver set off down the aisle, but was politely held back by Lütfi. 'Later, my young friend. First we complete the tour.'

The miniaturist continued down the remaining aisles. Each time he announced a subject, Anver found himself realising he had never heard of it. Yet despite so many new topics Anver was desperate to go back to the collection on wondrous automata.

When they reached the last aisle, Lütfi turned. 'Any questions?' he asked.

The young companions stood in quiet disbelief, mouths open, shaking their heads.

'Yes, coming here for the first time does have that effect,' Lütfi said.

16

LACKING DEPTH

THE COLOURS WERE TRUE, AS was the perspective, and the spatial arrangement within the painting could not have been better. The folds on the wedding dress were in precisely the right places, the jewellery seemed to glitter and the backdrop was stunning. How could anyone deny the prodigious artistry on display? They could not, for only a fool would criticise such a masterpiece of miniaturist work. Fatma was no fool, yet in her mind there was something terribly wrong with the painting she had commissioned Master Lütfi to paint in honour of her upcoming wedding to the Grand Vizier Kanijeli Siyavuş Pasha.

'How is it, Your Highness?' Lütfi asked hesitantly, noticing how underwhelmed she was after he removed the cover from the painting on the easel.

'A work of genius,' replied Fatma in a resigned tone.

The miniaturist stood beside his work in the outer tulip garden. The late-afternoon heat was beginning to subside as a warm breeze blew across the Bosporus. Beside Fatma sat Ulyana, and close to the entrance to the adjoining conservatory, she knew, Fumu stood guard. He was an ever-comforting presence, not that she really needed to be watched over within the palace grounds.

'If I may say so, Your Highness ... I detect a certain uncertainty,' Lütfi said.

'I cannot fault the work, Master Lütfi. You have surpassed yourself with this piece,' Fatma said. As had been recent custom, she had privately commissioned the miniaturist to produce this painting for her wedding. This was only for her and her betrothed. It would never be shown to anyone else, unless she chose it.

Fatma rose from her chair and walked over to the image. In it, she looked so regal, perched upon a cushion, which lay flat upon a fine Persian rug, which itself was spread out in a forest, with birds and small creatures around her. The hoopoe bird was a graceful companion beside her, as was a black panther, which lay curled close to her feet. To her left was a cherry tree in full bloom and behind her, far in the background, was her father's Topkapi Palace in all its splendour, the river snaking beside it. The idealised painting was perfect in every detail – colour, shade, tone – this could not be denied. Yet it was defective – its flaw lay in portraying her as happy. The thought of marrying Kanijeli did not fill her with any delight; rather a deep sadness permeated her heart. Fatma reminded herself all royal weddings were matters of convenience and alliance-building. Blood ties ensured loyalty and diffused tension. They had nothing to do with notions of finding true love. She knew this, had witnessed it her whole life. Why, then, was she expecting it to be any different for her? The possibility of finding a man she truly loved was a dream, much like the painting before her.

'Yet you do not appear happy with the outcome?' Lütfi asked again, worried that his work might not be up to the standard she was looking for.

'Not at all, Master Miniaturist. The work is absolutely as it should be, of the highest artistic standards. I will take it as it is: you do not need to make any further changes to it,' said Fatma.

The miniaturist considered her one more time, before nodding quietly to himself. 'I will have it framed and sent back to you, Your Highness.'

Lütfi called over his apprentice who had been sitting some distance removed and out of earshot. The young man began to pack up the painting and fold up the easel.

'There is one other matter,' said Fatma, after waiting till the apprentice had departed. 'Our young Janissaries, the Rüzgar. It's been a few weeks now. What of their progress?'

The miniaturist hesitated: it was clear to Fatma he was not comfortable speaking about this matter.

'It is quite laborious work and there is much for them to get through. They are making progress, Your Highness.'

'They are here at this moment, in the palace library?' Fatma asked.

'Yes, Your Highness,' Lütfi replied, an element of reluctance in his voice.

'Then I will visit them. Take me there now.'

'It is, ah ...' Lütfi was saying, when Fatma cut him off.

'Do not worry, Master Miniaturist. I am quite used to slinking around the palace grounds into places where I should not be seen or heard at certain times of day. Ulyana, my robe.'

The handmaiden presented her with a long cloak with a large hood, which she pulled up to cover her features. 'Let us go. Fumu will accompany us.'

The miniaturist led her from the conservatory, back through the tulip garden, where Fumu joined them, and they headed towards the palace library, which was beside the outer wall of the compound. Some of the animals from the menagerie had been left to wander in this part of the grounds, and she noted the peacock that strolled with impunity across the flower beds.

Entering the library, Lütfi politely dismissed the sitting librarian, asking him to wait outside and ensure no one else came in. Fatma walked around the familiar circular structure, but could not see the Rüzgar.

'Where are they?' she asked.

'I will fetch them, if you would like to wait here, Your Highness,' Lütfi indicated the central reading area.

'I will come with you,' Fatma declared, for she wanted to know where exactly the young Janissaries were. Besides, she had spent her whole life waiting for others to come to her when she preferred action, going to places, meeting people, leaving things to random chance. There was a certain excitement to be garnered from such an attitude.

Lütfi's expression was strained as he gazed towards the back of the library. It was then that Fatma noted the room that was always locked. She had taken it to be a storeroom in which additional books were kept. Had he placed them in there? If so, that would be quite an uncomfortable place.

'Come Master Lütfi, what is the matter?'

'Your Highness,' Lütfi started, also looking at Fumu to ensure he heard what he was about to say. 'There is a room in this library that contains a collection of books kept under lock and key. I am not just one of the keepers of this collection you see around you, I am presently the only keeper of this unique collection, which is known as the *al-'ulūm al-khafiyya*, the Library of Hidden Sciences.'

'Hidden – from whom?' asked Fatma.

'Everyone.'

'Explain yourself, Master Lütfi.'

'These books are veiled, Your Highness, for the knowledge contained within this particular collection is erudition not for the ordinary person or even the regular scholar. It is knowledge that has been guarded, in some cases for thousands of years, for the misuse of such intelligence would do more harm than good.'

'I was not aware such books existed,' Fatma replied.

'Only a few are, Your Highness. As keeper of the current collection, I must ask Your Highness and all others present not to speak of this hidden collection outside these walls.'

Fatma paused before replying. 'Is my father aware of this collection?'

'Yes, he has used it on occasion.'

'Safiye Sultan?'

'No.'

'My brothers?'

'No.'

'I see.' Fatma realised she had placed the miniaturist in a difficult position with her demand to see the Rüzgar.

'This is not a matter of royal privilege, Your Highness, it is a matter of imperial secrecy.'

'Well, then, I ask you bring the Rüzgar out here.' She would have to return to her normal position of waiting for others to show up. The life of an Ottoman Royal involved just that: waiting.

'Thank you,' said Lütfi, visibly relieved she did not demand to go into the Library of Hidden Sciences. 'I will fetch them.'

She sat upon a chair with velvet armrests, next to the reading table. She was a Princess, but one enslaved by destiny. Some minutes passed before the Rüzgar emerged. It was many months since she had seen Awa, and the young woman seemed to have aged. Fatma was saddened but she should not have been surprised she told herself. Awa had been in prison and then on the run. That was going to take its toll. Then there were all of the adventures and sorrow they had experienced retrieving the Armour of King David.

The Konyan, Gurkan, another she knew by reputation, was with Awa. He was pleasing to look at and had a quiet swagger about him. The other one must be the Venetian, Anver, the young Jewish man who was by all accounts a genius. Meeting all three in person was exhilarating. These young companions did things, went to places, witnessed events she could only dream of, living within the Topkapi Palace. She would happily give up the life of a Princess if it meant she could become an adventurer like Awa. They approached with the miniaturist.

'Please sit,' Fatma motioned to the other chairs around the table. They remained standing.

'I am not the Sultan nor the Sultana, you do not need to stand for me. I insist you sit down.' Reluctantly they drew up chairs and sat, with Awa selecting the seat closest to her.

'I have not had the opportunity to meet you since the deaths of Commander Konjic and Master Huja. Both were great men and they are always in my ... thoughts.' She had almost said prayers, but that would be deceitful, for she had not prayed for an aeon.

'As they are in our prayers, Your Highness. They may be dead but not our memories of them,' said Awa.

The Songhai spoke with such sincerity and her faith in God was unshakeable, despite everything that had happened to her. Fatma envied the firmness of Awa's belief but could not bring herself to emulate it. 'Konjic's name and that of Captain Kadri will be cleared. It is only a matter of time,' Fatma announced.

'If I may ask, Your Highness, where is the Captain?' Gurkan asked. The Konyan's suave voice corresponded with his smooth features.

'Lying low, beyond the city.' She peered at Master Lütfi, who kept his gaze lowered.

'Thank you for helping us ... leave the city the previous occasion,' Awa said, looking over at Fumu and respectfully nodding.

'It needed to be done,' Fatma replied. 'Any news of Will?' After she asked the question about the Englishman she realised she had done it too enthusiastically and should have refrained from using just his first name. She heard Fumu grunt in the background.

'We have not heard of him nor from him, Your Highness,' Awa said. 'We were hoping you might have some news.'

Fatma shook her head. 'I do not. Our thoughts are with him.' Where could the young Englishman have gone, if even his closest friends had no news of him? Was he really dead? 'To more pressing matters then,' Fatma said, shaking the doubts from her mind. 'How are your investigations proceeding?'

Awa exchanged a look with the miniaturist before addressing Fatma. 'They are developing, Your Highness. There is much to read, more than an entire lifetime of study for all three of us. But, God willing, we will make a breakthrough soon,' Awa replied.

'Good. If I can do anything, then you need but ask.'

'You have already done so much for us, Your Highness. If there is anything where your help is required, we will ask,' Awa said.

The young Songhai warrior was always so regal and balanced. Fatma wished she had some of this young woman's poise.

'These demonic possessions,' Fatma leant forward, placing her palms down on the table, 'they are affecting all people, of all social standings, whether poor or rich, pauper or ... prince.' The last word made Fumu turn around and look at her, as did Lütfi. The Rüzgar exchanged looks with one another.

'Has someone in the palace been affected?' Anver asked.

Fatma hesitated a moment. 'Yes.'

Awa raised her hand to signal Anver not to ask the follow-up question, which Fatma expected to be about the identity of the individual.

'Your Highness, we will continue to work as hard as we can,' Awa declared.

'Thank you,' Fatma said. 'This plague will only get worse, I fear. The sooner you can be rid of this malevolent Jinn, the better for all.'

The young companions nodded their agreement.

The Princess rose from her chair, as did the others, and she bade them farewell. Before leaving the library, she spoke softly to Master Lütfi, who was following behind her. 'One day, Keeper of the Hidden Scrolls, I would like to see your collection.'

'Yes, Your Highness,' he replied, but Fatma did not detect any conviction in his voice. Perhaps ignorance of these particular books was a sounder course to pursue than familiarity with them.

17

HIDDEN HAND

RETURNING TO HIS POST, THE librarian continued work as though nothing had happened. The placid fellow was not a book to be read. Awa wondered how many government servants such as the guardian of knowledge were employed by the Ottoman court, sworn to secrecy and pretending not to notice. The Rüzgar went back to their library within a library and secured the door once more from the inside as Master Lütfi had instructed them.

Sinking into chairs around the table close to the entrance, the Rüzgar appeared exhausted. Books lay spread out before them, pens and paper scattered between the various volumes. Slender containers of *kahwa*, coffee, were at the far end of the table, away from the priceless and unique works they delved into.

'It was hard enough before, but with the news that the demonic possessions have reached the palace, I feel a heavy weight crushing me,' Gurkan stated.

Awa had to admit the pressure to find an answer had intensified. If the ruling family were to be possessed, then the Empire would crumble from within. Maybe, she pondered, that was a good thing. The only problem was what would emerge in its place. Seldom did any good result when rulers were forcibly removed. She reminded herself she had a task to focus on, one given to her because of her unique role in the chain of events that had led to the release of Zawaba'a the Jinn, and according to the consensus of the religious elders of all of the represented faiths who met in Istanbul, only she was going to be able to imprison the Jinn again. The single most important question remained – how? The unit worked on for a couple more hours.

'It's getting late. Let's go over the material before we call it a night,' said Gurkan, stretching his limbs.

Awa agreed; she had not been sleeping well since returning to Istanbul. There was a mood hanging over the city. Everyone seemed anxious, on edge. It felt like the energy in the air before a thunderstorm. You knew something was coming, you just didn't know how powerful it was going to be. It was so palpable she could almost taste it on her tongue and she knew it had begun to affect her as well. They had to focus on the task for which they had been called back from Konya. She straightened her chair and looked towards the Venetian who was about to say something.

'Jinn, according to these works, can be controlled by a number of methods,' said Anver. 'Prayer of the pious. Talismans. Stones as well as other objects.'

'Do we know why certain stones or objects work and not others?' Gurkan asked.

Anver shook his head. 'I imagine they act like a spark in a moonless night sky that draws the attention of the Jinn.'

'I read in a manuscript,' Awa thumbed through some loose sheets of paper, searching for the source, 'that the use of certain objects, combined with prayer, makes the Jinn aware that someone from the physical realm is reaching into the metaphysical one they primarily occupy,' said Awa.

'Precisely. This draws their interest and curiosity as a moth is drawn to a flame,' Anver continued.

'Most of the time the conjuror is a novice and the Jinn may entertain them with moving objects around, but this doesn't last. If, however, the one who summons the Jinn is an able magician then the weaker Jinn may fall under this human's control, whereupon they are enslaved, either for a period of time or until certain tasks are performed.'

'Such as in the tales from the *Alf Laylah wa-Laylah*, the *One Thousand and One Nights*,' added Gurkan, smiling. 'I love those tales. My mother would always read them to us on cold winter nights. Sinbad the Sailor and ...'

'Maybe you can recall the seven voyages of Sinbad on another occasion,' Awa interjected.

The Konyan wanted to continue but held his tongue, returning his gaze to the source document Awa held.

'However, formidable Jinn do not fall under the sway of a human,' Anver continued, 'unless that person happens to be a prophet, messenger or saint, or wields a particularly forceful talisman.'

'And that is the problem.' Awa puffed her cheeks out.

'We have neither prophet, messenger nor saint, nor any object that could control Zawaba'a,' Anver said.

'How, then, do we attract the attention of a mighty Jinn like Zawaba'a and ensure he heeds our wishes?' asked Gurkan.

'I did read about a hexagram in one collection, but I would need to look back at it to remind myself of the specifics,' Awa added.

'A hexagram might work,' said Anver. 'Fierce Jinn during the time of King Solomon, who were haunting villagers, would be drawn into an occult shape called a hexagram. It could be as large as a royal chamber or only a few yards wide. I read about a mystic close to Fez who was able to use this technique to bring to heel a nefarious Jinn who was terrorising a nearby village. When he summoned it into the hexagram, he could give it whatever instructions he wanted. In his case, he wanted the Jinn to leave the village, return to the forest and not bother any humans again in its lifetime. It obeyed. Another scholar in Seville makes a similar claim, but ...' Anver hesitated.

'Come on, my friend, what is it?' Gurkan enquired.

'It's not a foolproof system. I did come across a Babylonian who attempted it, only to lose control. He became possessed by the Jinn he was trying to control and ended up throwing himself from the second storey of a building,' said Anver.

'Wonderful, we will definitely need to be wearing the harness for the contraption you are working on, my friend,' Gurkan quipped.

Awa gave the Konyan a questioning stare.

'You don't know?' Gurkan continued. 'Anver here has invented ... well, I don't know what you call it, but a man can jump from a tall building wearing this thing and land safely upon the earth, like a leaf drifting down from the sky.'

'I haven't tested it yet. I was going to try it first using a lamb or sheep,' Anver said.

'Why waste a good lamb, when there are so many stray dogs in the city? Tie one of them to your device.'

'I'm not great with dogs.'

'A cat, then.'

Awa cleared her throat. Conversations between these two tended to spiral out of control, and they'd end up reaching for their respective puppets once more, though thankfully Gurkan had left his back at the village.

'Yes, of course,' said Gurkan, taking Awa's hint. 'So we light a spark by using some object, draw Zawaba'a to us, hope he enters the hexagram, where we have a chance of instructing him if we have the right talisman at our disposal. And then?'

'We tell him to ...' Anver looked to Awa. 'What exactly are you planning to do at that point?'

She bit her lower lip before replying, 'I do not know.'

'Sounds like a great plan,' Gurkan playfully slapped his hand on the table. 'I'll take two please!'

Thud. The Rüzgar turned in the direction of the sound. It came from one of the bookshelves.

'What was that?' asked Anver.

'No idea.' Awa scanned the library for any movement or the scurrying of a creature along the ground. Silence greeted them.

'No one else could have entered the room while we were out,' declared Gurkan, who rose, spotting his sword, before deciding against picking it up.

The companions followed the Konyan deeper into the library. They crept past the various collections and came to a stop beside the banks of bookshelves whose manuscripts were categorised as '*Azā'im*, the adjuration of spirits.

'There,' Anver pointed.

A single volume lay on the floor, its pages open.

Gurkan tiptoed forward, wary of any sudden movement. Awa could see nobody and wondered whether they had a large rat in the library. If so, it would no doubt have been gnawing the books, and they needed to remove it before it caused long-term damage. She and Anver waited. Gurkan reached the book, bent over to look at the pages and picked it up. He strolled back towards them, his eyes on the page as he came.

'What is it?' asked Anver.

'It is the diary of Ibn al-Nadim. It says he was commonly referred to as the Bookseller of Baghdad. He lived in the tenth century and ...' Gurkan paused, scanning the page.

'And?' Anver enquired.

'He seems to have written a number of works about the Jinn and how to trap them.'

The companions looked at each other and around the library. Who else or maybe *what* else was here?

They went back to the table at the entrance, and Gurkan placed the book down on it. The three of them crouched over it.

'Ibn al-Nadim seems to have been quite a character,' said Gurkan as he continued to flick through the pages. 'He lived a colourful life as a popular bookseller in Baghdad, with local and international clients who visited him with fantastic stories, tales he shared with others. His bookshop was also a place for coffee and conversation. He was a practitioner of the hidden sciences, particularly when it came to conjuring Jinn and other spirits.'

'There!' Anver placed his finger on one line in the text. 'Powerful Jinn can be cast back into the vessel they were originally released from.'

They looked at Awa. 'We are *not* going back to Jerusalem. What else does it say?' she announced.

Anver turned the page. 'Solomon is said to have trapped a powerful Jinn in a vessel of brass. There are other examples of brass being used. Here, this scholar did the same in Aleppo, and this one in Khartoum.'

They had found a key to the problem they'd discussed minutes earlier, but it still begged the question of who was listening. Was it another Jinn supportive of their cause, or was it Zawaba'a himself, who had chosen not to appear before them and instead lead them down a blind alley with talk of brass vessels? With no other explanation on the horizon, they would take heed of the advice of Ibn al-Nadim the flamboyant Bookseller of Baghdad.

'Brass it is, then,' said Gurkan. 'Plenty of that around. Should be no problem whatsoever.'

'There is still the question of how we get Zawaba'a into the brass vessel,' added Anver.

Gurkan scratched his head. 'Ah yes, an important element of the plan,' he turned to look at Awa once more.

'And there is this,' Awa pointed further down the page they were on. 'The brass vessel must be placed in the centre of a hexagram, with the triangle at the top pointing east and the triangle at the bottom pointing west.'

'That shouldn't be too much trouble! We just ask the Jinn to kindly step into the hexagram, and hope he doesn't notice the brass vessel in the middle of it,' Gurkan cried, smacking his forehead.

She was as much in the dark as her companions and yet the responsibility of what they were trying to do was falling upon her young shoulders. They were too inexperienced. On previous missions they had had the sage leadership of Commander Konjic, plus Master Huja when they retrieved the Armour of King David. Now they were flapping about in the dark, making it up as they went along. What hope was there? Then she reminded herself that beginnings and endings were celestially fixed, everything else depended on Divine Providence.

'One problem at a time, my friends, one problem at a time,' Awa said.

18

FLYING FLAGS

VESSELS FLYING THE FLAGS OF a throng of nations, some Ottoman allies, others foes, lined the pier of the Bosporus as the intense heat of late August started to wane and the first cooler winds of autumn intermittently blew along the coast. Ships queued up along the river, taking their turns at the dock to disembark their passengers and their loads. Dockhands worked around the clock greeting incoming vessels as they berthed, before directing them to moorings further upriver. The city wharf had never seen anything like it. Neither had Will. He leant over the guard rail of the *Defiance*, one of a half-dozen galleons to arrive from England. The others were already moored and their cargoes removed. He was on board the last English vessel to reach the city, accompanying the Earl of Rothminster and his schemer-in-chief, Sir Reginald Rathbone.

The previous time Will had sailed into the city, he was a galley slave, disembarking in fetters and taken to the Janissary fortress, where his fortunes changed after meeting Commander Konjic and Captain Kadri. He was still a slave but now wore invisible manacles binding him to the wickedness of the Earl and Sir Reginald. So much had been transformed in his life, yet nothing had changed – Will remained a slave to the whims of others. There was no easy path on this journey back to where it all started. Nonetheless, as the young Englishman scanned the river so familiar to him, he realised it had changed, as had he, and he took comfort in knowing this, if nothing else.

The tapping of a cane on deck caught his attention and he swivelled to see the Earl of Rothminster, lavishly dressed in a silk doublet, emerge from his cabin. Though it was warm, certainly for an Englishman, the scoundrel appeared as calm and unflustered as if it had been a winter's days at Leeds Castle. Beside him Sir Reginald, though a frequent traveller to the East, seemed hot and flustered. He wiped the sweat from his forehead with a handkerchief. Li emerged a short while later, gazing across the city and nodding in appreciation at what he saw. The cities of the Ming Dynasty in China, Konjic had told Will, were some of the greatest upon the face of the world. Konjic had in his youth travelled to Xian and told Will how he marvelled at the city's defensive walls, which were thirty feet tall, thirty feet deep and more than thirty miles long. By Chinese standards, Leeds Castle was the home of a dwarf.

Will returned his gaze to the pier, where cartloads of wares were piled high. It seemed the nations had responded enthusiastically to the Sultan's invitation and decided to attend what was billed as a world's greatest trade fair. Within the space of a year the Sultan had gone from wanting to declare war on the Moroccans or the Persians to inviting them and others to his city, demonstrating his benevolence. The Englishman had had only one encounter with Sultan Murad III, on the night of the attempted assassination, and as far as Will was concerned it had been one meeting too many. The ruler had ordered many innocents to be put to death following the foiled attempt, and having met his son, Mehmet, Will was not left with any sense of allegiance to the Crown Prince either, having nearly lost his head to the fellow's aggression. The future ruler had sworn he would kill Will the next time he saw him.

Will doubted the Earl of Rothminster would be able to do anything should Prince Mehmet take offence at seeing Will, and so the young Englishman told himself he was going to avoid all Royalty. If Will was lucky he would be able to lie low and keep out of the Crown Prince's way. Then again, neither Rothminster nor Rathbone would lose any sleep if Will were taken away and executed. They would even work out a way of crafting it to their advantage, claiming they had returned with a wanted fugitive.

'Heave!' came the instruction from the oar-master as the vessel began to pull up, slowing down as it drew closer to land.

'Get ready,' the First Lieutenant cried out.

Anchor was to be dropped as soon as they docked. The chains would be made ready by deckhands. Will knew the drill, having executed it on countless occasions himself. Wanting to avoid Crown Price Mehmet also meant not being anywhere Princess Fatma might be. Now he had returned to the city, she was present in his mind once more. Their last meeting felt like a dream, only it wasn't, since he still had the red tulip brooch she had given him. He removed it from his pocket and rubbed it between his fingers.

Will didn't notice Li approach, standing beside him, keenly observing the brooch and its striking red tulip shape. 'Almost back,' said Will, pocketing the brooch.

Master Li rarely spoke, and this voyage was no exception. Despite pondering it, Will wasn't able to work out why Li tolerated being around the English, who showed him general hostility and scorn, belittling him for being a man from Cathay. Few in England, perhaps not even the Earl of Rothminster and Sir Reginald Rathbone, understood China's commanding position in the world and England's fledgling one. Had it not been for the instruction Will received at the Janissary fort, reading about the great Chinese imperial past as well as significant world events such as the Battle of Talas that took place between the armies of the Abbasid Caliphate and the Tang Dynasty in the eighth century, he would also have been none the wiser.

Li gripped the rail, leaning forward; Will noticed a smile cross his face for the first time. Will gazed towards what had changed the Chinaman's mood. It was at the furthest end of the pier: a vessel, made of long wooden timbers.

'*Baochuán,*' whispered Li.

'Excuse me?' Will asked.

'Chinese treasure ship,' Li said pointing at it.

On board the vessel were dozens of Chinese crew members. Something inside Will felt happy for Li. After all, speaking your own language was a joyous experience. He himself was happy to converse in Arabic, but getting back to England and using his mother tongue had meant a great deal to him.

'Li,' Rathbone's voice cut across the deck, and the Chinese bodyguard scowled once more, looking at Will before making his way back to his employer.

'Here,' Rathbone ordered Li to stand beside him, as one would a trained dog. The Chinaman resumed his emotionless posture.

'So he does smile,' murmured Will to himself as the Englishman witnessed with admiration how nimble the Chinese crew members were as they moved, cat-like, across the rigging of their vessel.

Soon the *Defiance* docked and the passengers disembarked. The Earl of Rothminster was greeted by another Englishman, who begged him to follow him. Behind him trailed Sir Reginald and Li. Will followed after them with the remaining contingent from the English ship. They had been given a place at the far end of the pier, which meant they passed every other vessel as they walked towards the city. The Venetians were unloading their crafts, crates upon crates being heaved over the edge onto the quay. The pulley holding the weight of one of the containers split as it was close to the pier, causing ripe tomatoes to spill out and burst all over the pier before them, covering the Earl's and Sir Reginald's boots with tomato skin and sap.

'*Spiacente*,' a plump, overdressed Venetian said, approaching the Earl. 'Sorry.'

'*Idiota!*' retorted Sir Reginald. 'I will ...'

'I'm sure it was an accident, Sir Reginald,' said the calming voice of the Earl.

'*Si, signori*,' the Venetian said, looking apologetically at them.

'Let us be on our way,' the Earl said, before continuing, leaving tomato-skin-and-sap footprints on the wooden pier.

Will couldn't help smiling. '*Grazie*,' he added as he walked past the plump Venetian, who stared at him with a bemused expression.

Another nation that appeared to have arrived in force was Persia. It was the first time Will had set eyes on Persians in Istanbul, but in Marrakesh he had come across a few of them in the city. They were quite distinctive: strong and proud, elaborately dressed, with skin so fair you could mistake them for being from England or Spain. He had not mastered their language, but as he strolled past he picked up a number of familiar words that their language shared with Arabic. At least five vessels at this section of the pier were Persian, carrying heavy cargoes.

Will had not noticed them until now, but ahead was a parade of officials, surrounded by soldiers checking goods and passengers as they left the pier, before they were granted entry to the city. He sped up, moving through the English contingent, wanting to be as close to the Earl and Sir Reginald as possible, because it was unlikely they were going to be checked when presenting their papers. The local Englishman guiding them spoke with one of the officials and waved his hand behind him, pointing out the members of their delegation. The official counted the number and then signed a piece of paper, handing it to the Englishman, who ushered their party through the gates.

Immediately the salty smell of the sea was replaced by the intoxicating aroma of fried fish coming from a bazaar across from the pier. He noted some Janissaries wandering through the bazaar, and his thoughts immediately went to his friends – Awa, Gurkan and Anver. Where were they and what had become of them? Had Commander Berk kept his word and not executed them? If so, were they still rotting in that awful prison? Will had experienced so much since then, being out in the open air, visiting his mother on a number of occasions, sailing back to Istanbul. His heart sank to think they were still in the confined space he had left them in, with no chance to see the sunrise or wonder at moonlight in a cloudless sky. He would need to slip away at the first available opportunity to try to locate them.

Someone grabbed his arm. Will turned to see Sir Reginald.

'Reminding you of earlier days, is it, Ryde?'

'You could say that,' Will replied, shaking his arm free.

'Don't get too comfortable now that you're back in the city,' Rathbone snorted. 'There's always a knife at your back, ready to plunge through your heart. Remember that.'

It was then Will noticed Li, standing behind him. The Chinese bodyguard had sneaked up on him without making a sound. His dagger was against Will's back and he felt it cut through the first layer of his clothing. The bodyguard was expressionless, as ever.

'I will,' he replied.

If he was going to find his friends, he would also need to shake off Li, a tricky task, it would seem.

19

SLEEPWALKING

L EAVING THE PALACE GROUNDS BEHIND, the young Rüzgar unit melted into the throng along the crowded thoroughfare, heading towards the Fatih district where their upkeep and board was taken care of courtesy of the Society of Miniaturists. Master Lütfi had not accompanied them this evening. The Rüzgar had built a rapport with Yasin the duty guard, who took them to be apprentices of the miniaturist. They had been here every evening, and most of the guards recognised them. Occasionally Fumu also met them as they finished and walked out with them, signalling to the others the connections of the miniaturist and so by extension Master Lütfi's three apprentices as well to the senior Royals. Few questioned the Kikongo warrior and fewer quarrelled with him.

The range of books available to them still made Anver's mind go foggy, and he often found himself dreaming about the library, dreams that ended with him drowning in a sea of words or being sucked down into a whirlpool of ink. He had read through a few works from across the collection, including volumes on oneiromancy, alchemy, the occult properties of stones, geomancy, omens, magical talismans, the adjuration of spirits and, his favourite, the manufacture of wondrous automata and related devices. Daily he had to stop himself from spending his time browsing through the latter collection, as it was going to prove to be the least useful, he told himself, in combatting Zawaba'a. Whatever happened, whether or not they were successful in defeating the powerful Jinn, he was sure this hidden collection was not going to be accessible to them once their work was done. He desperately tried to commit to memory as much as possible, yet the volumes were too many, the topics too wide and the depth of knowledge more than he had capacity for. Most of all, what they all sorely lacked was a knowledgeable teacher who could take them through the compendiums, providing a running commentary and making connections with other publications and bodies of knowledge.

The unit pressed on, diverting onto the side streets to avoid the main thoroughfare of Fatih, still busy this time of night, and likely frequented by some off-duty Janissary loyal to Commander Berk. They were still on the run from the Commander and his cabal of Janissaries, and their mission, despite having the backing of many influential notables and religious scholars, was not officially sanctioned by the Sultan or the new Grand Vizier. If they were caught, they would be in trouble. Anver doubted the Princess was going to be able to come to their aid a second time, and he had no intention of ending back in the same prison, counting the bricks on the wall and floor once more.

'The city is getting busy,' said Gurkan, indicating the main thoroughfare, which ran in parallel to the narrow lane down which they presently charted their course.

'I saw a contingent of Venetians today. They were surprised to speak to someone in their native tongue,' Anver said.

'Did they ask you why you were here?' Gurkan asked.

'No, but they were keen on making me a commercial agent to sell their exports after the trade fair and asked me to come to their stand,' he replied.

119

'Will you?' Gurkan asked.

'Me, no, I would rather make the things they sell than sell the things others make,' Anver replied.

'Sometimes you need to do both,' Gurkan said.

'Not me. If people like my inventions so be it, if they don't then I'm not going to spend time convincing them otherwise. It will be their loss,' Anver said.

'If people don't understand what you make and their benefits, then you might need to do some selling,' said Gurkan.

'Then they aren't worthy of my invention if they cannot understand it,' Anver replied.

Gurkan was about to respond when Awa cut in.

'Moroccans are also here,' she added. Anver noticed her clenching and unclenching her fists when she mentioned them. He knew from Will what had happened to her nation, the Songhai, and he could guess how she felt about the Moroccans.

Gurkan tried to change the mood. 'I have seen Africans from the interior. As tall and broad as Fumu. They told me they were Yoruba and others said they were Hausa.'

'Old tribes with deep roots,' Awa said. 'As were we.'

It seemed to Anver that Gurkan's attempt to change the subject from the Moroccans and the loss of Awa's nation only made the injury more painful.

'Wait!' Awa said. The unit halted. 'Down there, do you see the faint glow?'

Further away from the thoroughfare to their left, down a set of broken cobblestone paths, Anver peered into the gloom to see what Awa was pointing out. There was the red-tinged glow of what looked like a brazier, but unusually it was moving. Braziers did not move. Neither did hearths or fireplaces. What was it then?

The members of the unit exchanged looks. They were on heightened alert for anything unusual, and spending days reading about hidden sciences only increased their sense of the paranormal. Without saying a word, Gurkan led the way. They crossed one path and jogged down a tight alley, leaving the main district of Fatih further behind. The glow disappeared from view, moving around a corner, before Anver was able to spot it once more.

'Stop,' Awa pulled them up once more. 'There are others following it. Over there.'

Anver looked right, towards another alley and saw a clutch of individuals drifting along seemingly in the same direction as them. Though in a group, they appeared completely different to one another, seemingly unconnected. One man wore his bedtime clothes; there was a young woman with a long robe; close to her was a much older woman. Two others in the group were about the same age as the Rüzgar. These people did not seem to know each other, nor were they of the same social standing, yet here they were herded like sheep, all going in the same direction.

'And over there,' Gurkan pointed. Down another lane they spotted an equally unusual cluster of Istanbul residents meandering towards the red glow from the other side.

The light disappeared from view ahead of them, and the Rüzgar ran to keep it in view. All of the pathways converged on a small circular open area, which at a push could hold fifty or so people, standing bunched together.

Crouching low, the unit came to the clearing where the others, of whom they could now see there were about twenty, had already assembled. Every person was staring up and slightly ahead to where the red light glowed. Anver couldn't see it clearly as the light was within an alcove in the wall. The light was deep and it glowed on the faces of the individuals before them.

'That's ...' Awa whispered to herself, drawing Anver's attention, before shaking her head. 'No.'

121

The group stood motionless, yet Anver realised they were straining as though trying to move, but unable to do so. Something was happening to their bodies. There was a perceptible crackling of some sort of energy in the air. It made the hairs on the back on Anver's neck stand on end. Gurkan pulled his sword from its scabbard and saw Awa do the same. Yet Anver did not think a sword was going to help them. The persons before them convulsed, each shaking as though having a fit whilst standing, causing the Rüzgar to collectively shuffle forward, still in their low crouching positions. The people's bodies spasmed, arms and legs jerking of their own accord. It was horrible to look at, and Anver never wanted to be subject to such a situation, where his mind did not have control over his limbs. Then the red glow went out.

Anver turned to his bemused companions, before shifting his gaze back at the people within the opening, all wearing bewildered expressions. These Istanbul residents looked about, trying to understand what they were doing and who they were with. Apparently, they did not recognise one another. Some were downright embarrassed to be seen in their nightwear, others confused, but most of all he saw the look in their eyes. None knew how they had got here. They had been sleepwalking and had just woken up, who knows how far from home.

The Rüzgar waited in the shadows, allowing the self-conscious crowd to quietly disperse and go back to their homes.

'What was that?' Gurkan mouthed the question they were all thinking.

The companions had no answers between them as they silently melted away into the shadows once more, leaving the bizarre scene behind them.

They failed to spot the glowing red eyes watching them from between the iron bars of the sewage drain at the edge of the courtyard.

20

IMPERIAL VULTURES

THE QUEEN'S PORTRAIT HUNG IN the entrance lobby of the English Consulate in Istanbul. Dignitaries and guests from the home country were wedged in various corners of the hallway, spilling out into the gardens. The great and the good who had sailed over from England were present in the Consulate, planning and coordinating mercantile activities for the upcoming trade fair. Representatives selling steel, iron, coal and cotton handed their requests to the staff of the Consulate, who were run off their feet.

Previously when Will had visited the venue, the pace was slow and he met the private secretary of the ambassador, Sir Edward Barton. The man known to him only as Grey had given him time and was keen to engage in conversation, even probing for more information about the inner workings of the Ottoman court. Seeing Will once more, this time accompanying the Earl of Rothminster, the fellow had given him a knowing wink, clearly assuming he had always been an English spy amongst the Janissaries. Nothing was further from the truth, but for now Will was happy to play along with this version. He needed to make the Earl and Sir Reginald believe he was with them and if this meant appearing to be an infiltrator within the Ottoman court, so be it.

Sir Reginald was noticeably absent, and Will assumed the man was not fully rehabilitated in the eyes of the establishment after the affair of the Staff of Moses. As a result of Commander Konjic's efforts Rathbone had been directly implicated in the theft and Lord Burghley had let it be known that Sir Reginald was not to be involved in affairs of the state concerning the Turks. The Earl, however, had escaped such scrutiny and had even been granted a commission to explore lands to the east of Ottoman territories. How he used Sir Reginald outside of England was, it seemed, his prerogative. However, bringing Sir Reginald to the Consulate would have been a step too far, even for the Earl, as such news was most likely to get back to Lord Burghley and the Elizabethan court, who were loath to upset the fragile Ottoman alliance. They needed the support of the world's premier power to counteract the persistent threat of the Spanish and the Hapsburgs in general.

Spain's royal treasury was flooded with gold stolen from the Aztecs and the Incas, indigenous peoples of the Americas. Will had learnt of this during the past months in England. Whilst the Spanish economy grew stronger and their appetite for conflict with England grew fiercer, the Queen and her court remained without means to generate as much wealth as their Catholic adversaries. The Ottoman alliance as well as a possible one with the Moroccans, was essential to the survival of his nation.

'Ryde,' a voice called out.

Will turned to see a skinny fellow with a grubby moustache calling him over. 'Grey said I'd find you here. You're wanted out back.'

'Thanks,' said Will, making for the rear of the building.

'No,' the moustached man said. 'You can't go through there: an important meeting's taking place. You'll need to walk out yonder and then come around the back of the building.' He waved Will towards the main entrance.

The young Englishman took the hint, leaving the front of the building and skipping down the stairs. He turned left and started to make his way around the vast Ottoman villa that had been gifted by the Sultan as a venue for the English Consulate. As he walked down a stone path, he could see into the study at the rear, where the resident Ambassador Sir Edward Barton was sitting in a high-backed chair, along with a number of notables, including the Earl of Rothminster. They were deep in discussion, a conversation that Will would have loved to hear. As he went by, the Earl looked up to see him, eyes narrowing. Will turned away and continued to the rear of the building, eventually coming to a steel gate that he pushed open, entering the gardens behind the building. On his previous visit this had been a wilderness, but now someone had decided to cultivate it there was a lawn bordered with marigolds.

A steady stream of messengers collected packets from a table, handed out by a plump fellow with blotchy red skin. Will joined the queue to await his turn. The line moved surprisingly quickly and he approached the rotund chap.

'Will Ryde,' he announced himself.

'Ryde, yes, message from the Earl of Rothminster for you to deliver. Instructions are inside.' The man handed Will a packet. Taking it, he moved towards the rear of the garden. Opening it, he saw the instruction: *Urgently deliver this message to Commander Berk and ensure no one sees you.* Will halted in his tracks. Berk! Was this some kind of trap? No, they wouldn't have brought him back to Istanbul merely to hand him over to Berk. It would have been easier to dispose of him in England. Besides, there was a mission they wanted him and Li to perform, the details of which remained uncertain at this time.

Finding Berk wasn't difficult. Waiting for him was. He regularly frequented the officers' club outside the gates of the palace and it was the same tonight. Will wore a cloak with a hood wrapped tightly around his head to hide his features. He observed Berk enter the club but was unable to reach him before he dismounted from his horse and was surrounded by other patrons in boisterous embraces. Will recognised the names and faces of a number of the officers who went in and out of the club that evening. Most were confidants of Berk's. He hoped to see someone close to Konjic, but there had always been few, and none tonight. He wondered what had happened to Captain Kadri, but most of all he longed to know about his friends.

Several hours went by before Berk re-emerged, this time with a large group of officers. All, it seemed, had decided to call it a night and head home. Their horses were being brought around from the stables in the rear. The group chatted and joked, Berk seemingly at the centre of the revelries. The group thinned as others left with their horses, till Will noticed a stable-hand present Berk with the reins of his steed. Will made a dash across the street: he had to reach him before he set off at a gallop.

Berk was about to dig his heels into his mount, when Will called out.

'Commander Berk!'

The Janissary officer wheeled his horse to face Will. Some of the other officers behind Berk turned to look in Will's direction.

'Who are you?' Berk barked.

Will kept his hood covering his face. 'I have a message for you.'

'Message? From whom?'

Removing the envelope from his pouch, Will said more softly, so only Berk could hear his words. 'The Earl of Rothminster.'

Will watched Berk's face contort into a smile. 'Indeed. Hand it here.' He held out his hand. As Will reached out the skin colour of his own fingers was exposed. He should have brought a pair of gloves, he thought. Berk hesitated a moment. 'Show me your face.'

It was now Will's turn to dither.

'Now,' Berk said more forcefully.

Will tilted his head up, so that only Berk could see his features.

'Welcome back, Ryde,' snorted Berk. 'You've been a useful go-between.' Berk snatched the envelope from Will's hand and started to turn his steed.

'My friends,' Will said, hiding his face once more within the hood, 'are they ... alive?'

Berk pocketed the envelope, pulling the reins of his horse so he was now sideways-on to the young Englishman.

'You don't have friends, Ryde.' Berk dug his heels in and his horse galloped away, leaving Will looking after him.

The remaining officers were speaking in hushed tones amongst themselves, no doubt about what had just happened. Will didn't wait around; he marched away, disappearing back into the narrow streets outside the palace district. It was a stuffy night and the hood was only making it hotter for him so he decided to throw it back. He continued to walk through predominately empty streets, heading back to the tenement beside the English Consulate where he was lodging.

As he made the final turn before the Consulate, a burly hand grabbed him by the shoulder and thrust him against the wall, before grabbing his collar and lifting him up against the wall.

Will looked down to see Fumu, Princess Fatma's bodyguard.

'Ryde!' Fumu snarled.

'Fumu!'

'What are you doing with Commander Berk?' Fumu asked, keeping Will pinned to the wall.

'Nothing,' Will said.

'It did not look like nothing,' Fumu replied.

'It's not what you think,' Will spluttered as the Kikongo warrior's grip tightened.

'What should I think?'

'I was just ... wait, what about my friends, where are they?'

'The Kikongo warrior loosened his hold a touch, allowing Will's feet to come back to the ground.

'Your friends ...' Fumu was saying, when the Kikongo warrior was pushed away into the wall on the other side of the alley.

Fumu whipped around fast, surprised at being propelled in such a manner.

Li! The Chinaman was beside Will, checking he was all right, before he took a crouching position.

'No, wait!' Will cried out, but neither warrior heard him.

Fumu rammed straight into Li, taking them both to the ground. The man from Cathay rolled with the assault and was first on his feet, striking out with the side of his foot, landing a forceful kick to Fumu's head, flooring the bigger man. Li leapt into the air, his leg ramming the bodyguard, who rolled away at the last moment. Li followed up with a straight punch, which hit Fumu in the chest but didn't achieve anything. Li roundhouse-kicked Fumu in the shoulder, but the warrior, now better prepared, shrugged off the blow.

'Stop, both of you!' Will called out once more.

Neither listened. They went for one another. Li thrust out with an open palm, which Fumu deflected with his elbow, before he hit his opponent with a felling punch to the stomach. It winded Li as Fumu followed up with a right cross, which missed by inches as Li ducked at the last moment. Fumu stood tall and advanced once more. Li sprang a series of kicks from the left and right, before he landed successfully with one that grazed the bigger man's temple, causing him to sway for a moment. Li followed up with a flat kick to the stomach, pushing Fumu back as he leapt once more and planted another hefty kick to the Kikongo warrior's head, sending him to the ground.

As the big man fell, Li whipped out a blade and went for the kill.

'No,' Will said, moving forward and kicking the blade out of Li's hands. He hesitated as the blade skittered down the alley.

Fumu kicked out with the sole of his boot, which sent Li rolling backwards, before he charged once more. This time the Chinaman met him and they both collided in a wrestling hold. Fumu's hands were tightly intertwined with Li's as the larger warrior brought his superior strength to bear on the shorter one. Li's left leg bent and he slipped. Fumu advanced, pushing him down further. Li switched his grip, unlocking his fingers and grabbing Fumu's wrists, before rotating up with his legs, the soles of his shoes smashing into the nose of the Kikongo warrior, sending him staggering back. The Chinaman used the momentum to somersault backwards and land on his feet.

'Damn it. Wait!' Will put himself between the two warriors.

'What's going on?' a voice called out from the end of the alley. It was a man on patrol, bearing two lamps.

'Hey, break it up.' The patrol advanced.

Li glanced at Will, before running to his left, planting his feet onto a crate, leaping, partially running up the wall and using it to somersault over Fumu, so that he landed on the side of the alley towards the Consulate. He collected his blade and disappeared around the corner.

With the patrol close, Will turned back to Fumu. 'It's not what you think,' was the only thing Will could say, before he also raced past Fumu and headed for the apparent safety of the English Consulate.

21

SHROUDED

THE BOOKSELLER OF BAGHDAD RECOMMENDED a brass vessel for capturing a powerful Jinn. Yet, upon hearing this from the Rüzgar, the Master Miniaturist Lütfi advised them that they should seek the advice of someone with more insight into the hidden sciences than him. A person who possessed not just bookish knowledge but also practical knowledge. He suggested they visit Sheikh Dawood, the mystic from the Bektashi Sufi order, but before doing that Lütfi said he needed to rendezvous with an acquaintance. As it was still daylight, Awa and her companions wore long robes with hoods, which they kept up. The late-August heat had lost its intensity but was still warm enough to cause her to sweat under the disguise.

The meandering route to the Sufi lodge took them twenty minutes. It was late afternoon, and the markets on the main thoroughfare were coming alive. The lodge itself was down one of the ornate side streets filled with tulips, red, pink, white and yellow. The road dipped down a hill, and in the distance the companions could see the harbour full of the ships of foreign nations. Awa wondered what she would do if she ever encountered any of the Moroccan soldiers or those responsible for issuing the instructions to enslave her people. Did she have it within her to forgive them? She knew she should, for her own well-being, but doubted she possessed the capacity to forgive and forget yet.

'Here it is,' announced Lütfi, pushing a wooden door carved with a circle on its face. They crossed an open courtyard with a garden before reaching a lodge. He knocked on the door, waited till it was answered by a wiry young man, who peered about before letting them in. The man ushered them towards the interior of the building, through a room with a low timber ceiling, before they came into a hallway, and he pointed to a door midway down.

Lütfi approached the door and knocked, announcing himself.

'Enter.'

The voice sounded vaguely familiar to Awa as the Rüzgar followed the miniaturist through into a space where there was cushioned seating set against the walls. A man rose up and greeted them.

'Salaam, my young friends,' said Captain Kadri.

'Captain!' Gurkan rushed over to embrace their superior officer.

'Hush!' he said putting his fingers to his lips. 'Captain no longer.'

'We thought you were ...' Gurkan stopped himself from saying it.

Kadri nodded. 'I thought so, too. If it wasn't for the personal intervention of Sheikh Dawood, who is a spiritual teacher to some of the royal family, I would be. Come, sit, my young friends.'

He ushered the Rüzgar and the miniaturist over to the divan, pouring them a cup of coffee each and offering dates.

Kadri had aged since she last saw him. His cheeks were flatter and he had more creases under his eyes. 'I have heard great

131

tales about your adventures – from Aleppo and Damascus, to Jerusalem and Azerbaijan. What I want to know most of all is about my dear friend, Mehmet Konjic. How did he die?'

'With courage and bravery,' Gurkan responded. 'Commander Konjic's name will always be remembered in the villages around the Karabach Plateau. For them and for us he is a hero, a selfless individual who saved their children and sacrificed his own safety, when others would have fled in the face of dire odds. He inspired entire villages to rise up against a brutal warlord called Azi Dahäg, named Lord of the Two Serpents.'

'That is what I heard,' Kadri nodded. 'Even in death he continues to inspire. He once told me, *Our actions are dyed with the colour of our thoughts.* Let us pray for him'.

The companions took a moment, and the members of the two faiths present in the room prayed in a language familiar to them for Mehmet Konjic, their leader, friend and mentor. Each sat in silence for some more time, reflecting on Konjic's life, before Kadri turned his attention back to them.

'May his soul reside in everlasting peace and his onward journey be filled with light,' Kadri said.

The young companions echoed him, as did Master Lütfi.

'What about you? How are you faring, Captain?' Awa asked, unable not to refer to him by the familiar title.

'I am no longer a Janissary; my benefits have ended. So, I have taken to pursuing the craft of my forefathers, who were stonemasons. It is arduous, but with the incessant building work taking place around the city, I have managed to find employment for myself and a few others.'

'You have your own business?' Anver asked.

'It's not as grand as you make it sound, but yes, you could say that,' Kadri smiled.

'It is a worthy profession,' Awa added.

'As long as I keep a low profile in the city, I don't expect anyone to bother me, least of all Commander Berk, who seems to have become bolder since the appointment of Kanijeli Siyavuş Pasha as Grand Vizier.'

'A snake if ever there was one,' snorted Gurkan.

'I agree, but a shrewd politician as well, which is why he is where he is and we are where we are,' replied Kadri before changing the focus of the conversation. 'You wish to see Sheikh Dawood?'

'I suggested it might help in our investigations, based upon what we know so far about how to deal with this Jinn, Zawaba'a,' replied Lütfi.

'I can take you to him, but the arrival of this Jinn in the city is causing the Sufi orders much consternation. The cases of possession and peculiar behaviour reported by family members have led to a spike in the workload; there are not enough qualified members of the order to deal with these cases. We were, as I remember it, warned about this matter on your previous visit to Sheikh Dawood, so expect a frosty reception from some in his inner circle. The Sheikh himself is untroubled, as he says everything is from God. Whether it is good or bad, it is for us to simply deal with the situation as best we can.'

'When can we go?' asked Anver.

'Now, if you are ready,' Kadri replied.

The companions nodded.

With the reunion over they silently departed from the Sufi lodge, to make their way to the madrasa, where Sheikh Dawood was currently to be found.

Awa recalled her previous visit and the intoxicating aroma of *oud* perfume as they walked down streets with canopies overhead, making the pathway seem like part of a cave system. Inside the building, the atmosphere was as she remembered it, with some students diligently undertaking devotional acts, others learning and some teaching. They passed through the same scent-filled passageways before coming to wait outside the quarters where the Sheikh held audience.

Kadri slipped inside first and emerged some minutes later, beckoning them to follow him into the inner sanctum. Sheikh Dawood, composed and calm, sat cross-legged upon a low divan, rosary beads in one hand and a soothing smile upon his face. The companions sat in a line before him, with the miniaturist to their right and Kadri taking up a position between them and the Sheikh, whose acolytes were pressed against the far wall, heads bowed in respect for their teacher. One, whom Awa took to be a scribe, held a pen poised over a pad of paper. Greetings and pleasantries were exchanged before they got to the matter at hand.

Awa noticed Anver topple forward, catching himself at the last moment by putting his hands out as he hit the ground.

'What!' he exclaimed, looking about him.

It was as though someone pushed him in the back. Awa soon felt a hand on her shoulder and someone pull her back. When she turned there was only empty space.

'Enough. They know they made a mistake,' said Sheikh Dawood to no one in particular. He seemed to look past them. 'Yes, they have come to redress what you told them last time.'

Awa remembered the Qareen, the Jinn of Sheikh Dawood, being present when they last visited and warning the companions about not releasing Zawaba'a.

'He,' the Sheikh nodded his head past them, though Awa couldn't see anyone, 'is understandably upset. Zawaba'a's arrival in the city has created great discord amongst the Jinn folk. Some wish to follow him, as he is immensely powerful, and they have pledged their support. Others in their community oppose him, for Zawaba'a is known to possess a fierce temperament, even by their own standards. They do not believe his incarceration by Prophet Solomon would have altered his innate nature. Most of the Jinn are indifferent to what happens in the world of men. Just as most people are indifferent as to what happens in their world.'

Though she was familiar with stories of the Jinn and knew they, too, lived in communities, it had never occurred to Awa that they might have divisions like people. She had just assumed they were a homogenous group.

'Tell me, young ones, what can I do to help you?' asked the Sheikh.

'We came across a book that contained the diary of the Bookseller of Baghdad, who says that during the time of Solomon the Wise, the Jinn were captured in a brass vessel. Is this something we can use to contain Zawaba'a?' Awa asked.

The Sheikh turned to look past them once more. Smiling, he turned his gaze back. 'I see. I believe you were given some aid in discovering this book.'

'It just fell off the bookshelf,' Gurkan said.

This could only mean that some of the Jinn, favourable to what they were seeking to do, were already watching them, and where possible assisting them. Awa wasn't sure what to make of it, so she remained silent and waited.

'Brass is a tried-and-tested vessel in which to capture a Jinn, no matter how powerful it is. This is true,' the Sheikh replied.

'Does it need to be of a particular size?' Anver asked.

'Size has nothing to do with it, when you are dealing with such beings, who belong to the realm of the metaphysical.'

'About this size then?' Anver made a space between his two palms, into which a kettle could fit.

The Sheikh nodded.

'How do we get the Jinn into the brass vessel?' Awa enquired.

'This is an altogether different problem, and it depends on many things,' Sheikh Dawood said.

Awa felt her shoulders sag. She had known it wasn't going to be simple, but being told so plainly felt like a heavy weight on her soul.

'Such as?' Gurkan asked.

'The age of the Jinn, the older the harder it is to bring it under control because of its inherent power. A very powerful Jinn will easily repel your efforts. And if it was previously imprisoned, who did this to it? The next person who attempts it must have an equivalent level of ability. This last point is important in the case of Zawaba'a, for it was Solomon the Wise who banished it.'

'That sounds impossible,' Gurkan interjected, forgetting who he was addressing for a moment. 'My apologies, Sheikh, but Zawaba'a is exceedingly old and terribly powerful, which are two factors. And as for the third aspect, who can be greater in the world today than Prophet Solomon was during his time?'

'It is a prickly problem,' the Sheikh agreed, rubbing his chin.

'An impossible one,' Anver added.

The companions sat in contemplative silence, each mulling over the new information. Finally the miniaturist, who until now had remained silent, cleared his throat. 'Perhaps, Sheikh Dawood, we must use a means that in any other circumstance would be considered utterly forbidden.'

'What do you propose, Master Lütfi?' asked Kadri.

The miniaturist surveyed the former Captain, then Sheikh Dawood. 'There is Faris Al Housani.'

Kadri's expression remained blank, which Awa took to mean he lacked knowledge of the person mentioned by the miniaturist. There was, however, a sharp intake of breath from the Sheikh.

'I know, his ways are … unconventional,' added Lütfi.

'Not to say, heretical and sacrilegious,' added Sheikh Dawood softly.

'I agree, but the geomancer may be the only one who possesses the knowledge to imprison Zawaba'a once more,' said Lütfi.

The Sheikh shut his eyes for a moment, pondering the matter.

'You know of his whereabouts?' asked Sheikh Dawood.

The miniaturist nodded.

'His knowledge is deeply forbidden. You know this, don't you, Master Lütfi?'

'I do, yet in times such as these, perhaps this is the only recourse remaining,' Lütfi replied.

'I cannot tell you to go to him,' said the Sheikh.

Lütfi's head dropped.

Then the Sheikh added. 'And I cannot tell you *not* to go to him.'

22

BETRAYAL

ANOTHER FULL DAY OF RESEARCHING in the library left the Rüzgar exhausted. Staying awake in the musty atmosphere of thousands of books was proving challenging, and Gurkan was always the first to slink away for a nap. Awa would also rest, and Anver found himself following the practice of his companions. They were working till late in the evening and were often up early, as the Fatih district, where they resided, came alive with activity soon after dawn. It was the convention of Istanbul residents to have an afternoon siesta in the summer and the team found themselves fitting in with this rhythm.

On this particular evening they decided to call a halt to their work earlier than usual, as they were going to set off to find Faris Al Housani, the geomancer, first thing the next morning. He was in a location east of the city. The directions were sketchy, but Master Lütfi, who had visited the man before, was going to accompany them. The Master Miniaturist had come across the geomancer many years ago, before his banishment from the city for his heterodox practices.

Departing from the Topkapi and bidding their farewells to the now friendly guards, who always enjoyed some banter with the young companions, they strolled back towards the city proper, walking along a pathway with the palace walls running to the right. Their route soon brought them to the main entrance of the Topkapi Palace. This evening the normally placid location was a flurry of activity, with hundreds of guards and guests.

'What's going on?' Gurkan said, loping along in the direction of the hubbub.

'Whatever it is, we should keep out of the way,' Awa warned.

Anver was inclined to agree with her. They were sneaking around the city most of the time, fearful they might be spotted by someone who knew them and was loyal to Commander Berk. It was a precarious position to be in, and this fanfare at the main palace gates seemed to be attracting a number of what were in Anver's view important foreign dignitaries.

The unit took a wide berth, finding cover under a sycamore tree where they remained, partially veiled from the soldiers and guards at the palace gates. The vantage point allowed the Rüzgar a clear view of who was coming and going. Carriages pulled up at the entrance, and an assortment of well-dressed international visitors disembarked from their transports. Following a quick conversation with one of the guards on patrol, the visitors were ushered through the main gates, to be met by one of the decoratively dressed stewards who took them up a sloping hill into the grounds of the inner palace.

'They look Venetian,' Anver commented, watching a group of regally dressed guests, mostly men and some women, descend from three carriages and enter the grounds.

'How can you tell them from other Italians?' asked Gurkan.

'The coat of arms on their carriage: it is that of the Doge of Venice,' said Anver.

'We met him only two years ago, at the opening of the Rialto Bridge,' Awa said.

'You met the Doge!' Anver exclaimed. This was news to him; his companions had not previously shared this information. 'What was he like?'

'It was only a brief encounter, but he seemed like all men who pursue political occupations,' Awa said.

Anver wasn't quite sure what she meant. He had been expecting her to tell him what he looked like, his characteristics, but she hadn't done so. Instead, she used language that was difficult for him to comprehend. He liked to hear clear-cut answers: black or white, night or day. Anything else left him guessing what the person meant. He decided to go back to watching the dignitaries as they arrived.

'Persians,' said Gurkan. 'I'm sure of it. I have seen some visiting Konya before.' Anver watched a group wearing black turbans get out of their transports. Their papers were checked before they were given entry. A small group of guards followed them at a distance.

'Franks!' Gurkan announced, about the next group of visitors.

'How can you be sure?' Awa asked.

'I can't, but do you have any other suggestions?' replied Gurkan with a smile. Awa shook her head.

Other carriages pulled up, bearing what the Rüzgar assumed were visitors from further east, many with dark-olive skins, others with fair complexions and elongated eyes. Never had Anver seen such people before. Were they Chinese? He had heard a great deal about the Ming Empire, and that the Chinese were some of the most knowledgeable people in their world, with records dating back thousands of years, but he had never encountered anyone from those lands before.

'We should head back. We have an early start in the morning,' Awa said.

The unit started to move away as another carriage arrived. Anver's curiosity got the better of him, and he lingered to see who would emerge. They looked like Franks, but there was something familiar about one of the men. In fact, he had seen this particular man in Venice when he had been thrown into the canal.

'Wait! Look there,' Anver pointed in the direction of the new arrivals.

'What is it?' Gurkan came back to stand beside him.

'I have seen that man before,' Anver said.

'Sir Reginald Rathbone,' whispered Awa. 'We saw him fall from London Bridge into the River Thames.'

'Is it his ghost?' Gurkan commented.

'No, for that is the Earl of Rothminster beside him,' Awa said.

'The scoundrel we encountered at Nonsuch Palace in England,' added Gurkan, advancing.

As Anver watched, a third man emerged. This one, Anver had no trouble in recognising whatsoever.

'Will!' the three companions exclaimed in unison.

Their former comrade was just across the other side of the road. He wasn't missing or dead, he was perfectly alive, but what was he doing with the Rathbone and Rothminster?

'Why is Will with them?' Anver asked.

'It can't be,' Awa spoke after a moment's silence as the shock of seeing their fellow Rüzgar with the enemy settled in.

'Is he their prisoner?' Anver enquired.

'It does not appear so,' Awa said.

'Then why else would he be with them?' Anver asked.

Gurkan and Awa exchanged glances.

'He is a traitor! He was always working for the English!' Gurkan exclaimed, pulling free his blade from its scabbard. 'Why, I'm going to run him through.' The Konyan prepared to set off for the other side of the road.

'No! Wait!' Awa tugged him back. 'There are too many soldiers. You won't have a chance.'

'Let me try,' Gurkan retorted.

'No, not now, not here. We'll find him, but when we've planned it. When the odds are in our favour.'

Gurkan pulled up.

'It's what Konjic would do,' Awa added in a reassuring tone.

The name of their late Commander settled the Konyan, who sheathed his blade and retreated into the shadows.

Confusion rolled through Anver's mind. He preferred a well-defined way of working and living. Seeing Will with their enemies left him paralysed. Only after Awa placed a hand on his arm did he tear his eyes away and reluctantly follow her back to their dwelling.

***

Royal functions with so many dignitaries from international lands were rare. In fact, they tended to happen once a decade, if at all. However, under the reign of Sultan Murad III, encouraged by Safiye Sultan, these were now more regular occurrences. Events that the women of the royal household also attended were usually unheard of, though under Fatma's father some had taken place.

Visitors from many regions of the world mingled freely in the Grand Hall at this very moment. Numerous polite conversations rippled around the room, a low murmur of noise in the background. Servers moved briskly through the throng, offering sherbets to the guests. Princess Fatma surveyed the dignitaries entering the Grand Hall from her position above the hall, in a viewing room where a finely meshed screen allowed her discreetly to observe the hall below without anyone spotting her. On the raised dais at the head of the hall was her father, Sultan Murad III, and beside him Safiye Sultan, a pillar of strength in the royal household. To the right of her father was Kanijeli Siyavuş Pasha, the Grand Vizier and her betrothed. The thought of marrying him made Fatma's stomach tie itself in knots.

The other twenty or so seats were taken up by senior advisers and some of her other brothers. Crown Prince Mehmet was noticeably absent. Rumours swirled at court as to his condition. The official story was that he was ill with a tropical fever, which meant isolation was necessary for fear of infection. Yet Fatma knew the true nature of his malaise. He had been, like many in the city, possessed by a demonic force.

The arrival of the powerful Jinn, Zawaba'a, was now an unspoken crisis at court, for daily the cases of this new infection, whether mild or aggressive, increased. The city was under siege, though she knew no conventional army was formidable enough to march its troops to the walls of the Ottoman capital. Amongst this otherworldly pandemonium the great Trade Fair of Istanbul was taking place. When announced, it had been met with surprise at court, then acceptance, before finally an excited expectation. Now they were in the throes of the fair, and rather than being entirely consumed by this grand event, the city and its rulers were secretly struggling to quell demonic possessions. The court still did not properly recognise the problem, and Fatma could see the additional strain on the face of her betrothed and his officials. Any efforts to deal with the situation, such as by the Rüzgar, were being carried out in an unofficial capacity.

If news that the Ottoman capital was under demonic siege leaked out, and she could not see how it would not, these foreign visitors would return to their own lands with this story on the tips of their tongues, ready to convey it to all who would hear it. The trade fair was meant to make a statement of imperial strength, according to the new Grand Vizier, and not shine a light on a cancerous growth within the Empire's capital city.

Beside Fatma, her handmaiden Ulyana watched the cosmopolitan gathering in the Great Hall.

'Even the Tsar of Russia has sent a delegation,' whispered Ulyana.

'Where?' enquired Fatma.

'To the back of the hall, on the left. They have fur on their robes,' Ulyana replied.

'Yes, I see them.'

It pleased the Princess to witness the diversity of nations present in the Great Hall, bringing together nations from around the Mediterranean that had been at war with one another for decades. Elsewhere she witnessed others from further east, such as the Chinese and Indians as well as those from southern lands of Arabia as well as Africa. Even western nations including the Hapsburg Empire were represented, along with the Franks. It was a unique gathering that she hoped set the mood for the future, a more tolerant one based on mutual benefit.

'Ulyana,' said Fatma. 'At the back of the hall, to the right, is that who I think it is?'

A moment later Ulyana spoke the name Fatma thought she would never hear again. 'Will Ryde. Yes, Your Highness.'

'He is alive!' Fatma said, relieved to see the Englishman living and breathing before her. But how was he here? Who had invited him?

'It seems so, Your Highness.'

'I think an explanation is required, don't you?' Fatma said, turning to leave the viewing gallery and signalling her handmaiden to follow.

'Yes, Your Highness,' Ulyana replied.

23

SCHOLARLY ENCOUNTER

RETURNING TO THE GROUNDS OF the Topkapi Palace filled Will with a sense of foreboding. Not because he had bad memories of the place - rather it was the thought of being recognised by someone he had encountered before and publicly humiliated. The last thing he wanted to do was run into the Crown Prince. However, Rathbone assured him, as part of the English delegation he was protected by a sort of immunity and all previous misdemeanours were forgiven. The young Englishman wasn't overly convinced and half expected that he was expendable. Part of him wondered whether the Earl was deliberately taking Will to the palace as an expression of Rothminster's deep hatred of the Ottomans. The longer Will spent with the Earl, the more he realised the animosity the Earl held for the Turks was based on deep-seated jealousy. The Turks were magnificently successful militarily and commercially, expanding their domain during the reigns of Sultan Selim and Sultan Suleiman, during which time his own nation was just learning to navigate safely across the Channel without being repelled by the French and others in Europe. Envy of Ottoman achievements was the fuel igniting men such as the Earl of Rothminster and his acolytes.

Emerging out of the Grand Hall into the gardens beside it provided much-needed relief for the young Englishman. It was blisteringly hot within the enormous public hall, crowded as it was with immaculately dressed guests engaged in jovial banter, feasting on kebabs and other delicacies. The Englishman did not find anyone to converse with and, despite what Rathbone thought, he maintained a low profile, avoiding any Ottomans, particularly Janissaries, who might recognise him. Not having run into anyone he knew, with the evening wearing on, he decided not to tempt fate any longer and headed into the grounds outside. It would be safer for him to sit out in the gardens and simply avoid all people. The terrace on which he found himself was adorned with elaborate man-sized vases leading out to a lawn where he noticed groups of people chatting away merrily. By their appearance, they were low-ranking personnel, not invited into the Grand Hall, yet they seemed happier than the wealthy folks he had seen inside. The truth was Will felt more comfortable with this crew than with the lords and ladies within the palace.

Casting his eye about by the light of countless flickering lamps, Will came upon a sight he never expected to see. Li, Sir Reginald's taciturn stoic bodyguard, was smiling. In fact, he was laughing out loud. Surrounded by a group of what Will took to be minor Chinese delegates, he was conversing in this own tongue and was in immensely good spirits. So the bodyguard *did* have a sense of humour! Will watched him from afar, hoping Li would not turn and notice him. He didn't. Will perched on the edge of a wall running between the terrace and the lawn, where the dim lighting kept him out of sight. Remaining in the shadows was a valuable skill he had learnt as a Rüzgar.

Li's brief respite was broken when Will spotted Sir Reginald march out of the Grand Hall. Looking annoyed, he cast his gaze about as though searching for someone. Was it him? Will was about to get up and show himself, but decided to stay put. Rathbone spotted Li and made towards him, breaking up the conversation the Chinaman was having with his countrymen. Rathbone was too far away from Will for the young Englishman to understand what he said to Li, but even at this distance Will knew it wasn't pleasant. Li's mood seemed immediately to change: he straight away assumed the demeanour of a servant once more, nodding vigorously at whatever instructions Rathbone delivered. Discomforted by the manner in which Li was humiliated in front of his own people, Will for the first time felt a sense of affinity with the man from Cathay. Having barked his orders, Sir Reginald stormed off, and Li was left to say hurried goodbyes to his fellow countrymen before scuttling back towards the main palace gate. Will wasn't sure what Rathbone had asked Li to do, but he hoped it wasn't to try and track him down. He already felt uncomfortable at the manner in which Li was treated by Rathbone as well as by other Englishmen. Will would never have imagined that he would assume a cordial bond of sorts with Li, since it wasn't too long since the Chinese bodyguard had held a blade to Will's neck, ready to slice his windpipe open at the orders of his master.

'Will Ryde,' a soft female voice called his name. Will stood up and searched around but couldn't see anyone. Had he just imagined it?

'Over here,' said the voice, and this time he caught its direction and picked out a silhouette under a hazelnut tree to his left. Hesitantly, he checked the area around him, to see whether anyone else was watching him. As it all seemed clear, he approached the person who had called his name. The woman he encountered was the handmaiden of Princess Fatma. Will felt a sinking feeling in his stomach at the same moment as a thrill coursed through his veins.

'Ulyana,' Will said.

She smiled in the mischievous way Will had come to expect of her, before she bade him follow her around the trunk of the tree, where he came face to face with Princess Fatma Sultan.

'Your Highness!' Will exclaimed, bowing respectfully.

'You have some explaining to do, Will Ryde!' Fatma said sternly as she signalled to her handmaiden to leave.

'I ...'

'Yes,' Fatma said more softly.

He wanted to tell her he had missed her, that he remembered her often, that their friendship or whatever it was meant so much to him. That every day he would hold the Ottoman brooch she had given him in the palm of his hand and fondly recall the short but sweet time they had spent together. Instead, formality took over.

'I heard about your engagement to the Grand Vizier. Congratulations,' was all he could say.

She seemed a little taken aback, judging by the way she straightened her posture, holding her head a little higher. He knew then he should have said what his heart desired and be done with formality.

'Thank you,' Fatma said, her tone also more formal. 'And how is it that you come to be here?'

'It's a long story.'

'Give me the short version then,' Fatma said, a hint of annoyance in her tone.

Will really wasn't sure what he should tell her, as he couldn't afford to compromise his own position and the safety of his mother. Should it get out that Commander Berk was in league with the Earl of Rothminster, it would put an end to their current trade mission and with it, instruction would be sent to England to end the life of his dear mother. He would not be the cause of her death.

'I am here as part of the English delegation, headed by the Earl of Rothminster,' Will replied in a reserved tone.

'Rothminster, the rogue Earl who stole the Staff of Moses from the palace?'

'He is leading the trade delegation on behalf of Her Majesty Queen Elizabeth.'

'And you are in his employment?' asked Fatma, anger rising in her voice.

'Employment' was not a word Will would have chosen. He was a reluctant slave bonded to the Earl and Sir Reginald Rathbone. Yet, for the sake of his mother's safety he answered, 'I am.'

Fatma's lustrous eyes narrowed. Even when she was angry, she still made Will's heart race. 'How long have you been working for the Earl?'

'Your Highness,' Ulyana returned.

'What is it?' Fatma snapped.

'His Majesty will be passing this way in just a moment,' the handmaiden said urgently.

'My father!' Fatma said, turning to see a delegation emerging to the right of them, which would take them on the path directly behind the hazelnut tree and expose this secret rendezvous. The Princess turned upon Will, giving him a stare like a pair of daggers coming in his direction, before departing with her handmaiden, heading in the opposite direction to the Sultan's entourage.

The young Englishman did not want to be seen by the Sultan and those around him, so hurriedly made his way back towards the terrace. He had wanted to tell her the truth, but he couldn't. He felt physically sick, flopping into a wooden chair tucked into the corner of a miniature garden with a maze at its heart. He buried his head in his hands. The look on her face had been one of pure rage. Whether Fumu had already relayed

149

their encounter to her he wasn't able to fathom, but either way he had broken the trust of the very people he felt closest to in this city.

The Englishman sat in this morose manner for some time, till he heard an avuncular voice that brought him back from his reverie.

'Even if the world is ending and you have a seed in your hand, plant it, for in that seed there is hope.'

Will looked up to see an African man, whose face radiated kindness and concern. His distinguished robes were accompanied by a rust-coloured *kufi* skull-cap upon his head, and he held a set of prayer beads in his right hand.

'So says our beloved Prophet. Whatever heartbreak you have, my young friend, it will pass,' the man commented. He looked to be in his late forties or maybe early fifties, but it was difficult to tell.

'Even if the world is ending and you have a seed in your hand, plant it, for in that seed there is hope,' Will said in Arabic.

'You speak Arabic?' asked the man. 'Yet you are a Frank.' The man drew up another chair and sat down beside Will. 'Tell me, my young friend, how is it you come to speak such refined Arabic?'

'I grew up in Marrakesh, serving the quartermaster, Hakim Abdullah, a decent man.'

'I, too, live in Marrakesh,' said the African.

'Then you must know of Hakim Abdullah, famed quartermaster of the Bayt Ben Yousef?'

'I'm afraid to say I do not. I have only recently ... started living in Marrakesh.'

The gentle manner of the man got Will thinking what his profession might be. He possessed a certain type of acuity that Will had not seen in many; he was clearly an educated man, yet his disarming demeanour made Will feel that he was being treated as an equal. For though this man did not say it, he possessed the quality of a thinker, a man of ideas.

'If I may ask, sir, where were you before?'

The man smiled. 'It is a long story, and I would not want to bore you with it, my young friend.'

'My name is Will Ryde, I'm from England – and you would not be boring me. I haven't exactly been spending time in chivalrous company lately. I would very much welcome hearing the tale of one so refined as yourself, sir.'

'I am simply the same as you, my friend. We are both souls on a journey back to the Creator,' the African smiled, before continuing. 'I have heard of the English Queen, for she defeated the Spanish who brought their great Armada to her shores. Abd Al-Aziz Al-Fishtali, the court scribe of the Moroccan ruler, Al-Mansour, honoured her with a poem. He wrote: "God sent a sharp wind against the fleets of the tyrant that broke up their formation and pushed them onto the enemy's lands, bringing down their flags and banners." The Moroccans have named her Sultana Isobel. And as for my name, it is Mahmoud al Jameel.'

'Al Jameel?' Will asked. He knew only one other person with this surname.

'Yes, there are many al Jameels: it is a common name amongst the people of West Africa.'

It couldn't be. Will sat up straight as an arrow. 'Which tribe are you from in West Africa?'

'The Songhai,' Mahmoud replied.

'And did you live in Timbuktu?' Will continued.

The man looked Will up and down. 'I did, but how does an Englishman know so much about the Songhai?'

Now for the question Will needed to ask. 'Do you have a daughter?'

151

Mahmoud was taken aback by Will's question. His eyes narrowed, and Will realised how it must have seemed. 'I did,' Mahmoud replied, 'but she died about two years ago.'

'No!' Will leapt up, grabbing Mahmoud by the arm and lifting him up with him. 'Her name is Awa!'

'Yes, but how ...'

'Dear Lord, thank you.' He hugged the Songhai scholar, before realising he must have seemed like a madman to this kind African he had just met, yet felt so close to. It also struck Will that he didn't actually know whether Awa was still alive. Had he just elevated this man's spirits only to knock them down once more?

'Will Ryde, please explain yourself,' Mahmoud said slowly.

'Awa Maryam al Jameel is a ...' Will didn't know how to describe the relationship between them. He was, after all, speaking with her father. 'What I mean is, I've met her, I know her, we've fought together, been on adventures.'

'What are you saying?' Mahmoud asked.

'She wasn't slain at the Battle of Tondibi,' Will began.

'Praise be to God!' Mahmoud exclaimed, cupping his hands together in prayer and looking up to the heavens.

'She was taken as a slave and was being transported to Morocco, but she managed to escape, and eventually I ... well, myself and the Ottoman Janissaries, we met her in Alexandria.'

Mahmoud once more stared at him. 'You are a Janissary?'

'I am ... I was, it's a bit complicated.'

'Alexandria, you say, so what was she doing there?'

Will bit his lip, as he didn't have the courage to tell Awa's father how he saw her fighting in a gladiatorial pit and decapitating her opponent. 'We were on a mission to recover an artefact belonging to the Sultan, when we came across her. Our Commander, Mehmet Konjic, was impressed with her martial abilities as well as her intellect, and he offered her a role as a sort of associate of the Janissaries. She accepted and we spent the next two years going on various missions with our unit.'

'My daughter, an Ottoman Janissary?' Mahmoud shook his head. 'I wanted her to be a scholar, but she always had this martial prowess that it seems could not be denied.'

'She is still more a scholar than nearly everyone else I have ever met. Her understanding of many topics is so vast and she always credits it to you.'

Tears welled up in Mahmoud's eyes.

'Where is she now?' he asked.

'I ... don't know,' replied Will, his shoulders sagging. 'In the winter we all returned to Istanbul after our last mission in Azerbaijan, but then some things happened and we got split up. I haven't seen her since then.'

'Is she ...?'

'Yes, of course, she's alive,' Will lied, for in truth he did not know himself.

'Then we must find her,' Mahmoud said. 'For if she is in Istanbul, then it is truly God's plan for me to find her, for why else would He have brought me here?'

Will nodded. Yet if Awa had already died at the hands of Commander Berk months ago, then surely it had nothing to do with divine fate. It was more a divine tragedy.

***

By the time the Rüzgar returned to their lodgings the anger at seeing Will with the Earl of Rothminster and Sir Reginald Rathbone had dissipated a degree or two, but Awa was still seething inside at his betrayal. They had to speak with Will to find out what was going on. Unlike Gurkan, she found it hard to believe that Will had been a spy for the English all along. She had experienced so many things with the Englishman, from the first moment he came to her aid in the Citadel of Qaitbay in Alexandria, where he could simply have walked away from a fight in which they were heavily outnumbered, all the way through to the moment before they were arrested upon their return to Istanbul. If he had been a spy all along, why would Will have assisted her at all? There was no reason to do so. No, there was more to this than met the eye. For now she was going to reserve judgement on the matter. They would hear him out first, before deciding whether Will was friend or foe.

More pressing matters weighed heavily on her presently. They needed to see the geomancer in the morning, with their guide Master Lütfi. It was to be an early departure, and she needed to get a good night's sleep to recover her strength. Spending days on end rifling through complex scholarly books was far more taxing than she had ever given it credit for being.

Passing the main entrance, the Rüzgar were about to go to their lodging above the workshop, when Awa noticed Lütfi's wife beckoning to them to come through the back door, which led to a small courtyard before the accommodation where the miniaturist and his family lived. The miniaturist's wife Anisa was an accomplished herbal doctor and ran a successful practice in the building next door to her husband's.

'Yes, Doctor Anisa, what is it?' asked Awa noting her grave look of concern.

'Come, all of you,' Anisa urged.

They followed her through the small courtyard before entering the residence of the miniaturist for the first time. The doctor took them down a narrow corridor to their left before they came to stand outside a wooden door.

Awa exchanged a look with Gurkan and Anver. 'What has happened to Master Lütfi?'

154

Taking a long deep breath, Anisa gently pushed the door open and went inside. They followed. The miniaturist lay on his bed, seemingly asleep, but Awa could see two hefty men either side of him, tying him down with ropes whilst an imam prayed close by.

'No,' whispered Awa. The plague of possessions had claimed Master Lütfi, and it looked to be bad, really bad.

Lütfi began to moan as they entered the room. As Awa approached his bed, the two men shuffled away, having done their work with the binding, leaving only the imam in the corner, Anisa and the Rüzgar in the room.

'Master Lütfi,' Awa spoke softly.

His eyes opened, causing Awa to take a step back and collide with Anver.

'Awa ...' His voice sounded different. It was considerably deeper and throatier. The miniaturist's hand strained under the bindings, and Awa feared he would have leapt up and throttled her had it not been for the restraint.

'Be warned, child ...' A guttural voice emanated from Lütfi's throat, but it was not his. 'I am watching you!'

Awa's heart pounded. Who was it that was speaking to her? It was the body of dear Master Lütfi, but was it the presence of another, of Zawaba'a? Lütfi began to cackle, before starting to shake, sweat pouring down his face. He looked to be trying to resist whatever had taken over his mind and body, to fight back in some way. Then he went limp and lay silent.

Immediately his wife approached, taking his pulse, holding his wrist for some time. 'He is calming once more. The fever burns high, the demonic infection is strong, but my husband is also tough and he is doing his best to fight it. He will pull through, God willing.'

Awa was amazed at the woman's calmness. 'Have you seen this before?'

155

'Yes,' Anisa replied. 'As a doctor I have encountered many patients this past month in this state, only I did not expect to return home and find my husband in the same condition.'

'Have your other patients ... recovered?' Anver asked.

'Some ... but they tend to relapse. Until this malevolent evil hanging over the city is lifted, I fear it will only get worse. Your task was always important; now as far as my family is concerned it has become critical.'

'We will do our best, Doctor Anisa,' Gurkan said.

'My husband said he was going to take you to see Faris Al Housani in the morning.'

'Yes,' Gurkan replied.

'I do not know precisely where the geomancer is exiled to, but I have heard my husband say it is in the place known as the "burnt plain", between the two black hills.'

'Thank you, Doctor Anisa,' Gurkan offered.

'Get some rest, young ones, for you have much to do and the weight of responsibility sits heavy on your shoulders,' said Anisa.

Taking their leave, the Rüzgar departed. All thought of contacting Will as soon as possible had left Awa's mind. The Englishman would have to wait; she would see him when she saw him. For now, there were more demanding matters to deal with.

24

GEOMANCER

LEAVING AS DAWN BROKE PROVED tiring but sensible for the companions, who made good progress in the cool of the early hours. Now they found themselves on the scorched plain between the two black hills. This was as much information as they had garnered from Anisa, Master Lütfi's wife. The journey north from Istanbul had taken them along the coast until they could see the black hills towards the west, at which point they turned inland. The midday sun approached its zenith, and the heat of the day took its toll on the Rüzgar, who broke for rest, continuing only as midday bled into early afternoon.

At the base of the valley was a dense forest, and the young companions now ventured towards it, winding their way down a track overgrown with tall grass, in places up to their waists. The ground underneath was mostly firm, but in parts was boggy, and it was difficult to tell when the footing underneath would become too soft to traverse.

'Wait,' said Gurkan. Awa turned to see the Konyan bending over before coming back to his full height. 'Yuck! My boot is full of mud. The land in some places turns to bog. Be careful where you step.'

Seeing the terrain from amidst the thick wild grass was difficult, but there was no need to make life any more difficult than it already was. Awa slowed and took some tentative paces, feeling her way through the grass. To her right Anver did the same and further to her left Gurkan moved with caution.

Awa heard the flapping of wings overhead. Instinctively ducking, she twisted to see a kestrel swoosh by and up into the air.

'What was that all about?' Gurkan asked, surveying the sky overhead. 'Look out, here it comes again.'

The kestrel dived at Anver, who dropped to his knees in the grass as the bird soared up and away from them once more. Awa nocked an arrow to her bowstring, but was reluctant to bring such a graceful creature down. She watched the feathered fiend approach again and fired an arrow as a warning shot. It flew past the kestrel which at the last moment swerved and darted over and away from them, back into the forest below.

'You missed! You never miss,' Gurkan announced.

'I was trying to scare it, not kill it,' Awa replied.

'Arghh!' Anver cried out.

'What?' Gurkan rushed towards their Venetian companion.

'I'm sinking.'

Awa trod to her right to approach the Venetian from a different angle. His legs were totally submerged and she watched the bog rise past his navel and over his chest. He thrashed his arms about in panic.

'Don't move,' Awa ordered.

'But I'm sinking,' Anver moaned.

'She's right, stay completely still,' Gurkan added.

The Venetian obeyed and the rate of his descent slowed. He was still drowning in the bog, only more gradually.

Awa noticed the ground under her feet soften. She put her arm up to ensure Gurkan didn't follow. Instead, the Konyan looped around her and came to the other side of Anver, whose arms were now sinking.

'Hurry,' Anver cried out.

Gurkan uncoiled a rope and threw the other end to Awa.

'We're going to lower this. Reach out and grab it. You'll only have one chance. If you miss it, you'll sink,' Gurkan said.

Anver moaned.

Awa looked up, as she thought she heard the flapping of wings once more, but the sky was clear. With Gurkan holding one end and Awa the other, they lowered the rope, so that it was right in front of the drowning Venetian.

With considerable effort Anver yanked one arm out of the bog, fingers scrabbling for purchase on the rope. He gripped it tight, but as he did, the weight of his descent accelerated and he shot downwards, neck and head disappearing from view.

'Anver!' Awa cried out.

Silence. A single bubble came to the top; the rope they had thrown to Anver lay on the surface. There was no movement.

'*Anver!*' Awa screamed.

Fingers broke the surface of the bog and desperately clutched the rope.

'Let go of the rope, Awa,' Gurkan instructed as he began to pull on it, hauling the Venetian in his direction. Awa watched in horror as the rope slipped through Anver's hand. They were going to lose him. Then his fingers tightened, his grip firm.

'Faster,' she cried out to Gurkan.

The Konyan heaved. Anver's arm now emerged, followed by his muddy head, then his shoulders as he managed to release his left hand and grab hold of the rope with it. As Gurkan pulled him, the Venetian slithered like a reptile on a muddy riverbank.

Reaching safer ground, Anver spluttered, spitting out mud as he wiped his eyes.

'Learning how to swim didn't help much, did it,' he said, grinning through the muck. Awa smiled and Gurkan broke into a laugh.

'That's the spirit of my friend,' Gurkan slapped him on the back. 'If we aren't facing death at every turn then the Rüzgar are not doing their job properly.'

After so many near-death situations, Awa would have been happy to avoid them for the rest of her life.

'We need to find a different way down into the forest. The ground here is untrustworthy,' said Gurkan, looking around.

The forest was still a few hundred yards from their current spot and the bogginess was likely to get worse, should they continue down this route.

'Let's circle around,' Gurkan motioned for them to go right.

'Ready?' Awa asked Anver. The Venetian hauled himself to his feet as more remnants of mud fell away from him. He looked a sorry sight, but, despite almost dying, his mood was upbeat.

After a while the tall grass gave way to a shorter variety and the soil below them firmed up. It was easier to traverse this terrain, and Awa felt she was skipping along, walking becoming so much easier in this part. They soon drew close to the forest. Thick, gnarled trees, their roots like veins on an old man's hand, wormed their way along the outer edge, creating an imposing vista. As they reached the first trees, it became apparent that little sunlight penetrated the wood. The young companions exchanged looks with one another, before taking a hesitant step forward and through the outer perimeter.

Past the first row of trees, the air cooled, the temperature dropping. Overhead, Awa saw a thick canopy of branches where the sky should be. Streaks of sunlight pierced green-and-brown thickets of foliage. The land underneath was soft, mushy in places, wet in others. A coolness filled the forest, along with a stillness, which for one recently grown used to the bustle of the city was unnerving.

The Rüzgar carefully trod through the forest, negotiating the trunks, stumps, bushes and thickets. All the while they ventured deeper into the abode of the geomancer. A low-level growl startled Awa, as she swung her gaze to the left. Another followed from the right, closer to Gurkan's position.

'I don't like dogs,' murmured Anver.

An enormous dark-brown mastiff reared its head over the mound to Awa's left and a similar beast of disquieting proportions emerged on the right. The Rüzgar drew their blades.

'And I don't like killing dogs,' said Awa.

'Well, when you felled the beast in Leeds Castle, it was only one. This time we have two,' Gurkan mused.

'One for you then,' Awa replied, facing the canine as it approached through the foliage of the forest, its eyes fixed on her.

The hounds loomed, baring their teeth, saliva dripping, as Awa planted her feet and went into a low crouch. Speed was going to be of the essence if she was to have any chance against such a ferocious creature.

'Tread with care for you tread on the dead, and the dead stare at what you cannot bear.'

The voice echoed around the forest. Awa was unsure whence it emanated, but it froze her on the spot.

The Rüzgar turned, trying to identify the location of the person who spoke, without success. The dog nearest to Awa bared its teeth and barked once. Was it about to attack? She gripped her dagger more tightly, sweat dripping off her fingers. She heard the second beast padding closer to Gurkan.

'We seek Faris Al Housani,' Gurkan announced.

Silence met them. The dogs drew closer.

'Master Lütfi, Chief Miniaturist, sent us,' Gurkan added.

'What brings children of the top-soil to the forest?'

Awa watched as a man with a hood over his head, wearing flowing black robes, approached from a position at a ninety-degree angle to where the dogs were. She could not see his face, for it was covered and the darkness of the forest hid it.

Awa lowered her blades and stood up to face the man, mindful of the approaching dog. 'A powerful demon, named Zawaba'a, has been possessing inhabitants of Istanbul. Master Lütfi is one such person. We need your help,' Awa said.

The hidden figure seemed to contemplate them more closely, remaining silent. 'Please,' Awa added. 'We need the geomancer.'

The man whistled, and drawing the two dogs to him. The hounds abandoned their aggressive postures and moved obediently to wait beside their master. The kestrel flew down from a nearby branch and perched itself on the man's outstretched wrist.

'Then you shall have him,' replied Faris. He turned around and walked deeper into the forest, the dogs padding along beside him and the bird of prey taking flight once more.

'I suppose we follow him?' Anver said.

The companions sheathed their blades and made their way after the geomancer.

25

INTERPRETATION

THE GEOMANCER, FARIS AL HOUSANI, brought them to what Awa assumed was his home, deep in the forest. On the way, she was soon disorientated. The sun was hidden for long periods, and as it began to set she lost her bearings, for even the stars were difficult to visualise through the cover of the forest. The geomancer settled the Rüzgar outside his wooden cabin and disappeared inside for some time. When he emerged his hood was lowered so they could gaze upon his face for the first time. Awa smelt something cooking in the background.

Faris Al Housani appeared to be in his late fifties, but it was difficult to tell. His thick, swept-back hair, grey at the sides, curled in places as it fell about his neck and a thin beard ran across his chin, which was strangely pointed. His eyes were vibrant, and Awa imagined that in his youth he had been a very handsome man. He retained much of this elegance even now, and Awa wondered how a man such as he had become an exile and ended up living in a place like this with only animals for company.

The fire in the centre of the dwelling close to this cabin crackled as Faris laid more logs on it. The Rüzgar sat close by as the temperature had dropped considerably. The geomancer tucked in his robes and settled on a wooden stool directly before them, as though he were a teacher about to start a lesson.

'Now, tell me about Zawaba'a,' he demanded.

Awa cleared her throat. 'It is a powerful Jinn, caged by Solomon the Wise and kept imprisoned till ... last year, when we released it in Jerusalem.'

The geomancer raised an eyebrow but did not say anything, nodding at Awa to continue.

'Since his arrival in Istanbul, Zawaba'a has been possessing many inhabitants of the city. Some become passive, others aggressive. What he plans to do is uncertain, but we have been asked by ...' She didn't know who it was that really asked them – was it Safiye Sultan or the former Grand Vizier or the religious figures? '... people in authority to help cast it back.'

'By your hand and tongue was it released?' Faris asked.

Ashamed at her part in this affair, Awa nodded.

'A heavy burden it is to bear when innocents fall into despair, and you know it was your hand that caused this trauma in the land,' Faris mused, more to himself, it seemed to Awa. 'Continue.'

'We understand such a powerful Jinn as Zawaba'a can be imprisoned in a vessel of brass, but we do not know how. Master Lütfi said you would know.'

'Knowers are seekers until they grasp what it is they seek,' said Faris.

Awa gazed over at Gurkan and Anver who both shrugged their shoulders. Faris seemed to speak in riddles.

'Will you help us?' Awa appealed to him once more.

'No,' Faris said, rising.

Awa felt all hope crushed.

The geomancer gathered his robes close around his body and set off towards his cabin. He paused and partly turned in their direction. 'Not until we have eaten,' he announced.

Faris disappeared into his cabin.

'I like him,' whispered Anver as one of the dogs silently padded over and began to lick the Venetian's ear. 'Yikes!' Anver jumped up.

'It's all right,' said Gurkan, reaching over and stroking the hound's brow. 'He just wants to get your scent, so if you ever come back he knows you aren't a danger to his master.'

Anver crouched and tentatively patted the enormous animal. 'Good dog. Don't bite.'

The other mastiff lay beside Awa, tucking its heavy body in beside her feet. She tickled it behind the ear as it closed its eyes and dozed. In Timbuktu her uncle kept a dog to help him herd his goats. She had liked the animal, though chose not to look after one herself. Her father was not fond of having animals near his person. Where was he now? Every day in her prayers she thought about him, prayed for his safety. All this time with no word as to his whereabouts. Were her hopes simply in vain? For all she knew he might already have joined her mother in the next realm.

The geomancer prepared a stew of meat and barley that the Rüzgar ravenously consumed, having been travelling most of the day. In Awa's estimation food always tasted better outside the city, unpolluted by a bustling conurbation, which often led to a drop in quality in favour of volume. Following the evening prayers, the geomancer summoned them to a clearing behind his cabin. A circle marked an open space, in which the natural foliage of the forest was completely cleared, leaving a sort of blackened volcanic earth, which appeared as though it was scorched clear of all vegetation. Overhead branches were trimmed back and, in some cases, stripped of leaves, and for the first time that evening Awa was aware of stars filling the night sky. They sat on what looked to be former tree stumps, now carved into makeshift seats. Placed in a ring a few yards

165

apart, they formed part of what Awa assumed was to be some type of unorthodox ceremony that the geomancer was going to perform. This was precisely the sort of exploit forbidden by orthodox scholars, no doubt with good reason. Awa once more had a sinking feeling in her stomach. Were they about to make matters a lot worse?

'Apparently geomancy originated with Prophet Enoch,' Anver whispered.

'Idris,' said Gurkan.

Anver nodded. 'The library has a book called *Opening the Locks* by al-Zanati, which explains its origins. He was shown the science by the Archangel Gabriel.'

The companions were silenced when the geomancer approached. 'Whatever happens, whatever you see, whatever I do, do not move, unless I tell you to, for you know not where you will end up,' Faris declared, standing over them.

'Why?' Anver asked.

The geomancer stared incredulously at the Venetian. This ended the conversation.

The geomancer drew his hood over his head so his features were once more hidden from view.

'I'll sit here then,' Anver whispered.

'You,' he pointed at Awa, 'must come with me into the circle.'

'Why?' Gurkan asked. 'Why Awa?'

She felt touched by the Konyan's protective attitude towards her, but she knew the answer the geomancer was going to give.

'She has seen what I must see, or else this will all end in blasphemy,' Faris announced.

Awa didn't like the sound of this. She did not want to compromise the tenets of her faith in order to seek out the answer by unconventional means, yet here she was about to enter a ceremony that was, to say the least, heterodox.

166

A sudden gust of wind blew through the trees as the geomancer's robe whipped out behind him. The unexpected phenomenon made Gurkan stare about, unsure what was coming their way. Ready and alert, the Konyan rested his hand on the hilt of his blade.

'Wait here,' Faris instructed.

She scrutinised the geomancer as he moved into the open space before them, a long staff in his hand. Further gusts of wind moved through the trees, causing lamps to flicker and the geomancer's robe to billow out. The staff he gripped was a simple wooden object, with a thick copper ring at the top. With the bottom tip of the staff, he outlined one circle, which was large enough for three people to stand in. Faris sketched out a series of smooth lines in the soil, each one starting from a point around the circumference of the circle and branching away. He completed one, all the while praying, raised his staff and then progressed to the next, completing it and moving on. In total, Awa noted, he drew sixteen lines, crisscrossing at various intervals. She couldn't hear what he was saying, but some of the words were from the Holy Book. She was unsure of the source of others, or even what language he uttered them in.

The geomancer left the pattern he made upon the ground and strode away, carefully resting his staff against the side of his cabin, before returning with a large wooden bowl. He scooped out a series of wood chips and threw them in what appeared to Awa a random manner across the shape he had etched into the blackened earth. The geomancer continued pacing around his design, taking fistfuls of wooden chips and casting them across the pattern. Blasts of air burst through the forest, sending some chips much further than he had thrown them. She was sure a few even changed direction and came back behind the geomancer to land in odd positions. The lines in the earth formed a cross-section of grids. Once the bowl was empty, he set it beside his staff and walked into the very middle of the pattern, where he had originally drawn the first circle.

'Approach,' Faris instructed her.

Awa focused on the anxious faces of her companions, then went across to stand opposite the geomancer.

Darkness enveloped the forest as the air fluttered oddly around her like the flapping of a pigeon in front of her face. She had the strange sensation of being poked in the back and shoulders by the wind. This close to him, Awa heard the geomancer praying, the words unfamiliar to her ears, once more in an unintelligible tongue. His face remained partially hidden within the folds of his hood. Faris stretched out his hands and placed both sets of fingers on her temples. He shut his eyes, but Awa kept hers open. The geomancer continued babbling in the alien language as draughts of air surged around them from different parts of the forest, whipping the geomancer's robes about. He spoke forcefully, raising his voice so it could be heard over the wind as it circled the clearing. Was this the language of Prophet Idris, who was a Babylonian? If so, very few people in the world could understand what was being said.

Despite an escalating sense of dread, Awa remained statue-still, her gaze tied to the face of the geomancer, who still had his fingers upon her head. His touch was soft on her temples, yet she was sure she felt a surge of energy flowing through his hands. What was going on?

A blast of wind smacked her in the face, as if she had been hit with a wet cloth, causing her vision to blur for a moment. She blinked. When she opened her eyes once more and was able to refocus, she noticed that staring back from the darkness of the forest were two narrow eyes, glowing a fiery red. Instinctively, her hand reached for the pommel of her sword. She noticed another set of eyes focusing on the geomancer from a different part of the forest. More eyes lit up in other locations. Panic

168

mounted within her. Was this part of the ceremony? Did the geomancer know they were surrounded by strange beings, possibly powerful Jinns or other demonic spirits? The glowing eyes remained where they were, not revealing the bodies that held them.

The geomancer took no notice of the change in their surroundings. He let go of her head as a blast of wind threw back his hood, rippling through his windswept hair. The blacks of Faris's eyes were gone: only white shone back at her. Awa stumbled in shock, tripping, then falling on her back as she took in this bizarre scene. As the voice of the geomancer thundered about her, filling the entire clearing, she counted eight pairs of red eyes, sixteen eyes, the same number as of the lines drawn in the earth by the geomancer. The geomancer's arms were raised aloft, sleeves flapping, the wood chips scattered from one grid to another, but all the time remaining within the pattern he had drawn on the ground. His face was a terrible thing to look at, contorted, horrific, brow furrowed, the whites of his eyeballs glowed. The ancient Babylonian language continued to spout from his lips as his gaze pierced the area around him.

Fear of what surrounded them crept up Awa's spine. Her gaze shifted from the geomancer to the red eyes watching the proceedings. She wanted to leap up and do something, but Faris's instructions were clear. Stay put.

The geomancer fell to his knees, arms reaching up to the heavens, head tilted back. Agony etched on his face, his words now came between panting breaths. She wanted to help him, reaching forward, but hesitated. His voice was now drowned out by the wind as it whipped about them, a vortex within this small clearing in the forest. Leaves, twigs, branches, earth twisted around the clearing, as though they were in the centre of a cyclone. Dust flew into her face. Blinking, she looked about. The red eyes drew closer to the circle. The bodies they occupied remained obscured.

'Awa,' Gurkan said, motioning to the imminent threat circling them.

'I know,' she replied, drawing her weapon.

'Can we move now?' Anver asked, getting up.

The lights from the lamps and the cressets went out, plunging the area into darkness. Even the sky above appeared like a blot of dark ink; the light of the stars was gone. Awa whirled around, the red eyes nearer now. She started to see the dark shadowy forms of their owners, but the intensity of the wind made it difficult to get a clear view of what was actually happening. Out of the darkness a hand stretched in the direction of Gurkan. The Konyan ducked out of the way, then drawing his sword slashed down against it.

'*Arghh!*' the geomancer screamed.

Awa whirled to see Faris fall to the ground only a few feet from her, face first, arms flung out. Immediately, the wind ceased. The red eyes were gone. They were alone once more in the forest. Starlight beamed down into the clearing. Gurkan and Anver raced over to help the geomancer back up. His head lolled before he seemed to come to his senses. As he blinked Awa was thankful she could see the pupils of his eyes once more.

Faris spoke in a croaky voice. 'Unite the Emissaries of God. Let followers proclaim in a single voice. Then will a Demon's touch be unmade.' The geomancer passed out, his head drooping to one side.

Awa leant forward to check his pulse. 'He's alive. Come on, let's get him into his cabin.'

They carried Faris inside and placed him on his bed. She checked once more, but he was sleeping, his breathing returning to normal. He didn't seem to be in danger. They sat down on a set of chairs inside the cabin as the dogs returned to guard their master's bed.

'What were those things?' Anver made the shape of eyes.

'I don't know, but they were getting close,' Gurkan said, glaring at Faris.

'He told us not to move, but when we did, those things went away,' Awa said.

The hours passed, and the companions waited for the geomancer to rouse from his slumber. He eventually did in the early hours of the morning, when his movements woke the Rüzgar who had fallen asleep in their chairs.

Sliding his legs off his bed, Faris held his head, eyes squinting, till he noticed the three young companions nervously watching him. 'I told you not to move!' His voice was crackly.

Gurkan poured him a glass of water and handed it to him. The geomancer accepted it and sipped the contents.

'So close to being in my control,' he said.

'Those things with the red eyes?' Gurkan asked.

Faris remained silent.

'What were they?' Awa asked.

'Jinn,' Faris replied.

'What did you need them for?' Awa probed further.

'If you had not slashed out with your weapon ...' Faris trailed off, shaking his head, not answering Awa's question. She didn't like the sound of this. Why was he trying to gain control over these other Jinn?

'Did I say anything before I passed out?' Faris asked.

'Unite the Emissaries of God. Let followers proclaim in a single voice. Then will a Demon's touch be unmade,' Anver replied.

The geomancer looked down at the water in his glass before finishing the rest of it and placing the glass on the table beside his bed. 'That is all you need to know.'

171

'What does it mean?' Gurkan asked.

'Enough. You leave at dawn and do not return.'

They were not going to get any more explanation from the geomancer beyond his proclamation, which made no sense to her. How were they going to use this to defeat Zawaba'a?

Yet something else gnawed at Awa; the geomancer had somehow used her experience of encountering Zawaba'a to summon other powerful Jinn. To what end? There was more to the geomancer than he was letting on. The sooner they left this godforsaken forest the better.

26

COLD RECEPTION

GUARDS MOVED ASIDE WHEN THEY realised who was marching along the corridors of the Topkapi Palace. The Princess was not in a charitable mood. Fatma had woken this morning feeling furious. Two days ago she had met Will Ryde, the Englishman she had believed was a friend, who now turned out to be a foe working for the wretched Earl of Rothminster. Stories about the diabolical Earl had circulated at court after his failed attempt to steal the Staff of Moses. How was it such a man was given access to the city, let alone the palace? She needed answers. She needed to speak with her father, the Sultan.

She turned a corner and strode down a long marble corridor at the end of which were the chambers of her father. His plans and his whereabouts were a guarded secret, so trying to obtain an audience with him was challenging at the best of times – even for his daughter. He would see her when he wanted to see her, not when she needed to see him. Since the Sultan's family was large, it was a rare occurrence when he actually summoned one of his children to spend time with him, unless they happened to be the successor, her brother the Crown Prince Mehmet. Yet the future heir was presently out of circulation, possessed by a demonic force, driven mad or something in between. When

Fatma went to see him, he attacked her. If it were not for the guards stationed within his chamber at the time, Fatma feared what the outcome might have been.

The two sentinels close to the door of the Sultan's chamber exchanged stares as she came closer, unsure what to do, as this was not typical protocol.

'Move aside,' she ordered in the most formal voice she could muster.

'Your Highness, the Sultan is currently busy,' the guard on the left announced.

Fatma turned slowly to face the man. Eyes narrowing. 'Open the doors, or you will be relieved of your duties permanently.'

The two men looked at one another, before moving away from the door, allowing her to reach for the handle and walk through to what she knew to be the outer entrance hall before the main chamber in which the Sultan rested.

Once inside, she closed the door behind her and turned to find her fiancé the Grand Vizier Kanijeli Siyavuş Pasha sitting at a desk, reading a set of papers. He looked up, surprised to see her. His stern face softened a touch, but she could detect the irritation in it. He didn't like her and she didn't like him. Mutual antipathy would be the perfect backdrop to their politically motivated marriage.

'Fatma, how nice to see you.'

He had taken to calling her by her name after their engagement, dropping the title 'Your Highness'. It didn't sit well with her.

'Kanijeli, always a pleasure to see my betrothed,' she lied, a smile on her face.

'What brings my dearest to see the Sultan, when our beloved ruler is currently out on a hunting party with some of his guests?' he asked.

She had not expected her father to take such an active role in spending time with foreign dignitaries. She had never seen him take an interest in anything other than his menagerie of exotic animals and his book of lurid dreams, which the miniaturists turned into pictures. Maybe, at long last, he was thinking about his legacy, for his reign would always be compared to that of his grandfather Suleiman the Magnificent and his father before him, Selim the Grim.

Now that she had met her betrothed, rather than this being a wasted trip, perhaps she could still get something out of it. Ignoring any pleasantries she cut straight to the point.

'Why are the English here?' she asked.

Kanijeli remained seated behind his desk. He had not offered her a seat, which added to her irritation. This was, after all, *her* father's chambers. Yet in truth she never felt close to the Sultan nor anything he did. Why God had chosen for her to be born a Princess she did not know, but there was no wisdom in it as far as she was concerned. With her adventurous spirit, she would rather be a common villager living in the countryside where the forest and land were at her disposal. Or better still she would be a Rüzgar like Awa, out in the world on dangerous missions.

'One could ask this of many nations: the Persians, the Moroccans, the Venetians, the Hapsburgs. All have been foes at times. Your father the Sultan seeks to rise above these historic differences. *Trade not war* is his mantra.'

'We cannot trade with men such as the Earl of Rothminster,' Fatma said.

Kanijeli arched an eyebrow. She hated it when he did that, and he did it frequently. 'There are many men we do not wish to deal with, but the reality of politics is we must deal with them.'

'He stole the Staff of Moses,' Fatma pressed on.

175

Her betrothed tilted his head to one side and smiled. It was a condescending gesture, and she took it to mean what it was. 'Matters of state are best left to those of us with a talent for such things.'

'Do you deny he was behind the theft?'

'The Earl has been implicated, but in the interests of building an alliance with the English, the matter has been overlooked. The English are a plucky upcoming people, who are useful to us, for they are a perennial thorn in the side of the Spanish. It is convenient for us to have the English close for this reason.'

Kanijeli pushed back his chair and rose to his full height. He was a man with a strong build for a politician. His hair was black, yet speckles of grey had started to take root around his temples. The age difference between them was noticeable. He clasped his hands behind his back and sauntered around the desk, drawing closer to her.

The Princess remained where she was. Her chin up.

'Tell me truly, what is it that irritates you most about the English?' he asked.

'The theft. They are untrustworthy,' Fatma replied.

'Others have done far worse things to the Empire than steal a religious artefact, yet they are here in Istanbul and I do not hear you protesting about their presence. What really inflames you, dear Fatma?'

The use of her name infuriated her once more, particularly when he put 'dear' before it, knowing all too well she meant nothing to him. At least he did not call her 'child', which she suspected he wanted to.

'As I said, they are thieves, rogues. They should not be in our capital city.'

Kanijeli narrowed his eyes. 'Or is it a particular Englishman, a former insignificant Janissary. What was his name? Yes. Will Ryde.' Her betrothed observed her face carefully and for all her efforts, she could not disguise her look of surprise. 'Is he the cause of this touchiness?'

'He is nothing,' Fatma spluttered.

'I know. A mere servant. Some say he was a slave.'

'Maybe.'

'And what is it that causes an Ottoman Princess to meet secretly with this young Englishman?'

Fatma opened her mouth to protest, then shut it once more. 'Am I being watched by your spies?'

'We are all being watched, my dear, this is the nature of the Ottoman court. You know this. There are no secrets, no private liaisons, no clandestine gatherings. All news, no matter how petty, comes back to me. As the Grand Vizier, I am the adviser of the Sultan, so I must know everything that takes place in the city and beyond its borders.'

This meeting wasn't turning out as she had planned and it was getting worse by the minute. 'I will take my leave.'

As Fatma turned to go, Kanijeli reached out and took her wrist. The look on his face was a serious one; gone was the mocking humour.

'Your reputation is the only thing you have, Fatma. Do not sully it, for you will end up living a lonely life as a spinster in a room with no windows and die a miserable death without being remembered by anyone.'

She wanted to respond, but the appropriate rejoinder escaped her. Instead she shook her hand free, gathered her dress about her and made for the door.

27

TRADE FAIR

P ART OF THE WESTERN CITY had been cleared as a
venue for the trade fair, the first of this scale witnessed
in the city of Istanbul. More than fifty nations and tribes
were represented, each with its own pavilion. Residents were
encouraged to explore the riches of the world within the confines
of the capital. Visitors were welcomed from other parts of the
Ottoman Empire and further afield. The Sultan had truly opened
the doors to trade and wanted to see as much commercial activity
as possible. Will wondered whether the Earl of Rothminster was
correct in his observation that the Ottoman treasuries must be
running low for the Sultan to initiate such a spectacle.

Pavilions and marquees representing the various trading
nations were scattered across what was previously an open
field in the western quarter. Special carriages were laid on to
shuttle people to the venue, though most walked, as had Will
when he arrived a few hours earlier. The flaps to the pavilions
were pulled open, enabling visitors to move freely from one
venue to the next. Small flags flew on the roof of each unit,
designating the national or tribal origin of their merchants.
The European nations were clumped together in one quadrant,
each having its own marquee. The Germanic ones had built an
impressive pavilion, and at the entrance there was a gold-plated

carriage, in many ways depicting their engineering and design brilliance. Will discovered many tradesmen with technical skills, particularly metalwork, many of which he had had little knowledge of previously. Remembering his friend Anver fondly, he expected the Venetian would be enthralled by the skill of the Germanic metalsmiths.

Having spent most of the morning running errands for Sir Reginald around the European pavilions, Will finally had time to himself and wanted to explore further afield. He was particularly keen to go east in a global sense and see what was there. He was not disappointed, coming across a grand pavilion housing representatives from the Mughal Emperor of India. Of course, anyone who knew anything about recent world events knew of the great Mughal Emperor Akbar. His fortunes and those of his court were famous in the writings of the Ottomans. Their wealth seemed to match that of the Ottomans, and they were known for building lavish palaces and courtyards. At the entrance to the Mughal pavilion was a beast Will had only read about. An elephant. It had a long trunk and two tusks of ivory. The animal was decorated with fabrics and tassels of sparkling gold, silver and red. Will approached it, noticing its trainer sitting close by, whom he acknowledged with a curt nod.

'You're a big lad, aren't you?' Will said to the elephant, placing his hand on the animal's trunk.

The skin was like hardened leather, almost rock-like. If this beast decided to charge at an army, Will couldn't see anyone getting in its way. The elephant eyed him warily. Will picked up the brush that the trainer used and scrubbed the animal's leg. To Will's surprise the elephant nodded its head, as though appreciating the gesture.

'And intelligent,' Will added.

Leaving the elephant behind, Will entered the Indian pavilion. A young man ran up to him.

'*Barfee* for you, sir,' the young lad offered him a bowl and Will picked up one of the sweets.

'Thank you.' The lad disappeared to serve the next customer as Will savoured the milky dessert. It rather tasted like *halu*, which he had often enjoyed in Marrakesh. The Indian pavilion was crammed full with Europeans, gawping at the wealth on display. Jewels, heavily guarded but openly displayed, sparkled from every section of the pavilion.

Musicians in one corner played on instruments resembling the flamenco guitars Will had seen on every street corner of Marrakesh. The Indian instrument was longer and rested upon the crossed legs of the musician, who was perched on a cushion. Alongside him was an equally adroit fellow whose fingers tapped rhythmically on a type of drum.

As Will moved deeper into the pavilion, he saw it was awash with fabrics and craft items. The Indian traders were rushing about, servicing the demand from their European customers. It seemed there were too many customers and too few items to purchase. Someone caught Will by the elbow. He turned to see a familiar yet unwelcome face.

'Ryde,' snarled Sir Reginald Rathbone.

'Sir.'

'Look at those fools,' Rathbone motioned to the buyers. 'Fawning to the Mughals. Pathetic, I'd say.'

'How do you mean, sir?' Will asked.

'They, the Mughals with all their riches, should be buying from us. Not the other way around.'

'Seems to me, sir, they have what others want.'

'Rubbish, boy. It's just a question of perspective. They have the raw materials, but that doesn't mean we can't make the finished items and then sell them back to others, including the Indians. After all, buying from England will be a lot cheaper than going all the way to India.'

180

'I think the Indians might not want to do that, sir.'

'Who cares what they want. Military industrial power is what will make the difference in the new century, Ryde. Not horsemen with bows and swords. And we will have plenty of industrial firepower to play with soon. The tide will change. We will rule over these Indians one day, and they will buy everything from us – from steel to cotton. Mark my words, Ryde.'

The noble was mad as far as Will could see, and thankfully he soon turned away from Will and marched out of the pavilion. Evidently, he had seen enough to satisfy himself that his ideas – however outlandish – were right. Will continued to savour the delights of the Indian pavilion before deciding he would head over to the equally impressive Chinese marquee. The Chinese Emperor was just as rich and fabulous as the Mughal one. His nation was said to be even bigger, its books of knowledge and statecraft the oldest in the world. Will expected that Li might covertly have already sneaked off to the Chinese stand – and who could blame him? Speaking in your mother tongue was like having honey in your mouth ... sweet and soothing.

'Will, Will Ryde!' a voice called out. He turned to see Mahmoud al Jameel waving to him and making his way in his direction. Will hadn't discovered anything further about his friends and had been occupied all day with the sinister work of the Earl of Rothminster and Sir Reginald Rathbone. There was no time to go snooping around the city. The previous encounter between the Princess's bodyguard Fumu and Li also made him wary. He had a feeling Li was his tail wherever he went, as Rathbone didn't trust him. And he never would, which was why Will needed to find a way out of his current predicament. Somehow, he had to get his mother to safety and out of the clutches of these despicable rogues. Yet first he needed to know why they had brought him to Istanbul and what they wanted him to do.

'*Sidi*,' Will replied, using the term of respect Awa's father would be familiar with.

'How are you, young man?' Mahmoud asked.

'Well, thank you. And you?'

'Troubled. Since you told me my daughter might be in the city I have been ranging the streets, asking about her. No one seems to have seen her or even heard of her.'

In truth, Will couldn't be sure Awa was in the city or even alive. But he didn't have it in him to shatter her father's hopes.

'I, too, have failed to find any traces.'

He hadn't found anything because he had not really looked. He was kept on such a tight leash there was no way for him to get close to the Janissary fort or Commander Konjic's former base at the Rumelihisari Fort.

They continued to stroll down the central path, passing the Chinese pavilion, which Will made a note to come back to, as some of the food smells emanating from it took his fancy. The lane curved and led back towards an open square covered by an enormous canvas canopy, beneath which hundreds were milling about in a sort of vast meeting area. Traders and diplomats from an array of nations were in open dialogue with one another, all on Ottoman soil. Will caught sight of the Earl of Rothminster deep in conversation with Spanish representatives, which was odd, considering the Spanish were mortal enemies of the Elizabethan crown and the Armada they had sent was a recent memory. The Persian delegation was in animated discussion with Italians, who, if Will remembered correctly, would be under the rule of the Roman Catholic Church. The Moroccans were chatting with the Turks, when for so much of their recent history they had been sworn enemies. Remembering his time in Marrakesh, he knew the Moroccans felt pure disdain for the Turks. Until Will arrived in Istanbul, he had not appreciated that much of this was driven by envy. Everyone was speaking across adversarial lines. In one way it was heartening to see and in another it was just politics. Will recalled Commander Konjic instructing him that Socrates the great Greek philosopher said that the best of men were engaged with ideas and principles, lesser men with politics and the least capable with the affairs of others.

'I must leave soon, to visit scholars in Konya,' said Mahmoud.

'What exactly is it you do for the Moroccans?'

'I am a scholar at the court of al Mansour. As such, I advise on matters to do with my research area and seek out and document other scholarly works found in different countries and collect these for the Moroccan court.'

'Do you enjoy it?'

'Yes, for I am a scholar who has been sponsored to do his work. And no, for I would prefer to have been a resident scholar in my own city of Timbuktu, where I was already given patronage and lived in my ancestral home,' Mahmoud smiled. 'Yet God decrees what is to be and we must make the best of this.'

Will could see the familial connection with Awa. He imagined her saying something like this as well.

'I will try and return to Istanbul, but it might be my journey takes me elsewhere. I do not know. Here.' Mahmoud passed Will an envelope.

'What is this? Will asked.

'It is a letter for Awa. Should you see her before me, then give this to her. It contains the details of where I reside in Marrakesh and how to find me. Tell her I love her and will be waiting for her.'

Will nodded. 'I will give this to her.'

He just hoped she was still alive by the time he found out where she was.

183

28

NO ACCOUNTABILITY

P EDESTRIANS STROLLING ALONG PAST THE
Society of Miniaturists were few and far between.
Despite the early hour, more residents would normally
be going about their day by now. Sitting with her chin cupped
in her hands, staring out the shop window, Awa wasn't sure
what they had learnt from their trip to see the geomancer.
Other than using her encounter with Zawaba'a to summon
other Jinn, what else had he done? The one thing she felt sure
of was that he was not a man to be trusted.

The young companions deliberated over the words uttered
by the geomancer before he passed out, yet could not fathom
their meaning. Much could be indicated or nothing at all.
Perhaps, Awa speculated, the words were coded in some way,
or they might lead them down a fruitless path, exposing their
efforts to Zawaba'a.

Awa decided to let her mind work on the problem in the
background as she turned her immediate focus to a page of
text she had copied in the Library of the Hidden Sciences.
The passage was attributed to Solomon the Wise: *The one who
frees a Jinn after it has been cast into captivity, remains sheltered
from its dominance.* The text gave her a degree of hope as she
read it for the tenth time. Yet did such words apply to one as

powerful as Zawaba'a? There was only one way to put this to the test, and if she misunderstood the passage or it had not actually been uttered by Solomon, then there would not be a second chance.

Outside the window a carriage pulled up on the other side of the street; two men got out and went inside the haberdasher's shop.

'Here, drink this,' a soothing voice said as Doctor Anisa brought her a warm cup. 'It's basil-and-mint tea.'

'Thank you,' said Awa, taking it.

'I'm sorry I was not awake when you returned last night. Looking after Lütfi and treating my other patients left me exhausted.'

'I hope we didn't disturb you when we came in.'

Anisa shook her head. 'Were you able to track down Faris Al Housani?'

Awa nodded, sipping the soothing concoction, observing the haberdasher, a short, thin man with a drooping moustache, who was leaning on a staff. With a keen eye he was investigating the contents of the horse-drawn cart outside his shop. Pointing with his staff, he was indicating that the two men should unload certain items onto his own handcart, which the young man who was with him, who Awa took to be his apprentice, had pulled up onto the street.

'Yes?'

Awa rubbed her chin, sitting up straighter as she looked at Anisa. 'He performed a ceremony that summoned other Jinn then interpreted the signs he read from the lines and circles he drew. But his words make little sense.'

'What did he say?'

'He told us: "Unite the Emissaries of God. Let followers proclaim in a single voice. Then will a Demon's touch be unmade." We're not sure what it means.'

Outside, the haberdasher's handcart was quickly filled. He continued to order new items to be taken out, his staff directing the delivery men with great precision. Though Awa was not able to see the precise contents of the smaller boxes being removed from the horse-drawn cart, she supposed they were items related to sewing, knitting and dressmaking. The young apprentice placed the boxes with great care in the handcart. Watching them, she fondly remembered the dressmakers of Gao, who were famous amongst her own people, including the scholars of Timbuktu, who would make their way to Gao to buy items needed for sewing clothes for special occasions.

Anisa held her cup firmly, lifting it to sip the tea. 'The Emissaries are the prophets.'

'Yes,' Awa replied.

'Their followers are Jewish, Christian, Muslim or other faiths where a prophet or messenger came with a revelation. God says he sent a prophet or messenger to every nation or tribe upon the earth, perhaps as many as one hundred thousand messengers. We only know the names of a few.'

'Yes.'

'So when the prophets unite and their followers speak with one voice, the demon will be vanquished.'

'It would seem so. But there are no prophets or messengers in the world today. How can they unite? Followers we can bring, but people are so divided – what would it take to unite them in a single voice?'

Outside, the haberdasher had finished supervising the items to be unloaded and bade the delivery men farewell. Clapping his apprentice on the back in a fatherly way, he threw a cloak over his back. The apprentice wrapped the cloak about him and took hold of the haberdasher's staff, lifting it into the air in a dramatic gesture. The old haberdasher laughed, before his apprentice returned the old man's staff and the two of them pushed the handcart back into the shop.

'Wait!' Awa leapt up, almost spilling her tea.

'What is it?' Anisa asked.

'Prophets aren't in the world anymore, but the items that belonged to them are. The Pot of Abraham, the Turban of Joseph, the Staff of Moses, the Sword and the Armour of David, the Scrolls of John the Baptist and the Seal of Muhammad – peace be upon all of them.'

Puzzled, Anisa stared at her, before she and Awa blurted out at the same moment.

'Unite them.'

They would need to trap Zawaba' a inside a circle of these holy items. And then? She wasn't sure of the last part of it, but perhaps they had the makings of a plan.

'We need to see the former Grand Vizier, Sardar Ferhad Pasha,' Awa said.

'I hear he is teaching at a madrasa beside the Obelisk of Theodosius in the mornings.'

'Teaching?' Awa enquired. It didn't seem like the sort of thing Ferhad would do, but then who was she to judge others?

'People change, sometimes for the better,' said Anisa with a smile.

Fetching her two companions, Awa led the Rüzgar to the Obelisk Madrasa. The walk took them past many people who simply appeared weary and beaten down, as though they had enough of the unseen terror stalking their city. The usual chirpiness and energy was missing; even the stallholders had lost their voices, sitting passively waiting for customers to approach as opposed to praising their produce and offering warm invitations with friendly banter. Doctor Anisa had told her about the increasing number of residents losing their minds; it was getting worse, this illness, as some called it, though others preferred plain idiom and said straight out it was possession. Every stratum of society was affected. There were rumours circulating that some of the Royals were also infected or possessed by a demonic force.

Zawaba'a was reaching all people; there were no walls or barriers to stop him. What were the demon's plans, if there were a plan at all? Did it just intend to infect the whole city and drive them all to madness? Awa imagined residents would soon be leaping into the fast-flowing Bosporus, to be carried out to sea to their deaths. Contending with the Earl of Rothminster, who desired wealth, or Azi Dahäg, who wanted power, was much more straightforward. What did Zawaba'a want?

'How many objects are there belonging to the prophets in the Topkapi?' Anver asked.

'I don't know,' replied Gurkan. 'The collection was last held by the Mamluks in Egypt. It's grown since it arrived.'

'It has?' Anver asked.

'Why, of course, my Venetian friend. We, the famed Rüzgar, recovered the Armour of David.'

'Indeed,' Anver smiled. 'I wonder how many more objects there are in the world that can be traced back to a prophet.'

Awa tried not to remember the events that led them to bring the Armour back to Istanbul ... the terrible deaths of Master Huja and Commander Konjic; and the schism that took place in their unit when Will became possessive of the object, something Konjic had feared, which is why he never used it in his fight with the Lord of the Two Serpents. It could have saved his life, but he retained his integrity to the end. He would die as himself, not become someone he wasn't.

Arriving at the Obelisk Madrasa, they enquired after Sardar Ferhad Pasha and were told he would shortly be finishing a class. The young companions were asked to wait in an empty classroom. They sat cross-legged upon cushions on the ground, looking at a line of books at the front of the class, where the teacher would sit on a high-backed chair. A young boy soon came in with some tea, which they received gratefully and sipped in companionable silence, pondering the next phase of their mission.

There was a noise at the door, and they looked up to see Ferhad's imposing figure. He raised an eyebrow.

'What happened?' he asked, entering the classroom and shutting the door behind him, before joining them on the floor. Awa had expected him to take his place on the teacher's chair, but it seemed that losing the title of Grand Vizier had left him more humble than before. A good thing as far as Awa was concerned.

'We visited Faris Al Housani,' Awa said.

'The geomancer!' Ferhad whispered, surveying the area behind him.

'We were told he possessed certain knowledge that could assist in our investigations,' Awa continued.

'And did he?'

'Yes,' Awa considered her companions. 'We think so.'

'Go on,' Ferhad encouraged her, having got over the shock of their visit to the geomancer.

'We need access to all of the prophetic items in the Topkapi Palace,' Awa said.

There was a sharp intake of breath, before Ferhad asked, 'Why?'

'Something Faris Al Housani told us. We need a way to unite all of the prophets' relics, to trap Zawaba'a within ... imagine it to be a ring of sorts.'

'All right, and then what happens?'

'We're still working on the bit that comes after that,' Gurkan chimed in, diverting Ferhad's intense gaze away from her, for which she was grateful.

'Why can't you do what needs to be done at the Topkapi Palace itself, where the items are safely housed?' Ferhad asked.

'We don't even know where Zawaba'a is. There is little chance we can lure him into the Topkapi, since we have no means of attracting his attention. No, we have to find him then trap him in his own lair,' Awa said.

Ferhad nodded in agreement. 'Do you have an inkling as to where he might be?'

Gurkan raised his finger in the air. 'I feel we are close to discovering it.'

'You feel?' Ferhad asked.

'Yes,' Gurkan replied. 'We've searched a number of locations already. We're working through others. Sooner or later, we are bound to find his lair.'

'So you plan to venture into the demon's lair with the priceless objects belonging to the greatest prophets of all time, items that are irreplaceable, are worth more than any amount of gold, and you are going to do *what* exactly?'

'As Gurkan said, it is a plan in progress,' Anver responded.

Awa was surprised at his boldness, compared to when she first encountered him. It seemed their adventures had toughened him.

Ferhad shook his head, staring towards the vast array of books at the front of the classroom.

'Matters are getting worse each day, with more and more people affected by this sickness. Some are calling it the demonic plague. Others say there is a curse upon the city, a punishment from God, for the Sultan inviting all his enemies to Istanbul. We know the truth – it is Zawaba'a. Still, we cannot have civil unrest in the streets and must return matters to their normal state as soon as possible.'

The companions remained silent, letting the former Grand Vizier work through the arguments in his head.

'Very well,' Ferhad said finally, 'if it is possible to get you in, for security is, as you know, extremely tight in the Hall of Religious Relics. By God, you were part of that security protocol that Commander Konjic introduced after recovering the Staff of Moses! Well, let's just imagine you are able to bypass the security, after that you are on your own. If you get caught, then I will accept no responsibility, and it's likely you'll find yourself back in the same gaol as before. This time they won't wait till the morning to execute you. Do you understand the risks?'

Once more Awa asked herself why was she doing this. She could just leave Istanbul right now and head south. But where? As far as she knew, her dear father was dead, or at least lost to her forever in this world. What more did she have to live for if not this cause? To make good something they had done wrong by letting the demon out in the first place?

She exchanged a look with her companions, sensing their hesitation but at the same time their determination. It seemed to her the Rüzgar had had many falls, but their greatest attribute was the unstoppable determination to get back up every time they fell. They were, after all, like the wind, an untethered force.

'We do,' Awa replied.

29

HOLY REQUEST

THE BLACK BEAR COFFEE-HOUSE off the main street of the Kumkapi district, home of the Armenian community, appeared to be attracting a steady flow of patrons this evening. They were mostly tradesman, artisans and some coarse types from the port. No one important as far as the authorities were concerned. *The perfect place for a meeting*, mused Will as he approached, with Li by his side. He pushed open the door and went inside. The customers, an irregular bunch as far as Will could make out, paid little attention to him, but a few stares did linger on the man from Cathay. However, soon enough, the shaggy crew returned to their conversations or games of cards. Will scanned the large open room with its low ceiling, but saw only locals. Had he and Li come to the wrong location?

The Chinaman nudged him and motioned ahead, taking the lead and walking past the coffee servers towards the back of the building. One of them nodded at Li as he went past. The bodyguard had been here before; Will decided it was best to keep quiet and pretend he knew what was going on. They left the main serving area behind and passed down a narrow corridor with private meeting rooms on either side. Will detected voices coming through some of the doors but wasn't able to tell what they were saying. Li stopped at the very last room and knocked four times in quick succession.

'Enter.'

Will let the Chinaman take the lead and followed him into the room, where there was a table capable of seating six. On one side, wearing smug expressions, were the Earl of Rothminster and Sir Reginald Rathbone. Uncertain as to their intentions, Will remained constantly vigilant when close to these two rogues. They had barely spoken with him since arriving, merely asking others to send him on errands. Mostly these tasks involved dispatches and documents that needed to be taken to certain individuals by particular times. Nothing untoward as far as Will could tell.

The two English gentlemen acknowledged his arrival, before staring back at the documents laid out before them. Rathbone raised his coffee cup to his lips, taking a sip. Even from this distance the coffee smelt enticing and flavourful to Will who had grown accustomed to drinking the brew whilst living with the Ottomans. Li told him to stand to one side of the door, and the Chinese bodyguard took up a position on the other side. Will was rather hoping they would invite him to sit down and have a cup of coffee with them, but no such civility was offered. It seemed they were waiting for someone else to arrive.

Several minutes passed like this, the Earl and Rathbone sipping their drinks in silence, ignoring Will and Li, whilst Will's nerves became more frayed by the minute. He had been on his feet most of the day, running about the city delivering packages, still unable to locate his friends. Li was his constant companion these days. Evidently, Rathbone did not trust him as far as Li could throw him and made sure the Chinaman maintained a watchful eye on the former Janissary.

A knock at the door startled Will out of his reverie. Rathbone glanced at the Earl, who took a moment to clear the papers laid out before them, before nodding to his accomplice.

'Come in,' said Rathbone.

A figure wearing a long-hooded robe entered. It was impossible to see his features. The man seemed to take Will in before he turned towards the gentlemen seated at the table.

'Good evening,' said the newcomer.

'And to you, dear sir,' said the Earl, gesturing towards one of the seats.

The man moved round the table, so that when he sat he would be facing Will directly. He paused a moment, before lowering his hood to reveal the features of Commander Berk, the Ottoman Janissary officer responsible for the weakening of the Rüzgar and the man guilty of destroying the reputations of Commander Konjic and Captain Kadri. Will felt an urge to leap at Berk and strike him down before he settled in his place at the table with the Earl. Seeing Will's startled expression, Berk sneered at the young Englishman with a look of pure and utter disdain. To Berk, Will was nothing more than a slave, to be used in whatever grand game they were playing.

'Is the pup behaving?' Berk asked.

'He has no choice,' replied the Earl.

'As it should be,' Berk said.

Will noticed Rathbone observing him keenly, and it was hard not to let his true emotions show. Berk was most likely responsible for the deaths of his friends. Yet Will could not touch him: he was a bizarre ally of the Earl's, and while Will's mother remained under the Earl's 'protection', as Rathbone liked to put it, Will's hands were tied. He bit his lip and lowered his gaze, before Rathbone turned away, ensuring Will clearly understood his lowly status amongst those gathered in this room.

'Are you ready?' Berk asked.

The Earl glared at Li and then Will. 'Yes.'

Ready for what? What was the Earl going to get Will to do? It seemed from Li's body language he knew, but whatever plans they had, they were kept veiled from Will, leaving him tense and exasperated by the whole situation.

'Then here is the schedule,' Berk said pushing a piece of paper towards Rathbone, who unfolded it, looked at it, then tucked it away inside his doublet.

'And the day?' the Earl asked.

'Saturday,' Berk replied.

Whatever was being planned was only two days away. Searching the faces of these rogues, Will wasn't able to understand what they were talking about. Even when they spoke it was in a sort of code, and unless you knew the context of the conversation, which he didn't, there was no way of following it.

'What of your regiments, are they in place?' enquired the Earl.

'My regiments are my concern, and they will be in place. Just make sure the items are no longer in the city. They are the spark that will ignite the fire,' said Berk.

'They will be on a ship, and our men will rendezvous with your men at the appointed place so the items can be handed over, undamaged.'

Berk leant forward, eyes boring into the Earl. 'A lot is riding on this. We are about to end the reign of the monarchical Sultans and inaugurate the rule of the Janissaries. The Ottoman Empire was founded by men who knew how to fight, and it will be given a new lease of life by fighting men. The Sultans have become insipid and weak, unable even to take to the battlefield.' He paused before continuing. 'Don't fail me. For if you do the world is not large enough for you to hide in it, Rothminster.'

The realisation of what was afoot hit Will like a punch in the gut. The Janissaries were going to overthrow the monarchy and establish a military elite to rule the empire. He had heard about the Mamluks, who had been slave soldiers, doing such a thing in Egypt. Now the Ottoman Janissaries were about to repeat this. What would happen to the royal family? What was going to happen to Princess Fatma? Rebellions never ended well for those in power nor for the ordinary people: when blood started to flow, it had a habit of gushing in all directions. He couldn't stand by and do nothing. But why was he concerned? Did it really make any difference to him who the rulers were?

The Earl smiled in the roguish manner Will had witnessed on many occasions.

'In this new military order you'll need allies who are also fighting men. Our Queen will be dead soon, and our new monarch will support you in your struggles against the Hapsburgs. He has already assured me of this. We will be your partners in the West.'

'A partnership is made of equals. The English are not our equals,' Berk retorted.

Rothminster was momentarily caught off guard, before replying, 'Very well, the English will be your supporters and helpers.'

'Let it be so,' said Berk. 'And may our resolve be firm. My men will wait for the items on the agreed island.' He got up to go. The Janissary Commander was making for the exit. This was Will's only chance: he had to know.

'Are they alive, my friends?'

Rathbone shot him a disdainful look. The Earl glared at him.

Berk drew closer to Will, till he was only a foot away. 'Would it please you if I told you they were?'

'Yes, of course,' Will replied.

'Then I will not tell you.' Berk tucked his robes about him, lifted his hood back up and left the room.

Will wanted to chase after Berk, put his elbow into the man's throat and beat the truth out of him, but he couldn't; looking back at the Earl of Rothminster he realised he was already out of line as far as the present nobility were concerned. Rathbone got up from his chair and crossed the short distance to Will.

'Did we ask you to speak?' Rathbone asked.

'No, sir.'

Without warning, Rathbone drew his blade from its scabbard and smashed the pommel into Will's chin, knocking his head back against the wall. His eyes welled with tears as he tried to adjust his vision, expecting a barrage of blows, but by the time his head was clear, Rathbone was sitting calmly back at the table sipping coffee as though nothing had happened.

The Earl held the paper that Berk had handed to him, reading it over. He turned to Will, a smile upon his polished features. Will wiped the tears from his eyes, standing up straighter.

'You should know this, Ryde, that there is one reason and one alone why we brought you to Istanbul, for in truth neither of us trusts you nor do we like being in the presence of a lowly servant,' the Earl announced. 'You are familiar, very familiar, in fact, with the Hall of Religious Relics within the Topkapi Palace. You know where every sacred object is kept, where the guards are posted, what traps are placed to catch a thief. And it is to this end that you are here.'

It began to dawn on Will what they wanted him to do.

'Saturday evening,' the Earl said, holding up the piece of paper, 'you and the Chinaman will make your way into the Topkapi Palace, with the help of this schedule of when the guards rotate. You will remove all of the religious artefacts belonging to the prophets and be on a boat out of the city before the alarm is raised.'

Destiny seemed to have tied him to the Staff of Moses and the other sacred items. He was going to be transporting these artefacts once more, this time not bringing them to Istanbul but out of the city gates.

'King Richard the Lionheart may not have been able to capture the Holy Land in his Crusade, but I will capture what is holy,' said the Earl.

By the sound of it, the Earl had no intention of rendezvousing with Berk's men and handing the artefacts over to them. He was planning to take them back to England.

30

CISTERNS

MUNCHING AN APPLE, WITH A scrapbook in his other hand, and a pencil tucked behind his ear, Anver cut a curious, out-of-place figure, strolling down the lane in the Armenian-dominated Kumkapi district, packed as it was with tradesmen, artisans and dockhands. Business was done for the day, and these traders and artists were more interested in socialising than reading. It mattered little to the Venetian, who, whilst flicking through his notes, kept a watchful eye on approaching pedestrians, careful to avoid them and carry on.

It didn't help him avoid the hooded man who suddenly emerged out of the Black Bear Coffee-House, knocking into Anver.

'Imbecile,' the hooded man snorted, losing his balance.

Anver caught his scrapbook as it headed for the ground but lost his apple in the process: it rolled away into a narrow trough on one side of the road. *Shame*, he thought. It was a tasty piece of fruit, but he wasn't going to retrieve it from where it ended up.

The hooded man straightened and remained motionless for a moment.

'You!' he pointed a finger at Anver.

'Me?' Anver replied meekly.

The man lowered his hood. Anver immediately recognised the face of the person who had sent them to the utterly unpleasant prison. Commander Berk of the Janissary force.

'Yes, you're the Venetian, the Jewish lad. Whatever your name is.'

Anver gulped. This was not good.

'I think you have me confused with someone else, sir,' Anver replied, shutting his scrapbook.

'No, I don't. I never forget a face. You were with the West African girl, Awa, and the Konyan, Gurkan, and the ...' he paused, looking back at the coffee-house from which he had emerged, before continuing. '... the Englishman, Will Ryde.'

As gently as was possible in his frazzled state, Anver took a stride back, then some more. Berk smiled. 'The irony of it. Now I can finish you and your friends off.' The Janissary Commander waved across the street, where Anver noted two waiting accomplices. Both were heavy brutes, dressed in civilian clothing, but if they were with Berk, they were most likely Janissaries and would know how to handle their weapons.

The Venetian rotated on the spot, noticing two more men making a beeline for him. This didn't look promising. He removed the sack from his back, fingers groping about inside. Where was the thing? He knew it was here someplace. The men were getting closer. Berk waited where he was, smiling, putting his hood back up. Anver's fingers discovered the object he was looking for. He removed the glass vial with its black powdery contents. Rapidly, he struck a flame using a tinder box before he lit a short fuse on the end of the vial and launched it at the ground next to the two men behind him.

Boom. The gunpowder went off. The Janissaries leapt to one side. The explosion was harmless, but enough to startle his assailants and buy him some time. Anver shot through the space they'd left by diving to the side, as dark-grey smoke swirled about in the area. Running past them, he threw the other glass vial he had prepared and it went off with an equally satisfying bang. The two men crossing the street briefly paused but noting the minimal impact of both explosions, plucked up the courage to give chase.

'Get him!' Berk shouted as Anver slung the sack over his back. He sprinted down the street, cutting right down a cobblestone alley. The space narrowed to the width of three men, before it opened up into a courtyard, with residential dwellings on every side. Narrow arterial pathways led off in a multitude of directions, giving him too many options. He knew from past experience that these paths sometimes circled back in the same direction they came from, and the last thing he wanted to do was run into Berk once more. Instead, he set off in the opposite direction, heading towards the second hill of Istanbul, in the direction of the Forum of Constantine, an area he had never visited. It was not one people recommended, particularly after dark when strange goings on were often reported.

'There!' One of his pursuers had spotted him before he was able to disappear down the side street. He should have been quicker. He cursed his timing. It must have been down to losing the apple; he still had its taste on his tongue. He really wished he hadn't dropped it and wondered whether a street dog was going to eat it for its evening meal. That thought left him feeling a little better, though he had never been keen on dogs.

The street before him sloped downwards, accelerating his progress. Navigating around the items people left in streets was never easy, and in this one there were too many to count. He almost clattered into an abandoned cart, which stuck out from behind a shed someone had decided to build outside their dwelling and which blocked off half of the street. In avoiding it, he shifted his weight to the left and grazed his elbow on the wall. It hurt. He pressed on. The footsteps behind him were closing in. Anver was not a runner at the best of times and there seemed to be a lot of it involved in his job as a member of the Rüzgar. But he never complained, because the job allowed him to try out his inventions and ideas and he fitted right in with the rest of the crew.

At speed, he approached a junction and made up his mind to go left as his bodyweight was already veering him in that direction. His lungs were burning now from the effort of the chase and the exhilaration of it. He risked a quick look back. The men, of whom there were now four, were closer than before. He couldn't outrun them: they were professional soldiers after all. He needed to hide someplace. Lie low, let them race by and then sneak back to meet the others at the Society of Miniaturists when the coast was clear.

He first had to get out of their sight for a few seconds. Anver cut right into a lane. It smelt really awful, and he almost retreated but could hear the men approaching. Up ahead the lane curved around a corner out of sight. They knew he had come this way and would assume he'd followed the bend in the lane. As he rolled under a set of carts standing flush against the building on his right, he noticed there was a narrow water channel in the ground behind the carts which seemed to run the length of the street. This was an outflow of waste from these buildings. Unlike in other streets, this one wasn't covered. No wonder it smelt so bad. God knows what he was crawling about in.

'What a stink,' one of the Janissaries shouted as they thundered past.

Anver remained completely quiet, his heart racing, his forehead pouring with sweat. He cupped his hand over his mouth and breathed out as slowly as possible.

The other two Janissaries also went past, taking the bend in the road up ahead. The smell about him really was revolting. He was about to get up, when he noticed a flicker of light come from below ground and reflect up into the water channel. Strange, he thought. On all fours and moving as silently as possible, Anver shuffled forward, the slime a constant reminder of the filth he was crawling through. It seemed that in Will's absence, falling into bogs and crawling through hideous places was now his calling. He wasn't pleased to be doing this and was trying very hard not to throw up. Drawing parallel with where he had noticed the flicker of light, he realised the channel came to a halt, then rounded a bend, moving under the building above him. It became narrower still, but enough to fit his slender frame. He threw a look back along the street. Still no sign of his pursuers, but it wouldn't hurt to descend to a deeper hiding place which they couldn't spot from the street if they decided to double back.

The crawl led him to an opening into which all of the sludge from the water channel flowed. This was still further underground. Peering down, Anver noticed a walkway. There must be someone down there, but who? He heard voices from the street and saw the feet and ankles of the four men standing by the opening to his channel.

'You sure he headed this way?' one of them said.

'Yes, but where did he go?'

Silence.

'All right, you two double back, in case he somehow gave us the slip. We'll look here: there's so much junk on this street, he might be hiding behind one of the carts or barrels.'

If they decided to look further they might find him. There was little choice left. Anver slithered through the narrow opening which led into the lower walkway, dropping to the floor, before taking in his surroundings. He was in some kind of underground tunnel beneath the roads and lanes of the city. There was a walkway, and alongside it was a narrow channel of running water. He wondered where it flowed to. A few cressets lit the way. Other than the sound of his footsteps there was silence around him. He headed in the direction of the flowing water, intrigued to see whether it led to the Bosporus and an escape route from his pursuers.

He continued walking for nearly twenty minutes before the passage led to another, which guided him right, then further right, before he saw the first inhabitant of this underground settlement. The man was a sentry, weapon by his side. He looked bored. More importantly, what was he guarding in this abandoned place? Anver decided he'd make things a little more interesting for the fellow. Searching through his sack he soon found what he needed. Lighting the harmless but extremely bright firework, he threw it to the left of the fellow down the corridor. The light flared and the sentry did what Anver expected: he went to investigate, leaving the route open for Anver to slip further into whatever the sentry was there to block.

The bland, smooth walls soon gave way to ornate carvings from an older period. The Byzantine patterns were in line with what he had seen above ground at the Column of Constantine and other relics from the past. The ceiling dipped before he emerged through an archway into an enormous chamber with a high ceiling and arches running all along the sides. In the centre were large pools of water. It looked like some kind of old bathhouse from Constantinople's past. Strange orbs of light scattered throughout this grand chamber radiated a low glow giving the subterranean surroundings an eerie radiance. Keeping low, he scuttled forward, aware of a group of men, all armed, up ahead. They all had their backs to him and seemed to be listening to someone.

Anver had rested his hand on a cold surface before he realised it was a statue. Above it was a cylindrical pillar, similar to the hundreds of other pillars that stretched from floor to ceiling, connecting the arches spanning the roof of the structure. Taking a closer look, he jumped when he noticed the statue at the foot of the pillar. It was the head of a figure he had read about from Greek mythology – Medusa. He certainly had no intention of being turned into stone, yet looking about him, all he could see were stone statues. He quickly removed his hand from Medusa's head and eased forward to hide behind the next pillar, deliberately making his way closer till he could hear the conversation clearly.

The men wore long black robes, with hoods covering their faces. They looked like the hermits he had seen outside Jerusalem but – unlike those men of faith – he doubted the piety of these fellows. Peeking around the next pillar, Anver detected a red aura before the men. He couldn't see what was emitting it, but he had come across this before. Yes, when they were fleeing Istanbul, there had been something luring him into the narrow side street. Was this the same phenomenon? Heart thumping in his chest, he reminded himself to remain calm. What would Awa do in this situation, he asked himself. She would investigate. He would do the same: whatever was going on here had something to do with their mission to stop the Jinn who was terrorising the city.

He was only two pillars away from the huddle of black-robed figures when he decided he couldn't get any closer without giving himself away. He peered around the current pillar and through an opening between two of the robed men he saw what his friends had witnessed in Jerusalem. Zawaba'a.

The Jinn throbbed with power, its hulking form sending a shudder down Anver's back. He felt the hairs on his arms stand up at the sight. Anver whipped his head back and hid behind the pillar, frozen with fear, his back pressed against the cold stone. How were they going to capture such a being? He prayed for courage then tentatively peeked out once more.

Before Zawaba'a on the ground were rows upon rows of black obsidian rocks in all shapes and sizes. Some looked like they had been detached from jewellery, others from weapons, others still were just rocks.

'Is this all?' Zawaba'a's face was incredulous, looking at the rocks before him.

'Oh, Great One, this is all we could find in the city,' one of the robed men said.

'Cities have become larger but are filled with useless objects and worthless people,' Zawaba'a said. His voice was a low growl, the words seeming to hang in the air after he had spoken.

The cadre of robed acolytes bowed their heads. Anver was unsure what the Jinn was doing with these men, but they must have been his agents in the city. The Venetian went back to observing the fragments and pieces of obsidian laid out on the ground.

'Place them in the cauldron,' Zawaba'a ordered.

The disciples immediately picked up the obsidian stones from the ground and did as instructed before moving back to their positions. Anver had to shuffle across the ground and hide behind a new pillar to keep watching what was happening.

'Do not touch any of these till the morning,' Zawaba'a warned the men.

'Yes, Great One,' they replied.

With the cauldron in front of him, Zawaba'a plunged his muscular arms inside it, and Anver thought he heard a hissing sound coming from within the vessel. The Jinn's face was hidden in shadow, only its burning red eyes visible to Anver. The cauldron began to rattle, as though the insides were boiling. Anver could see the strain running down the Jinn's arms. He seemed to be sending some type of energy from within himself into the obsidian. The sound of stones pinging around the inside of the vessel grew louder as the robed priests retreated. Anver gripped the statue beside him; this one seemed to be of a fish.

Smoke poured out of the cauldron when Zawaba'a stepped away, stumbling as he did so. Whatever he had just done had clearly drained an incredible amount of energy from him. The Jinn slumped to one knee, catching at the side of the cauldron with one outstretched hand to keep himself from toppling over.

The black-robed follower who had spoken previously hurriedly advanced.

'Oh, Great One ...' he said, but Zawaba'a lifted himself to his full height and backhanded the man so that he flew through the air and landed flat on his back, his head hitting the ground with a crack, right beside Anver. His eyes were closed.

'Do not dare approach me without my command!' Zawaba'a snarled.

The Jinn turned slowly about, disappearing into the deeper recesses of the chamber. The glow of his aura faded. Anver looked across at the sprawled follower and realised his companions would soon be coming to check on him. He had to get out now. He sprinted for the next pillar, then the next and kept going, moving from one to the other, till he was back under the side arches of the chamber. He distracted the sentry who was there with another harmless but intriguing set of fireworks before finding his way to the walkway that he hoped had an outlet somewhere close to the Bosporus.

31

REVEALED

THE SOCIETY OF MINIATURISTS WAS quieter than usual these days. It never bustled with patrons like a souk, but on a typical day a steady stream of discerning and well-to-do residents made their way through the wood-and-glass doors, through the workshop and into the welcoming room at the rear of the building reserved for entertaining customers who could speak freely with the Master Miniaturist Lütfi Abdallah. Those days were gone, for now at least, so long as the master lay in his private quarters, in the grips of demonic possession, seemingly neither in this world nor in the next but trapped somewhere else. Other than his primary apprentice, who remained, Doctor Anisa had given his other staff time off with pay.

Every time Awa heard the moans of the miniaturist emanating from the rear of the building, it only strengthened her resolve. She missed Lütfi's wise counsel, for the man was well versed in many of the manuscripts they were reading as well as having had previous dealings with the geomancer, whose own intentions remained a mystery to Awa. The more she recalled the incident, the more it appeared he had used her memories to bring together other powerful spirits and demons and was looking to bind them to his will. To what end she did not know, but harnessing such a force could only lead to an evil outcome.

Sipping her coffee, she examined the sheets of paper spread before her. Despite all the research they had done they weren't much closer to knowing how to imprison Zawaba'a than when they started. Notionally he could be imprisoned in a brass vessel, such as a vase or urn. They might be able to use the sacred objects left by the prophets to bind him, but beyond that there was no telling how they were actually going to get him inside the brass prison. She went over the words uttered by the geomancer once more: 'Unite the Emissaries of God. Let followers proclaim in a single voice. Then will a Demon's touch be unmade.' How were they going to get their followers to unite, when nations were so divided? Even amongst Muslims there was a division between the Sunni and Shi'a, and amongst Christians it was even worse, with the bloodletting going on between the Catholics and Protestants. Even the Jews had their divisions, between the Orthodox and those such as Anver who lived in European cities like Venice. She rubbed her forehead with her knuckles, trying to ease some of the tension.

'I feel the same,' Gurkan said. The Konyan slouched in a chair in the corner of the underground room. He looked like he was half dozing.

'I'm sure,' Awa replied, a hint of sarcasm in her voice.

'No, really,' Gurkan continued. 'It's why I'm resting at this very moment. The sheer scale of the problem is weighing me down.'

'So you're sleeping.'

'I would say I'm letting my mind wander.'

'To what end?' Awa asked.

'I don't know, it depends where it goes.'

'Daydreaming you mean, of heroic deeds and chronicles written about the great Konyan swordsman Gurkan.'

The Konyan smiled. 'Not at the moment, but, yes, I admit, I do indulge in that sort of thing as well.'

'Better to live life in the spirit of service and let others write what you did,' Awa replied.

The Konyan was about to come back with a response, when the door at the top of the stairs leading up to the main building opened, revealing Anver.

Gurkan looked up. 'You look awful,' he said.

'Are you hurt?' Awa asked.

The Venetian half fell down the narrow stairs, before coming to stand before them.

'Oh, you smell worse,' said Gurkan, holding his nose.

Anver surveyed his clothes, regarding them for what seemed the first time.

'Really?' said Anver. He smelt his sleeves. 'Oh, that's bad.'

'What happened? Awa asked.

The Venetian was distressed by his appearance now that Gurkan had brought it to his attention and needed further coaxing from Awa to continue.

'Zawaba'a!' Anver blurted out. 'I found him.'

Awa and Gurkan exchanged glances. 'Where?' Awa asked.

'In an underground place, with water, sewage.'

'What were you doing down there?' Gurkan asked.

'Running away from Commander Berk and his thugs.'

'Berk!' Gurkan repeated.

'I bumped into him on the street outside the Black Bear Coffee-House in the Kumkapi district. Janissaries chased me, but I gave them the slip by crawling into a sewer.' He pointed at his clothes.

'Brave man,' Gurkan commented.

'I discovered an opening that led to underground tunnels. There was this enormous Byzantine-period chamber with arches, pools of water, the head of Medusa.'

'Medusa, the ...' Gurkan wriggled his fingers around his head to give the appearance of snakes.

'Yes, that Medusa. But most of all there were these men in black robes, as if they were in a cult. They kept addressing Zawaba'a as their Master. He then poured his energy into a batch of obsidian rocks. The effort seemed to weaken him. I got out at that point.'

The Jinn was far more organised than they had expected. He wasn't operating alone but had built that following of humans the former Grand Vizier had informed them about when he first approached them with the mission. What was he planning to do and what were these obsidian rocks for? There were too many questions, adding to the existing complexity and making solving this problem additionally thorny. Awa was beginning to have a sinking feeling that they were too far in over their heads, operating without a Commander, without even the kind of wise counsel Lütfi had offered. They knew so little, and it seemed their enemy was always one step ahead of them. But what was Zawaba'a planning?

A knock at the door to the stairs broke her train of thought. It was Doctor Anisa, calling down to them.

'Young ones,' Doctor Anisa said. 'This message just arrived for you, from Sardar Ferhad Pasha.'

Gurkan bolted up the stairs to collect the message, thanking the good doctor and returning with it to the others. Opening it, he read through the message.

'Saturday,' Gurkan said. 'That's when Ferhad wants us to take the prophetic items from the Topkapi Palace.'

They were soon going to be the guardians of the most sacred items belonging to some of the greatest of prophets, yet they still did not know what they needed to do with them. Awa felt herself sinking further as a heavy weight seemed to haul her down into a pit of uncertainty.

32

BREAK-IN

I T TOOK THE YOUNG COMPANIONS longer than
they expected to find their way through the inner palace,
despite using a detailed map of the corridors and the
locations of guard posts, but eventually they came upon the
Hall of Religious Relics. Anver had never guarded the relics
himself but Gurkan and Awa had had plenty of experience.
Being in the vicinity of such revered items was regarded by
many Janissaries as a blessed situation.

The team split, moving to their designated positions. As
they did they placed black hoods on their heads, with slits for
their eyes. Should they be spotted, which was highly probable,
identifying them would at least be harder, so long as they
escaped. The only problem, as Anver saw it, was that donning
hoods made it pretty obvious why they were in the palace at
this time of night. Anver watched Gurkan scoot around the
outer perimeter and up a flight of stairs so that he was on the
same level as the sentry whose job it was to patrol the upper
tower as well as to maintain a watchful eye on the sentry who
stood guard outside the locked door to the Hall of Religious
Relics, a sealed room with no other entrance to it.

Treading softly, they approached the guard outside the Hall
of Religious Relics. Anver kept count of how long the man

stood in one position before moving to the next. Awa had told him it was about five minutes, and at three hundred seconds the guard reversed and moved to other end of the side of the door about ten yards from his starting position. The sentry settled into his new standing position. He was clearly bored, having drawn the short straw for night duty, but his life was about to get very interesting. Anver did feel a touch sorry for him.

The change of position triggered the new countdown, and he knew Gurkan was able to observe the same sentry as he was watching through the dyed muslin sheet that acted as a fabric-wall shielding the corridor from dust at night, but which also enabled the higher-placed watching-sentry, whom Gurkan had gone to deal with, to track the movements of the guarding-sentry as his silhouette was made visible by the light of the lamp throwing his shadow onto the white fabric strung up in the corridor.

Anver removed the figurine from his sack and placed it on the wooden box. The spine of the figure, dressed as a soldier, he clipped against a metal pin protruding from the box and then turned it softly to wind up the mechanical parts within the box. They had practised this dozens of times; he just hoped it would work now, as they needed time to get in and out of the Hall of Religious Relics. They estimated it was going to take them more than five minutes, so this little mechanical wooden doll would provide the illusion of the guard still patrolling his position, which the watching-sentry would be able to observe from his lofty position.

He looked up and gave Awa a hand signal indicating he was ready. She sent a similar message to Gurkan who nodded. The seconds ticked by and the guard coming to the end of his five minutes on one side, marched across the ten yards back to his other position. Anver observed the watching-sentry notice the other guard's movements, after which the distant sentry replicated the steps up on the watchtower. This was then an indicator for another sentry in a different watchtower that everything was in order. This system allowed the Janissaries to patrol large areas of the palace without having too many boots inside, which the Sultan and his family were wary of. Anver had noted the friction between the palace and the Janissaries many times; it seemed to be a love-hate relationship, each needing the other but neither willing to accommodate the whims of the other side.

Awa gave the go signal to Gurkan, who initiated a distraction on the upper tier by rolling a round pebble, causing the watching-sentry to move away from his guard post momentarily. When he gazed elsewhere, Awa jumped up from her hiding place, hood temporarily off, and blew a tranquillising dart from a blowgun. The projectile left the pipe, and the sentry dropped, his knees buckling as the drug took its effect. Anver peered back up at the watching-sentry, who was still out of position. The Venetian scuttled across the marble floor, placing his mechanical walking doll contraption on the ground, and placed a lamp against it, so that its image was projected back against the fabric wall, giving the impression the guard was still in position. Awa ran around the other side of the fabric wall, ensuring first the watching-sentry had not returned to his position, before checking that the shadow of the wooden doll was clearly projected onto the fabric wall, to make it appear that the Janissary was in position.

This was the easy part. Anver had wound the contraption up and the internal clock mechanism was set to five minutes, after which the wooden-doll figure would imitate the guard walking ten yards, as the mechanics within would move the pin holding the doll to the other side of the wooden base before stopping. The device was only built to perform this once; it

214

could not turn around and have the guard walk back. Their ten minutes to break in and get out had started.

Anver joined Awa by the fallen sentry and lifted him by the arms, placing him in a sitting position, his legs splayed out before him. He would wake, but not for a few hours. They waited for Gurkan, who had the most important item they would need to get inside.

They heard footsteps running and withdrew into the shadows, only to emerge once they sighted the Konyan.

'You have it?' Awa whispered.

Gurkan removed a set of keys from his tunic, smiling as he did. 'Of course, my smooth tongue and sleight of hand can relieve the most mindful of their possessions.'

The Konyan strode past them and fumbled through the set of keys, trying to find the one that opened the doors to the sacred Hall. It took a precious minute before he got it open. Once they had passed through the door, Anver swung it shut and gazed around, noting the precious items displayed in various glass cases dotted around the complex. The Destimal Chamber contained the principal prophetic items they sought, with the Audience Chamber and the Chamber of the Blessed Mantle holding other important religious artefacts.

***

Her family had been using this entrance for at least a generation. It might have existed in the time of her grandfather, but Fatma was not convinced. The smooth walls and straight floor were testament to the ingenuity of the Ottoman builders who seemed as adept at building below ground as above it. Before it was too late and she was questioned as to where she was going, she had decided to take a stroll: there was only one place within the palace where she liked to spend time in contemplation, where

215

she had the opportunity to reflect and put things in perspective. Her upcoming marriage to the Grand Vizier weighed heavily on her. To add to the prospect of the unwelcome marriage, Fatma had been told that the state of her brother Mehmet's mind had deteriorated further.

'It is so much cooler here, is it not Ulyana?'

'Yes, Your Highness.'

They walked on for a few more minutes, enjoying the chill air that existed at a lower level during the summer months. The spiral stairwell leading to the Hall of Religious Relics was right before her now. Taking the stairs, she and her handmaiden unlocked the door at the top and went through, entering the sacred Hall, having used the secret entrance built only for the Sultan and his family so that they could come and go as they pleased without others knowing about it.

She felt it as soon as she came out into the main hall. Someone else was here, her father, perhaps. No, he wasn't known for spending evenings in such a place as this. Who, then? The hidden door leading into the main entrance hall was disguised as a wall panel, and Ulyana shut it, the door clicking into place. Fatma placed a hand to her lips.

'I can hear someone else,' she whispered to her handmaiden, whose eyes opened wide in excitement.

Displayed within the entrance hall were objects belonging to saints, neatly placed in glass displays. These were a mixture of mainly personal items: robes, rosary beads, prayer mats and other items of clothing. Moving between the displays, dark shadows concealing their approach, Fatma was able to come to a position by the threshold of the Destimal Chamber that housed the prophetic items. She froze as she noticed three hooded figures wearing masks, carefully removing the holy objects and with a good deal of reverence placing them on a central circular table before opening up other glass cabinets and removing more objects. Whoever these thieves were, they must be highly skilled to have broken into one of the most secure places in the palace. A bolt of excitement followed by a shot of fear went up her back. The sensible course of action would be to alert the guard, who would be stationed just outside the main door. But surely that was the way the thieves had entered, so they may have silenced the guard. She desperately wished she had her sword with her.

'What shall we do, Your Highness?' Ulyana asked in her ear. What, indeed?

33

FAMILIAR DUEL

PLACING THE GRAPPLING HOOK on the summit of the primary defensive wall surrounding the vast palace kitchens, Will peered back down the brickwork he had scaled. It had taken Li mere seconds to scramble up, whereas he had spent much longer than one minute reaching the top. Now he was here, his arms and legs ached from the ascent and he was reminded of the time the Rüzgar had broken into Leeds Castle. He seemed forever to be breaking into the strongholds of powerful men who could have him executed without thinking twice. He knew he was walking a tightrope, but what choice did he have? Dressed all in black, with a hood over his head, only the eye slits showing, the Englishman inspected the Chinaman, also dressed in garb more befitting a Japanese Ninja.

The sun had recently set and Maghrib prayers were ending across the city. Will was filled with a sense of guilt at what he was about to do. The former Janissary's knowledge of the Topkapi Palace's defences allowed him to breach the part of the wall that was the noisiest but where the racket was more a distraction for the guards. The royal kitchen was below them, and what person would not be seduced by the delectable aromas pouring out of the stone structure and its chimneys. Will was already salivating at this height. Li sniffed the air and nodded, as though adding his appreciative gastronomical thoughts to what Will was already thinking.

The guard rotation plan given them by Commander Berk ensured that they arrived during the few minutes this part of the wall was not patrolled. The patrol tended to linger longer outside the royal kitchen at this time in the evening, hoping to catch some leftovers from the evening meal. Will recalled Huja informing him that the palace ensured no food was wasted by distributing it to all who needed it inside and outside the palace. His wise old friend often reminded him about the principles of his own Islamic faith, which was to serve the poor and the needy. Will tried to ignore the delicious smells and concentrate on leading the way, staying low against the outer battlements and scurrying along the walkway built into the wall. They were hidden from anyone on the outside, but they needed to be watchful of guards down below who might spot them. Will pulled up as he noticed two sentries move about in the kitchen courtyard, before passing through an archway.

The two unusual companions continued to skirt the upper wall to the edge, before the next sentry gate, where they jumped down a level as they approached the treasury building. The Englishman and the man from Cathay took a set of stairs down to ground level. From here on Will knew they were vulnerable. Berk's timetabling got them only so far; even he would not be able to make the sentries and guards within the palace disappear or turn the other way. Here he would need to rely on the guile of the Chinaman, who seemed to be a master of stealth.

'We need to get to that side,' Will indicated the direction across from the Treasury.

Before them was a manicured lawn with mature trees and flower beds. To the right was the dormitory building and straight ahead was the Hall of Religious Relics, their destination. Crossing this open area was not an option, as guards were stationed along the rooftops and they would be seen by the light of lamps dotted around. Li nodded, before setting off at a run, crouching close to the ground, his fingertips touching the blades of grass. Will followed, less magnificent in his passage than his Oriental comrade. They halted beside a cedar tree, concealing themselves behind its trunk. Outside the dormitory building two guards lounged, each taking a long draw on his pipe. The smell of tobacco wafted into Will's nostrils. It was surprisingly good. He told himself he would one day take to the pipe but not till he arrived at a grand old age, though considering his profession, he might not even reach middle age. Maybe he could consider taking to the pipe a little earlier in life, if he got out of here alive.

The two waited, biding their time in silence, Li not making a sound and Will feeling like a clumsy oaf compared to the soundless Chinaman.

'Wait here,' instructed the Chinaman in a soft tone.

Will was more than pleased to let Li do whatever he needed without getting in the way. Crouching on all fours, staying below the glow of the lamps, Li made his way across the lawn like a reptile, scuttling unnoticed. He stopped, holding himself in position on his fingers and toes, body lifted effortlessly off the ground. When the two guards turned their heads away, he rolled to one side, disappearing behind a hedge. Will squinted through the murk, unable to spot Rathbone's bodyguard. When he next sighted him, he was already beside the two Janissaries on the raised floor outside the dormitory, and in a move unlike any he had seen, he seemed to half pinch and partly jab the two men one after the other in the neck, so they slumped forward unconscious. That was a useful little move, Will thought to himself; he would need to ask Li to show him how he did that.

Taking his cue, Will ran along the edge of the lawn, coming up on the platform, and lugged one of the Janissaries away, holding the man under his arms. Li gave Will some rope, instructing him to tie the man's hands and feet, and gag him so he couldn't raise the alarm. They left the two unconscious Janissaries by the dark corner of the dormitory building. Surveying the space back inside the doorway to the dormitory, Li gave the all-clear and they shot past it, heading towards the Hall of Religious Relics.

Will had kept Li out of sight of the patrols on the roof, but was met by a most peculiar sight when they reached the outer door of the Hall. He was expecting to see another guard, but there was none. Instead, he found a wooden block with a mechanical doll placed on it, and a lamp shining to one side, projecting the image of a soldier standing against the dyed muslin fabric curtain that kept the corridor clear of dust in the evenings. In all his days patrolling here, he couldn't recall seeing this deceit, so what was going on? As he observed the contraption he realised there was something familiar about the mechanical doll.

Gripping the handle of the door to the Hall of Religious Relics, Will softly turned the knob and, as he expected, found it locked. He made way for Li, who removed a small box from his inner pocket and took out a set of thin metal rods with grooves etched into the tips. One rod was hooked at the end, the other bent at a right angle. Will stood guard as Li set to work, picking the lock. The Englishman focused on the mechanical doll. Very familiar.

Li pocketed his tools and placed his hand on the knob, turned it and pushed the door open. They entered the dimly lit outer entrance hall, containing the lesser religious relics, belonging to saints. The Destimal Chamber displaying the prophetic items was slightly ahead of them to the left and Will motioned for Li to follow him.

221

Before they were able to turn the corner, another person dressed all in black, with a hood to cover his face and only his eyes showing emerged. The man froze when he noticed Will and Li, dressed in similar attire. Will tensed, his hand going to his sword. The other fellow, sensing his intention, whipped out his blade, and launched himself at Will, whose own sword came out in a flash and parried the thrust. The hooded swordsman was nimble, darting at Will, attacking from unorthodox angles. It reminded Will of someone else he knew. Will stumbled back, noticing Li about to enter the frame. Will motioned to him that he could take care of this fellow. Li had been doing all the hard work this evening and, as he had never seen the Oriental wield a sword, the least Will could do was put down another swordsman.

His opponent jabbed forwards once more. Will moved, twisting his body at the last moment, and knocking the other man to the ground as he went past. The attacker rolled with the fall and stood up, taking up a defensive stance, expecting Will to attack. Will should have gone for the fellow, but he marvelled at the smoothness of the manoeuvre. There weren't many people he had seen pull off that type of move before.

As he was about to attack, two other shorter figures, also dressed in black, faces hidden by masks, ran out of the Destimal Chamber, carrying a satchel filled with what Will assumed was religious loot, plus the Staff of Moses, which one of them held, tip to the ground. Will could honestly say he wasn't pleased to see the Staff of Moses again, despite its holy status, for every time he encountered it, it meant trouble was coming his way. The swordsman, plus these two others. Wait a minute.

'Gurkan!' Will exclaimed.

The swordsman froze in his tracks, as did the other two, who looked from the swordsman to Will. Will turned to the two shorter figures.

'Awa, Anver?' asked Will.

The swordsman whipped off his hood. Gurkan. 'By God, is it you, Will?'

Will removed his hood, smiling at the Konyan. The Englishman lowered his blade, advancing to embrace his friend. Gurkan was about to do the same, when he glared at Li, then hesitated, retreating, his sword still up.

The other two had removed their hoods and Will saw Anver's beaming expression and Awa's dear face as they came up to stand beside Gurkan.

'We thought you were dead,' Anver exclaimed.

'I thought you were dead,' Will retorted.

'Where in God's name have you been, Will?' Gurkan asked, keeping a watchful eye on Li, who seemed confused by the exchange, standing in a tense position as though he was about to attack but unsure who to go for.

Will was about to say something, when another voice cut through the air.

'He's been with the Earl of Rothminster, that's where he's been.' Will whirled to see Princess Fatma Sultan and her impish handmaiden Ulyana emerge from behind a display. What were they doing here?

'Rothminster,' Gurkan seemed to spit out the name. 'The fellow who nearly had us killed, and whose castle I was tortured in.'

'The very same,' Fatma said. 'Will now works for the Earl of Rothminster.'

His three friends exchanged looks with one another, shock and despair upon their faces. They looked back at him with hopeful eyes, imploring him to deny it. He couldn't.

'Is it true, Will?' Awa asked, her voice firm, eyes searching for the truth.

Will looked from Awa to the Princess. There was no denying it.

'Yes,' Will said.

There was a moment of silence. Time seemed to stand still, Will could hear his heart beating loudly in his chest as his ears burnt with humiliation. He had betrayed them all, everyone he had called a friend these past few years.

'Traitor!' Gurkan yelled, launching himself forward, blade aimed at Will.

The next moves were a blur as Li shot past Gurkan, but as he did, twisted the Konyan's wrist into an uncomfortable position, forcing Gurkan to drop his blade. The Chinaman pulled Gurkan back towards him, lifted the Konyan and slammed him flat on the ground. Li leapt back up, striking Gurkan in the face with the side of his foot. The Konyan's head cracked back, hitting the ground, knocking him out.

Awa was moving, daggers drawn, in Li's direction, but the bodyguard leapt wide, touching down momentarily on the dais of a statue, three feet off the ground, then using its height to leap up and propel himself in the direction of Anver, who dropped his satchel containing the holy relics and backed away. Li swept it up, and motioned for Anver to give him the Staff, which the Venetian did without hesitation.

Will grabbed Awa, pulling her close to his chest, so that the top of her head rested upon his chin.

'Don't, Awa, he's dangerous,' Will said.

With an incredulous stare, Awa gave him a look that hurt more than any physical injury he had suffered.

'Who *are* you?' she hissed, wriggling to break free. He didn't want Li hurting his friends; he had seen what the Chinaman could do without weapons. With weapons, his friends stood no chance.

'I'm still Will, the same,' he replied.

'Were you always working for the Earl?'

'No, never. It's complicated,' Will said, taking the daggers from her grip and nudging Awa away from him. The Chinaman had come back to join him, giving him the nod that he was ready to go. Will shot a look at the disappointed faces of Princess Fatma and Ulyana, then back at his friends, Awa and Anver. Gurkan was still out. He didn't want to do this, but they had his mother, he couldn't compromise her safety. If he told them, Li would inform the rogue, Sir Reginald. This was the only way. It was best for them to forget him.

The unlikely duo of the Englishman and the Chinaman had started to back away from the stunned onlookers, when Will remembered something.

'Awa,' he said, still retreating.

She stared at him hard, fists balled up in anger. He couldn't blame her. In her eyes he had betrayed the Rüzgar, broken their bonds of friendship, gone against everything their dearly departed Commander had taught them – valour and integrity – two virtues that even your enemies should know you by, as he used to say.

'Your father, Mahmoud al-Jameel, is here as part of the Moroccan delegation,' Will said.

'My father,' the words barely escaped her mouth. 'Here?'

'I met him only days ago, at the palace,' Will peered across at the Princess, who like Awa was tense as a cat about to pounce.

Awa turned to Princess Fatma. 'Is it true?'

Fatma shrugged her shoulders. 'I do not know. There are many scholars who have come with the Moroccan delegation.'

'Wait,' Will called out, remembering the letter Mahmoud had given him. He took it from an inner pocket. 'Here, this letter, he gave it to me to give to you.' Will placed it on the dais of where a bronze urn was displayed.

225

The eyes of his Songhai friend focused on the letter. As Will withdrew, following the retreating Chinaman out of the door, Awa called out to him, 'Zawaba'a the Jinn is also in Istanbul.'

The Chinaman yanked Will by the arm, shutting the door behind him. Zawaba'a! The Jinn they released in Jerusalem. He remembered the loss of his friend Huja and their narrow escape from death beneath the Tower of David. He had heard rumours of an increase in demonic possessions, every street corner buzzing with small talk on the subject. There was even speculation that some Royals had been affected.

He didn't have time to think about it now. They had to get out of the Topkapi before the alarm was raised. Will gritted his teeth, following Li, who was disappearing into the shadows around the dormitory. He had a feeling it was going to be a very long night.

34

HYSTERIA

TUCKED INTO A HIGH-BACKED CHAIR in her chambers, a sensation of nausea swept through Fatma, making her stomach churn and her legs wobbly. Less than half an hour ago she had gone to the Hall of Religious Relics to search for some solace and reflect on the major upheavals that were affecting her life – her unwelcome marriage being the most pressing matter. Instead, she had returned far sooner than expected, utterly devastated.

Before her eyes some of the most prized religious relics in the world had been stolen by a man she had at one time held an affection for; she had even thought that in a different time and place, were she not a Princess, it could have been more. Will Ryde broke that trust tonight. He plunged a dagger through the very heart of such a notion and revealed himself to be nothing more than a thieving scoundrel, much like other English pirates she heard stories about. It grieved her more to witness the callous manner in which he treated his closest friends, the very individuals who were members of the famed Rüzgar unit. There was nothing else to say, but to declare him an enemy of the Ottoman Empire.

Yet, there was something more. She could feel it. He was not boasting nor did he take on the mantle of one proud of what he was doing. There was a sorrow, a remorse in his eyes, and most of all those eyes lacked the conviction of a mischief-maker.

'Ulyana, can you fetch me some fennel tea?' Fatma called out to her handmaiden, who was most likely in the next room laying out their evening meal, sent over from the kitchens.

The Ukrainian might not have heard her, for there was no reply.

Fatma rubbed her forehead with her fingers. She could feel a low-level headache coming on, which some fennel tea would see off. Pushing down on the armrests, Fatma rose and walked over to her balcony.

Being based on the second floor of the palace had its disadvantages, such as the climb up the steep staircase, but it had significant advantages when it came to the stunning views she could take in from her balcony every sunrise and sunset. The night sky was pitch black this evening, with the new moon still not visible. The canopy of stars sparkled above the slumbering kingdom of her father, yet as she cast her gaze towards the city, there was an unusual haze over it. From a distance it looked like smoke, yet it had a red tinge. In the rainy season one part of the city could be blanketed with low-level cloud, while others were clear of the haze. Was a part of the city burning? Yet there were no flames. In the distance screams echoed out. This was altogether something else.

Fatma turned to gaze at the furthest point she could see and realised the smoke curled like the body of a serpent, winding its way through the city streets below, eventually making its way into parts of the palace. In fact, she could now see wisps entering the very building she occupied. It was unlike any fog she had ever witnessed, for close up it was as black as night but seemed possessed of streaks of red within it. This was no natural phenomenon.

'Ulyana,' she called out to her handmaiden.

Still no response. Unusual that the girl could not hear her voice. She would need to go and check where she had gone to. Fatma was about to leave the balcony when she heard the sound of a high-pitched scream, followed by another, then several more. These were not far away; in fact, this shrieking was coming from within the palace walls. Whatever was happening out in the city was also taking place in the palace. More yells and cries came from the other buildings, and when she stared down she noticed a Janissary racing across the courtyard. How odd, for the man was making the most awful racket. Soon after, two more soldiers ran by. They were followed by two other Janissaries, but these two seemed to be howling, bawling at the others, as though they were chasing them and the first three Janissaries were fleeing. These men would be court-martialled. Such behaviour within the palace grounds was not to be tolerated. Now other screams and the sounds of metal crashing and glass smashing rang out across the grounds of the palace. All very close.

'Ulyana,' Fatma called out, concern in her voice.

Half a dozen women raced by below in their nightwear, chased by another crazed man. However, this man was soon joined by a demented woman, hair trailing out behind her, fingers out like claws. She also seemed to be chasing the fleeing women. What in God's name was happening?

'Uly ...' the name of her handmaiden caught in her throat as Fatma turned around.

Ulyana stood motionless in the doorway, silhouetted by the lamplight.

'Ulyana, what is it?' Fatma said.

The girl remained silent.

There was something not quite right. Her loyal servant's head was tilted to one side, and her fingers were tensed like

229

the claws of a raven: in fact, her posture resembled that of the madman and mad woman Fatma had seen from her balcony.

'Ulyana!' Fatma added some steel to her voice.

The next moment her handmaiden hissed like a cat, and with a short running jump pounced at the Princess. Fatma leapt to one side, clattering into her chair, rolling off its armrest and landing on the ground. Ulyana's head whipped around, tracking Fatma's movements, and she attacked once more, this time landing on top of the Princess. The handmaiden went straight for Fatma's throat, seizing it in a vice-like grip – and squeezing.

Ulyana's mouth foamed and her feverish eyes were wild and feral. She was possessed!

As the Ukrainian squeezed, the air constricted in Fatma's throat. She held off her handmaiden's attack as best she could, but she could not deny the difference in strength. She had to try something else. Was this going to be how her life ended? Darkness crept in around the corners of her vision as her energy dissipated and she started to lose strength. Fatma was blacking out, and there was nothing she could do about it.

Clang. The noise reverberated in her ears.

Air returned to her, the hold on her windpipe gone, as Fumu came into view, holding his sword. He had whacked Ulyana with the flat of his blade, halting her attack.

'Your Highness,' he said, crouching down beside her.

The Princess gulped down air, taking huge and painful breaths as she lifted herself up on her elbows. Her neck was sore and would no doubt be bruised. A few more moments and she wouldn't have survived.

'Can you get up?' asked her bodyguard.

'Yes,' she replied, her voice croaky.

Fumu helped her up, and Fatma collapsed into her high-backed chair as the room continued to spin around her. More screams and sounds of fighting came from outside, reminding Fatma the world around her was inflamed with a demonic possession. She looked over at the form of her dear handmaiden. Was she possessed? And if so, how did Zawaba'a reach her? What had happened to make so many sane people lose their minds at the same time?

She pushed herself up from the chair, still unsteady on her feet. Fumu gripped her elbow, steadying her.

'Thank you,' she whispered, before moving out to the balcony once more. Below her in the open space, men tussled with one another – some she took to be possessed; others, not. In some fights women were involved. It was chaos. Fires raged around the royal kitchens, and she could hear shouts coming from every corner of the palace.

'What is happening, Fumu?'

'I do not know, Your Highness, but we must get you to the safety of the inner palace. It is fortified and cannot be breached.'

'Let us go,' Fatma said, turning a little too quickly and feeling her surroundings spin. She steadied herself against a chair, taking slow, deep and painful breaths. She grabbed her olive-coloured riding cloak and followed her Kikongo bodyguard out of her chambers. She glanced one last time at Ulyana, praying that when her handmaiden woke up, she would be her usual self once more.

Outside her chambers the corridor was empty, but Fatma heard the sound of a struggle taking place inside one of the other rooms. She hesitated, but Fumu shook his head and she continued behind him. They came to a set of stairs and tentatively descended. There was a body lying at the bottom, a soldier who wasn't moving. Fatma felt fear well up inside her once more and wrapped the riding cloak about her person.

Outside the building she saw horses bolting and people running in all directions. The stables within the palace

231

grounds must have been opened. She immediately thought about the menagerie and some of the wilder beasts kept there. She wouldn't want to escape from the mayhem caused by the possessed only to be mauled by a tiger. They travelled deeper into the palace, towards the private quarters of her father, the Sultan. On the way, she passed the chambers of her brother, the Crown Prince. The two guards who were stationed outside were missing. There were signs of a struggle, as a chair had been knocked over and a sword lay on the ground. Had her brother escaped? *Whack!* The enormous thud of a body slamming against the inside of the chamber door startled her, and she jumped. Fumu immediately came between her and the door, weapon raised. However, he was not needed: the door was reinforced. Her brother Prince Mehmet, the future ruler, was not going to get out. He was saying something. Fatma wanted to know, taking a step closer.

'Your Highness,' Fumu warned.

She raised a hand to calm him and approached the door. The thumping had stopped and all she could hear was deep breathing. He knew someone was outside. She took the final steps and placed her ear against the door to make out what he was mumbling. At first it sounded like nonsense, the words running into one another, but then it became clear to her.

'I will kill my brothers, all of them. I will kill my brothers, all of them. I will kill my brothers, all of them ...'

Fatma staggered back, as though slapped in the face. Her breathing accelerated. Shaking her head, she moved away as fast as she could. As she did, the thumping of a palm against wood restarted. Her brother was truly insane.

Rejoining Fumu, a trickle of sweat fell off the bridge of her nose. She started to run as Fumu picked up the pace. They rounded the next corner, which would lead to an open courtyard, on the other side of which was the inner palace precinct and the secure keep for the Sultan in times of extreme threat to the palace from outside.

'No!' Fumu exclaimed.

Dozens of small skirmishes were taking place before the keep. It was an uncontrolled mêlée of men and women attacking one another with whatever they had. Horses darted through gaps between them.

'What has happened?' Fatma asked.

'The outer defences have fallen and they have secured the keep. Look, the black flag flies above it.'

'What does that mean?'

'They will not open the gates for anyone. The black flag can only be raised on the Sultan's direct order. It cannot be lowered without his express permission. We will not be able to get inside.'

'There must be a way,' Fatma said.

The Kikongo warrior shook his head. 'There is not, Your Highness. It is the most secure place in the palace, because of the protocols they put in place. You could be the Sultan's mother, but they would not open the keep once it has been locked from the inside.'

Fatma surveyed the mayhem within the palace grounds. If the most secure location within the palace was inaccessible to them, then there was nowhere left within the grounds that could be considered safe.

'Then we try our luck on the outside,' said Fatma.

Her bodyguard arched his eyebrow. 'Outside?'

'Yes, it's a big city, there will be safe places. There must be others who are sane of mind, like us. We need to find them.'

Fumu was shaking his head.

'Find me a sword, Fumu, and let's go. We need to get out of the Topkapi.'

35

SMOKED OUT

THE EVENTS OF EARLIER IN the evening weighed heavily on the young Rüzgar. The initial shock of discovering that Will was working for the nefarious Earl of Rothminster soon turned to anger, then sorrow and a sense of loss. Anver wasn't quite sure what he felt. Will was still his friend, he had no doubt whatsoever. Seeing him again had sent a wave of elation through the Venetian. He knew something had changed, but it was still Will, the same Englishman who had helped him out in Venice, the same person who had settled him in with his new friends. But it could not be denied that he was working for the other side, for the wretched Earl of Rothminster.

When Anver left the Society of Miniaturists for an evening walk to clear his head, Gurkan was nursing a bruise on his head that Doctor Anisa treated with ointment. Awa, meanwhile, had read and re-read maybe a dozen times the letter inked by her father and conveyed to her by Will. There was no denying that it was his handwriting and dated only a few days previously. Awa appeared elated and at the same time despondent about the choices Will had made. She had told Anver and Gurkan that she would look for her father the next day. The Songhai woman could not risk missing him; she had to find him. He was in the same city as her, somewhere in Istanbul, perhaps walking the very streets Awa passed along. Anver understood her desire to find him. His own parents had died when he was young, and though he had loved them dearly, his memories grew more blurred as the years passed.

The Venetian had taken to wearing a hooded robe after his unfortunate encounter with Commander Berk. He didn't want to be recognised on the street anymore. Yet when he turned onto the main thoroughfare of the Fatih district the sight he witnessed made him remove his hood in order to confirm with his own eyes what he was seeing. Ahead of him, some twenty yards away, was a volatile group of Istanbul residents, from all walks of life, judging by their clothing, surrounding a fine carriage drawn by two horses. The terrified passengers were peeking through the curtains. The driver had been dragged off the seat on top of the carriage by one of the crazed attackers and was being set upon by others.

'Run!' a portly man screamed as he scuttled across the intersection just ahead of Anver. 'Run for your life!'

Shortly after, two women, hair flowing behind them, fingers like talons, chased after him. Anver was sure he heard them hissing like cats.

Crash! Behind Anver there was a commotion. He saw a young man, about the same age as him, leap from the first floor of a building, landing on top of the canopy of a fruit-seller's stall. The fellow was quickly back on his feet.

'Gone mad!' he shouted, looking terrified. Anver looked at the window from which the young man had jumped to see a brutish fellow leaning out of it, clenching his fists and shaking them at the young man. When the brute saw Anver, he snarled at the Venetian. Everywhere around him, fights were breaking out, screams erupting, things being smashed and broken. What in God's name was going on?

Searching the streets, Anver noticed a black smoke creeping through them. It wasn't as thick as fog, which obliterated one's vision, but it was dense enough to cast anyone coming through it into shadow. There were also red streaks flashing like bolts of lightning, passing through the mist. It was then Anver spotted the dark hooded forms, moving from street to street, placing objects on the ground and igniting them with a torch one of them held. This was the same group of men who were with Zawaba'a in the underground tunnels. A man pushed past Anver, and the Venetian spotted a small mob of others running in his direction. He couldn't tell whether they were crazed or not, but he decided to go looking for the acolytes of Zawaba'a.

Anver darted down an alley as the black mist from the burning objects engulfed him. He froze. Was he about to turn into one of those crazies? He waited. He rubbed his fingers together, not daring to move, in case he should suddenly lose his mind. Nothing.

The mist passed over him. He had breathed it in long enough for something to happen. He was clean. Pressing on, he followed the trail of lit objects left by the cult group. Most were smoking too much for him to see what they were; however, one of them had just been lit, by the looks of it, as Anver spotted the dark robes disappearing around the corner. Anver went over to the smoking rock and realised it was an obsidian stone, black and shiny. He took off his robe and with it, he smothered the smoke coming off the stone. He patted it down and when he checked, the rock was no longer smoking, just smouldering. Cutting through with his knife, then ripping a piece of his robe, he wrapped the stone in the fabric, making sure it wasn't going to ignite, then placed it safely in his sack and slung it over his shoulder.

Anver realised he must have taken his eye off his surroundings, for he heard a deep growl. When he turned, it was to see the brute from the window standing a few yards away, baring his teeth at him. Dear Lord! Anver set off on a run, tripping as he did so. Stumbling around a corner, he ran straight into another crazy man, who tried to bite him. Anver pushed the scrawny fellow away, bouncing off the side wall and running down a narrowing alley. He heard a scream behind him and realised two women had joined the pursuit. Great!

The alley, with three-storey buildings on either side, twisted right, then curved left in an arc, ensuring Anver couldn't see what was coming around the next corner. At the last moment, he spotted another group of three possessed persons come racing around the bend, but not before he had dived right into an alley that was only as wide as two persons and seemed to contain small doorways. This looked to be the rear of a tradesmen's alley, where goods were brought in by wheelbarrow. Anver prayed it went somewhere, out into a more open place, as he now had a bunch of crazy residents on his trail.

'No,' Anver groaned when he saw the alley end in a wall too high to jump over.

Whirling around, he saw that his pursuers were just entering the long passageway and hadn't spotted him up ahead in the dark. They seemed to halt a moment when they didn't see him, before turning on one another. Slapping and biting, they fell into a weird frenzy. Anver slung his sack down and pushed his head inside. It was here somewhere, where was it? Had he left it at their base? Yes, there it was. He grabbed it and yanked it out. He had never even tested it, having just mocked up a prototype from the sketches he had made whilst in Konya.

Anver held up the arquebus-type contraption, around which he had coiled a rope. The crazies were still fighting it out with one another. He knotted the end of the rope onto a metal claw and pulled it tight. He was careful to tie at least three knots, as this was going to be all that held his weight. He wasn't sure if this was going to work, but as the sounds of the crazed pack grew louder, he also realised they were getting closer and he had no choice but to risk his neck. He pointed the arquebus style object high into the air, the metal claw facing upwards. The Venetian could just make out the edge of the roof of the three-storey building. His arm shook. *What am I doing?* he thought to himself.

'Aargh!' they had spotted him and were now running.

Saving my own life, he reminded himself.

Anver pulled the trigger. It was hard to press and he applied both hands and two fingers to press it. *Click.* The rope uncoiled at speed, flying skywards, the metal claw shooting out, heading for the top of the roof. To his surprise it went over and landed on the surface. He had almost run out of rope. Anver yanked it back. The claw slid along the rooftop, then caught on something. Good. He pulled down as hard as possible on the rope. The claw held in place. This would have to do.

He turned to see the first of the group coming after him. Anver gripped the rope and then, with his feet against the wall, began to climb up, his body jutting out at almost ninety degrees from the wall. He had seen Awa and the others perform this type of manoeuvre and had even practised it once himself. The first few steps were fine, then his legs began to burn with the effort. The first of the crazies had reached the spot he had been standing in moments earlier. The sight of their mouths foaming, teeth chomping and faces grimacing was enough to speed him up, and he accelerated despite the pain in his legs and arms. He was soon at second-storey level but then felt a tug on the rope. He looked down to see the brute from the window start to climb. Anver wasn't sure if the rope was strong enough for the weight of one person, let alone two.

'Get off!' Anver shouted, pulling himself up, but his muscles were exhausted. He couldn't go any further. It was easier just to fall back to the ground. The brute was gaining on him – his muscles were stronger. The wicked smile on the man's face was enough to convince Anver to try once more and he heaved himself up, reaching for the lip of the roof. He grabbed it, then hauled his body over it and fell onto the surface. He immediately set about trying to dislodge the claw, yet the fellow's weight pulling on the rope kept it firmly in place. It would not budge.

'Hurry,' Anver implored himself. Taking out his knife he started to cut away at the fibres of the rope. He saw the brute reach up and grab the lip of the roof. *Oh no.* Anver sawed away in desperation. The rope split, one end slithering away to the ground. The crazed fellow's knuckles went white as he hung there. Anver looked over the edge at his foaming mouth, teeth bared in animal fury. There was not going to be any negotiating with this chap. With his knife, Anver stabbed the man in the hand, causing him to lose his grip and topple back down two storeys.

The Venetian heard the crash and the cracking of bones as the brute hit the ground. Anver took a deep breath before walking away. He had had no choice, he told himself, and crossed the rooftop, shaking. He clasped his hands together, trying to compose himself. When he reached the other side of the roof, he could look out across much of Istanbul. The obsidian rocks, once ignited, burnt with unnatural smoke, a fire that had something to do with the power of Zawaba'a, who had cast a demonic fury into the stones. Red streaks passed through the mist. Fires raged in some parts of the city and black smoke hung heavily over the rooftops. But most of all it was the terrified howls, screams and shrieks that shivered Anver's bones.

The Jinn they had released in Jerusalem, the one imprisoned by Solomon the Wise for many millennia, had unleashed its fury on the greatest city in the world. Would the residents last the night, or was this the beginning of the end?

36

BREAKING POINT

THE STOREHOUSE ON THE DOCKSIDE was filled with long timber planks, some crooked, others straight. Tied by rope and twine or stacked one on top of the other, they created a world of wood, and it smelt like it. Will reckoned the location was used as an extra supply point for the city's builders, as Istanbul maintained a voracious appetite for new construction projects. The storehouse was vacant at this late hour, and Will didn't think it would be occupied till the morning.

He sat upon a stack of wood, his back resting against the side wall. What had his friends been doing in the Hall of Religious Relics and why was the Princess present? It felt so wrong not to be in the thick of it with them. He was one of those who fought to remove evil, not to contribute to its triumph. Yet there was no denying how he was going to be seen by his friends – as an enemy in their midst. The fury on Gurkan's face, the shock and disappointment on the faces of Awa and Anver, broke his heart, but he kept reminding himself why he had to stay committed, to keep his mother safe. He went over it all in his head once more. The Rüzgar were stealing the holy relics. Why? Zawaba'a had arrived in the city. How?

'Aargh!'

Will jumped down from the wooden platform on which he was perched. The scream came from outside, and it didn't sound as though it was too far away. It was unusual for there to be shouting at this time of night and particularly in a place such as this. Will went over to one of the few windows; it was more a narrow slit, crusted over with wood-chippings and sawdust. He cleared the glass with his sleeve and peered out. Nothing. Then he noticed something, a fellow running, arms waving about like a madman. The chap was chasing someone, perhaps the person who had screamed, but he couldn't tell from his vantage point. What in God's name was this all about? Anyway, the fellow would soon be dealt with, as the city patrols at night were firm in stamping down on any hellraisers. Will was about to go back and sit down when he saw a dark fog, or was it black smoke, drifting through a part of the dockside. He'd never seen the like of it before. Were his eyes deceiving him, or was there a sparkle of red within the blackness?

'Will Ryde!'

He whirled about. Sir Reginald Rathbone had entered the storehouse, with Li a few paces behind him. Rathbone had been inspecting the religious relics in the small room beside the storehouse, and Will assumed the noble was about to tell him he had forgotten something.

'Good work,' Rathbone said, much to Will's surprise.

'Thank you,' was all Will could say.

'Li here tells me you ran into some old friends of yours.'

'Yes, sir.'

'What were they doing in the Hall of Religious Relics?' enquired Rathbone.

'I honestly don't know.'

He wished he knew, but in all fairness ... Wait, he thought for a moment: Zawaba'a. They had used the Staff of Moses as part of the summoning ceremony. Why would they be taking all of the relics, including the Staff, once more? Was it to summon more Jinn? Surely not. Will spotted the small anteroom where the religious relics lay spread out on a wooden table. He wondered if they had been trying to banish the Jinn. Oh God in Heaven, what had he done?

Rathbone fixed him with a penetrating stare. 'Really?'

'I've been thinking about it, and God's honest truth, I was surprised to see them,' Will said, trying to conceal his mounting alarm. If the religious relics were the only things that could be used to imprison the Jinn, and these were about to leave Istanbul ... he began to feel sick in the pit of his stomach: his actions may have just condemned more people than he realised.

Rathbone tucked his hands behind his back and walked around a stack of wooden pallets, so he was partially obscured from view.

'Were you pleased to see them?' Rathbone pressed.

Will hesitated. 'I was pleased to know they were still alive.'

Rathbone nodded. 'Loyalty to one's friends is a noble trait. I can understand that. Look at Li,' Rathbone waved his hand towards the Chinaman. 'Loyal as ever, like a well-trained ... dog, I suppose.'

The English noble said it without even making eye contact with the man from Cathay. Will focused on Li, whose stoic expression gave nothing away.

'I must say, Ryde, the artefacts from the Hall of Religious Relics are quite a collection. The Staff of Moses we had ... seen before. However, to look upon Abraham's Pot, Joseph's Turban, David's Sword and Armour, the Scrolls of John the Baptist and Muhammad's Seal, why, it sent a holy shiver up my spine.'

'What are you planning to do with the relics?' Will asked, though he knew the answer.

'To England they go, under lock and key for now, but when the time is right, we will display them and I can already imagine pilgrims flocking from all over the England and further afield to pay their respects. Why, as custodians of the holy treasures, we are bound to find that these will be a significant money-spinner.'

Custodians of the holy treasures. The gall of it. It sounded to Will as if the plan was for the religious relics to fatten the treasuries of the Earl and Sir Reginald. The treacherous English nobles were going to profit from these revered objects. He felt his stomach dip further, as the implication of what he had done became apparent. Would his name go down in the history books as the thief who stole from the Sultan, conveying the goods to the Earl, who whisked them away to England? It was not a reputation he was going to relish. They would call him *Will Ryde – the Thief of Istanbul.*

'When do we leave?' Will enquired. He wanted to know if there was still time to go back, find his friends and explain what the situation was without Li overhearing his dilemma and reporting back to Rathbone.

The nobleman progressed towards Will and stopped a few feet away.

'Li and I will be leaving immediately with the religious relics. Our transport is waiting for us.'

Will felt the mood change in the room. He noticed Rathbone's expression darken. Li took a step closer to him. Will immediately drew back.

'And me?' Will asked.

'You, Ryde, won't be leaving Istanbul.'

'What do you mean?'

'In fact, you won't even be leaving this storehouse ... but your corpse will. We can dump it in the Bosporus.'

Will's hand went to the pommel of his blade, as both Rathbone and Li sought to corner him. He had only a wall behind him.

'But we have a deal!' Will tried to reason with him.

'*Deal*. The aristocracy don't make deals with servants like you, Will Ryde.'

Will's back was against the wall as the two started to block him on either side.

'But my mother ...' Will implored.

'Oh, don't worry about Mrs Ryde, she is a rather fetching woman for her age, and I'm sure I can find a role for her in my personal household. Perhaps to look after my bedchamber.'

Li hesitated, glancing sideways at Rathbone.

Will clenched his fists. The villain. He was going to take Rathbone out himself, if it was the last thing he did. Will launched himself at the aristocrat, but Li was faster, intercepting him and tumbling sideways with Will. The bodyguard rolled back onto his feet, placing himself between Will and Rathbone. Will got to his knees then stood up to his full height.

'Out of my way, Li. My fight is not with you,' Will said.

The man from Cathay remained stationary, taking up a fighting stance. Will would have to do this the hard way. Part of him didn't want to hurt Li, but where the life of his mother was concerned, he would go through anyone to protect her. Will drew his blade.

'Last chance, Li,' Will warned.

'A well-trained dog always protects his master,' Rathbone announced, from behind the bodyguard's protection.

Will plunged his blade forward. Li deftly sidestepped. Will was anticipating this and twirled, to swipe his blade across Li's chest. But when he twirled around Li wasn't where he expected him to be. In fact, standing before Will a few yards away was the sneering Rathbone. Will immediately made a dash towards him, but before he could reach him, the backs of his knees buckled and he fell to the ground. In the next moment, Li's foot struck his sword hand, sending the blade skidding across the stone surface.

Li made to chop Will on the neck, but the young Englishman saw the strike coming, and blocked it with his arm, whilst still on his knees. Will swung with his other hand, but Li twisted away, twirling Will by the neck, so that he now had his back to Rathbone once more. Will tried to get up, but Rathbone's leather soles smashed him in the back, sending him face first to the ground. His vision blurred as he tried to get up, scrabbling forward on the palms of his hands, straining to get out of reach. Rathbone followed up with a boot in his stomach, knocking the wind out of Will.

'Oh, I'm getting too old for this,' puffed the English noble. 'Finish him,' Rathbone ordered Li.

Will crawled away on all fours. He had to survive. Save his mother from the fiendish claws of Rathbone. Will started to rise once more as Li grabbed him from behind in a choke hold. Will's legs slid desperately on the ground, his heels slithering around, eyes watering as he tried to budge the Chinaman's iron grip. His eyes watered, black patches appearing before his eyes.

'I'm ...' Will gasped.

'You're nothing. Li will break your neck. I will return to England with the religious artefacts, and your mother will be my personal bed-servant for the rest of her days. Remember that as you die.'

Rathbone turned on his heel and strolled off.

'Li ...' Will said as the bodyguard continued to choke him, crushing his windpipe, 'Please ... my mother ... protect her.'

245

His vision darkened. It would be only a matter of seconds. Was this how he died? A failure?

'Li ...'

Everything around Will went black. The last thing he heard was the sound of something flying through the air, then a thud.

37

HARSH CHOICES

SCREAMS AND SHOUTS ECHOED DOWN the
street outside the Society of Miniaturists, causing Awa
to emerge from the building along with Gurkan. Dark
forms running in the shadows, arms waving about in mad
gestures, chased after others, who raced away. Further down
the street a man leapt from a first-floor window, crashing to
the pavement below. He rose, his leg bent at an odd angle, but
still managed to crawl away, as Awa spotted a woman with a
demented face hiss at him from the window from which he
had leapt. She also made the jump, and though her landing
was a touch smoother, she also seemed to be displaying the
same injuries as she hobbled after him. Behind her a woman
screamed and ran across the road, followed by another woman
who chased her. Two men were trading punches on the corner
of the intersection.

'What in God's name is happening?' cried Gurkan.

Awa stared back towards the private quarters at the rear of
the Society of Miniaturists. They had seen what had happened
to the gentle Lütfi Abdullah when he had become possessed.
Was this now taking place citywide, in every district, on every
street? Yet how? What was triggering this madness, causing
families and neighbours to turn on one another?

'Zawaba'a,' Awa replied in a flat tone.

In truth, her mind had only been on finding her father since Will gave her the letter a few days before, in this very city. She needed to find him, and soon, or else he might leave and their paths would never cross again. Yet the world around her was falling to pieces.

'How?' Gurkan asked.

She shook her head.

Her mind was pulled in two directions. Get away from this mayhem and seek out her father, or deal with this, since she was responsible for what was happening in Istanbul. Had they not released the powerful Jinn, the lives of all these people would not have been turned upside down tonight, nor in the previous weeks when families were placed under intense pressure after a family member became infected.

The shock of seeing Will working for the Earl of Rothminster was still registering in her mind. Was he always an English spy? She tried to remember all the occasions, many of them genuinely happy ones, when they were together, and there was nothing that indicated his loyalty was to anyone other than Konjic. Yet it could not be denied, for he confirmed it himself, that he was in the employ of the despicable Earl. She had known Will for too long, there was something else to it. He wasn't disclosing the full picture to them, but the truth was that the Englishman had stolen the religious relics, right from under their noses. To make matters worse, these were the only objects with a chance of stopping Zawaba'a, even though she remained unclear as to how.

Her father's appearance, Will's betrayal, the city falling apart. Her mind whirled. She just wanted to sit down, bury her head in her hands and let it all pass over her. But it never did. Inaction was never an option. Her father had taught her that. *Whenever you see an injustice, Awa, act to correct it*, he would say.

It was hard to act when the easiest path was to run away, flee to the hills and to wash one's hands of responsibility. If all the good people in the world took the path of indifference and apathy, then only the mad would rule. As she struggled with this internal turmoil, she noted a lone figure darting through the commotion and making its way in their direction. Her hand instinctively went to the hilt of her dagger. Gurkan stood guard beside her. As the person drew closer, she realised it was Anver.

'The whole city's smouldering,' the Venetian said, gasping for air as he came up to them.

'What?' Gurkan asked.

'I was chased by this crazy group of people, managed to get up on the roof, look across the city. Fires have broken out, there are scuffles on every street corner, there's even smoke rising from the Topkapi Palace,' Anver said.

'How is this happening?' Awa asked.

'From what I saw, the followers of Zawaba'a are lighting obsidian stones. When they ignite and begin to burn, a black smoke tinged with red streaks starts to pour out of them. Some people who encounter it, flip: they become wild, start attacking whoever is nearby.'

She was responsible for this mayhem. She was desperate to be reunited with her father, but this situation had to be dealt with first. There was no choice.

'Can you take us back to where you found Zawaba'a?' Awa asked.

'Yes,' came the Venetian's hesitant reply.

Gurkan looked at Awa. 'We don't even have the religious relics. What are you planning?'

She had no idea, but they needed to stall Zawaba'a somehow and retrieve the stolen items.

'Anver and I will go to find Zawaba'a: we need to keep him occupied. Gurkan,' she turned to the Konyan. 'You need to find Will and get those religious relics back. Without them, all we can do is play for time.'

Gurkan nodded. 'I will.'

Awa wasn't sure sending the Konyan after Will was such a good idea, for they had come to blows too often.

'And make sure you don't kill one another,' she added firmly.

The Konyan shrugged. 'As long as he stays out of my way, I'll stay out of his.'

She didn't like this plan at all.

'How will I find you, once I have retrieved the objects?' Gurkan asked.

Anver gave Gurkan detailed instructions for finding the underground cavern before turning back to Awa.

'Then it is agreed. Anver, get the brass urn. We need to go, now,' Awa said, her voice firm.

Gurkan placed a hand on her shoulder and one on Anver's.

'Together,' he said.

Before this night was over, she also wanted to get together with her father, and it was this desire that spurred her on. They would, with God's help, overcome this monster and banish it from the world once more. Then she would find comfort in her father's embrace.

***

It was exhilarating running through the streets of Istanbul, and it was terrifying running for her life out of the palace gates. The keep was secured and the rest of the palace was unguarded. Fatma stayed close to Fumu after they left the palace precinct. Her cloak was drawn around her and her hood was up. Fumu had managed to find two other men-at-arms, who flanked her now, ensuring they were protected from any attack.

The main thoroughfare outside the palace was anarchy: burning fires, fist fights, carts overturned. Street lighting was smashed, making the road appear even more eerie in the light of the flames. They crossed over without incident. As they entered a new street, the two men-at-arms were attacked by lone individuals. Fumu was set upon by another man who jumped on the Kikongo warrior's back and tried to bite him on the neck. The bodyguard threw the man over his shoulder and slammed his boot into the man's chest. Fatma heard something crack and the felled man didn't move after that.

Other attackers swarmed around them, leaping in uncoordinated ways. Reluctantly, Fatma drew the curved scimitar that Fumu had found for her and held it up. She had always wanted to be in a real fight, but now that she was she found her arms trembling uncontrollably and her throat parched. Her bodyguard cleared the way of assailants, kicking, pushing, slamming into them with his meaty palms, but eventually one got through. Nausea rose from the pit of her stomach, seeing the mad fury and violence around her. A thin man with wild eyes came straight for her, fingers out like the claws of an eagle. Fatma wheeled out of the way at the last moment, her cloak flapping, trying to smash the flat of her blade on the fellow's head as he went past. She missed, but the fellow tripped and hit his head against a street lamp, knocking himself out in the process. Feeling sorry for him, she was about to check whether he was all right, when a woman broke through behind her, and cannoned into her back, sending the Princess sprawling onto the ground.

Fatma was rising when she felt the woman being lifted off her back and, as the Princess turned to look up, Fumu threw the woman to one side like a rag doll.

'Are you hurt?' Fumu enquired.

'No, I'm fine,' Fatma replied, picking herself off the ground as another attacker got through: Fumu backhanded the man, knocking him out cold.

The visceral ferocity and carnage unfolding around the Princess made her start to weep. Terror clutched her by the throat.

'We must find a safe place, off the street,' Fumu exhorted her more gently.

The Princess met the gaze of her bodyguard, who smiled encouragingly, before she rose and followed him.

Rounding the corner, a wild pack of Istanbul residents, arms and legs thrashing, came thundering in their direction. The Kikongo warrior's face creased with unease.

'Hagia Sophia. Let us go there,' instructed Fatma.

Her bodyguard considered it, looked at the running mob, then nodded.

'Hagia Sophia,' he instructed the two other men-at-arms, who fended off other attackers.

'Run,' Fumu said, clearing the way before her as they headed south. He barged into and knocked aside any before them, Fatma tucked in close behind him and the other two soldiers to her right and left. The wild pack was on their tail, howling for blood. Her heart pounded. What was happening to the city of her forefathers? If one powerful Jinn could unleash so much destruction, what would a cohort of them be able to achieve?

The street cleared before them and they veered right, noticing the domes of the Hagia Sophia come into view. The street opened up into a main intersection as they drew closer to the ancient place of worship. Up ahead others were streaming towards the sanctuary. The gates around the Hagia Sophia were shut tight, with armed Janissaries patrolling. They were checking every person coming through. Only those not possessed were being allowed in.

'Don't announce who I am,' Fatma instructed Fumu.

'Your ...'

'No, Fumu, let us enter as the ordinary people do.'

There was a crush of fifty or more people at the gates, Janissaries checking each person before allowing them into the complex.

'Hurry,' a person cried out in the wedge of bodies ahead of her.

Fatma and her men-at-arms came up to the rear of the throng of fleeing residents and waited as the unruly assembly shuffled slowly forward. It was taking too long. They should have opened other gates and allowed citizens through that way.

Wild howls came from behind her as an angry mob of the possessed rushed at the crowd seeking sanctuary inside the Hagia Sophia.

'They're here, open the gates!' a man shouted as others implored the Janissaries to let them in.

Fumu turned, whipping his staff with its wicked metal tip off his back and holding it out. Fatma, hands shaking, removed her scimitar from its scabbard, gripping the hilt with both palms, yet she was so terrified that the weapon still wobbled. The two men-at-arms readied themselves. A crowd of twelve charged at them, racing across the flat ground towards them. Fatma didn't want to be there; she was not cut out for this sort of brutality. She would rather hear about the courageous exploits of the likes of the Rüzgar than experience even a single day of what it might be like to be a Rüzgar. Her legs were shaking. The mob picked up speed, now only yards away.

They crashed into the four of them. Fumu's staff took one man out straight away; whirling it again, he knocked another back and into the fellow behind him. Fatma ducked as her attacker swung his arm at her in an uncoordinated frenzy, and then was about to thrust the blade of her scimitar into the

253

fellow's back, but hesitated and stopped at the last moment. The man turned, smashing her in the face with his elbow, sending her to the ground; her weapon went flying. A young man in the crowd waiting to get inside, immediately picked up her blade and drove it into the back of her attacker. Blood soaked through the clothes of her assailant and he collapsed.

'Are you all right?' the young man asked Fatma.

She nodded, scrambling back on all fours towards the crowd waiting to get through the gates, as the young man took her place defending the group from the attackers.

Other Janissaries now emerged from behind iron gates and fences, joining Fumu and the other three and using their superior skill to overpower the possessed, beating them down.

'Get inside,' one of the Janissaries ordered.

Fatma raised her hood over her head and with Fumu and her men, entered through the gate. The Janissaries came in, securing the entrance and placing a line of soldiers on guard, long spears at the ready to push back any attackers.

She entered the ancient building, through the entrance beside the Ablution Fountain, before making her way into the main prayer hall, which was already full of people. Some were praying, others sitting, others standing dazed by the turn of events. Yet they were people from all communities and all faiths. She noticed the Mufti of the Hagia Sophia in dialogue with the Christian Patriarch and the Jewish Chief Rabbi. Beside them was Sheikh Dawood, head of the Bektashi Sufi order. Members of his order were dotted around the complex, comforting others and praying with them, no matter what faith they followed.

Hundreds of nationalities and tribes were crammed into the building, and she reminded herself the Grand Fair of Istanbul was nearing its final days. It had brought many new faces, nations and tribes to their city. She could see a significant group of Moroccans and Africans as well as Persians, Indians and Europeans. Casting her gaze around it became apparent to Fatma that people from all backgrounds were within the Hagia Sophia.

All sought refuge in the same God. Maybe it was time she joined them. A tentative smile formed on her face, the first for a long time.

38

SMITE

VENTURING INTO DARK TUNNELS BELOW ground was part of the job for the young Rüzgar. The companions, armed only with their weapons and a brass urn, found themselves retracing the route Anver had taken. Circling back to the same location proved arduous, as they encountered many frenzied Istanbul residents on their way. Awa knew these people were transformed through no fault of their own, and she ensured they knocked them out rather than maimed them seriously. Most were ordinary folk, not trained to fight, and as a result they were easily overcome. A few were street thugs, and they presented a more significant challenge.

Following the path originally taken by Anver, they entered into a vast open area with columns and water, and most significantly the head of Medusa, of which Anver had spoken. It was an eerie sight, for they were in an old part of the city of Constantinople, with the new part having been built above it. Considering where they had entered and their direction and length of travel, they weren't too far from the Hagia Sophia. In fact, she thought that if she were to venture above ground now, she would be able to see it.

Anver stopped her before they turned the corner into the chamber.

'What's the plan?' Anver asked.

'We find Zawaba'a and stop whatever he's doing,' Awa replied.

Anver raised his head a touch. 'With what, a brass urn?' he said, motioning to the contents of his sack.

'We have to stall him and pray Gurkan and Will don't kill one another but actually make it back.'

The catacombs were empty. Cressets hung on walls, illuminating pockets of the enormous cavern, but much of it remained in darkness and shadow. A silence settled, as still as the water in the ancient pools.

'Are you certain they were here?' Awa asked, turning towards Anver.

The Venetian nodded vigorously. 'Right there,' he pointed to the spot where he had seen the malevolent Jinn.

'Come on, let's get closer,' Awa urged them as they went forwards, keeping close to the ground. They moved between the columns, shadows within shadows.

'Children come to play,' echoed a deep voice, the sound bouncing around the walls of the cavern.

She had heard the voice before. The first time she had, her blood froze, as it did now. 'Zawaba'a,' she whispered. She had to remind herself that Anver had not witnessed the Jinn in Jerusalem.

'Where is he?' Anver said, lowering the sack from his back.

'Everywhere!' Zawaba'a boomed.

The Rüzgar stood up, for there seemed little point in crouching when the Jinn already knew they were there.

'I don't see him,' said Anver, searching for something within his sack.

'There.' Awa pointed to a red glow disappearing down a tunnel off the main chamber. She started in its direction but came to a halt when a group of street thugs entered, wearing the black robes that Anver had said were worn by Zawaba'a's acolytes.

'Ah, six of them,' Anver said. 'Three each, maybe?'

The absent Konyan's confident tone before a fight seemed to have rubbed off on the shy Venetian. She liked that.

The thugs charged, expecting the young companions to scatter. Instead Awa leapt forward. The first thug swiped at her and she rolled under his punch, her dagger slicing his chest, drawing blood. She dropped to one knee and took out the next brute by wheeling around and burying her blade in his stomach. The man's shocked expression said everything about his over-confidence. Awa jumped back and dispatched the third foe by slicing the back of his knees, sending the man to the ground, allowing her to easily overcome him with a pommel to his temple.

She turned to stare incredulously at Anver. The Venetian was beaming.

'It works,' he cried.

Three thugs were writhing on the ground, fingers scratching at their eyes, their faces looking as if they had been burnt.

'What did you do to them?' Awa asked.

'Pepper and spice, apparently, make great immobilisers,' Anver said.

'You made a pepper ... what?' said Awa.

'I don't know what to call it, but it's like a ball of pepper and spices, which when mixed with the right amount of vinegar and gunpowder, creates this response.'

'May God protect us from such weapons,' Awa said, placing a hand on her companion's shoulder.

The thugs were down, but the Jinn was not.

They set off after him, with Anver close behind her. The tunnel curved into darkness, before it straightened, running for some fifty yards. They sprinted down it, skidding to a halt at the end, where it twisted right and veered steadily upwards.

She could now hear shouting coming from the streets above; they were not too far below ground, it would seem.

'Come, young ones, enter,' Zawaba'a's voice echoed around the stone chamber.

'Wait,' Anver said. 'It might be a trap.'

'We're already trapped,' Awa said, moving out into the open where the Jinn could see them. Anver pulled up beside her. With a sharp intake of breath, she whispered, 'God is Great.'

'As am I,' responded the Jinn.

He was seated high up on a dais, upon the most glorious throne Awa had ever seen – gold, silver, encrusted with rubies, emeralds, sapphires and crystals of all shapes and sizes. It sparkled in the light of the cressets. The pulsating body of the Jinn was shrouded in mist, but his upper frame was clear to see. He had a powerful chest and shoulder muscles. His face remained in shadow, but for the eyes, which burnt a fiery red. He appeared to be wearing a cloak of sorts, but one that rippled along with his body as he moved.

'It is as I remember it,' Zawaba'a drew their attention to the magnificent throne. 'My Master, Solomon the Wise, summoned one of my brethren to bring it from the palace of the Queen of Sheba. And here it is, well, a replica, but it reminds me of glorious yesteryears.'

Screaming from above drew Awa's attention. When Awa looked up at the ceiling she noticed an exposed drain cover. The inlet to capture the water remained as it was, however, the ceiling above it was ripped open in one place, and she could hear the footsteps of residents running overhead.

'The city is in turmoil, and it took me so little effort. Human minds are so frail, weak, it was almost ... boring,' Zawaba'a mused. 'If this is the greatest city on earth today, then humankind has indeed fallen low.'

Awa noticed Anver removing the brass urn from his sack whilst keeping it out of sight of the Jinn. She still had no idea how they were going to trap the monster inside.

'What do you want?' Awa asked.

'What everyone wants. Peace.'

'This does not look like peace,' Awa said gesturing up to street level.

'Oh, child, how naïve. To make peace, you must first make war. Destroy those who oppose you, then lead those who remain. It is always the way.'

'Why are you doing this?' Anver interjected.

The Jinn faced the Venetian, his eyes narrowing. 'When you have been imprisoned for thousands of years, and the world you knew was always just out of reach, well, when you are freed, why not have some fun?' The Jinn bellowed with laughter.

'People dying is not fun,' Anver retorted.

'People ... are a plague upon this earth, always taking, never giving. All other creatures will be joyous when humans are sent back into the wild where they belong. The Jinn reigned supreme upon the land and sea before the filth of humanity was introduced to this world. Today, we live in mountains, deep within forests, areas of the world where humans have not reached. Yet, why should we be driven away from the places we have called home for millennia before mankind appeared? Why? This is just the spark; my people will come around to this way of thinking when they see the greatest human city on earth crumble to nothing, its people driven mad with fear, tearing one another apart.'

The sound of fighting overhead increased. It seemed as though an entire mob of crazed Istanbul residents was heading in one direction, towards whatever was directly above the chamber.

***

One of the Janissary officers pushed open a door to the Hagia Sophia and marched inside the building.

'We need reinforcements. Anyone who has a weapon and can wield it, report at once to the front courtyard. If you don't have a weapon but can fight, come anyway.' The soldier marched off to another part of the complex and made the same proclamation.

Fumu, who had been resting on the ground with his two men-at-arms, stood up with them. He looked at Fatma. 'We will be back, Your Highness. For your safety, remain inside.'

Before tonight she would have disagreed, believing she knew how to handle a weapon and possessed the stomach for a fight, but now she knew this not to be the case. Practising with Ulyana was one thing, but a real skirmish, where the blood of another was shed – this, she realised, was not for her.

The Princess had decided to remain concealed beneath her hood, not announcing herself to the others around her. They would fret, and it was not a time for such fuss when all of their lives were at stake. Watching her bodyguards depart along with a contingent of thirty other volunteers, she felt her eyes fill with tears. *How stupid*, she thought to herself. The minutes passed, and her breaths became deeper and calmer. Those who were outside were now truly on their own. Fatma placed herself by the window of the entrance close to the Ablution Hall, as it provided her with a clear view of the courtyard outside.

261

The Janissaries beside the outer perimeter were using lances to push back the possessed residents, who were now a colossal swarm. Their heads bobbed up and down in the evening light, growls and screams emanating from them. The grand mosque, which at one time had been a church, seemed to be a magnet for those infected by the demonic possession. Should the iron railings around the perimeter be breached, then the horde would be at the outside doors within seconds.

She could see Fumu towering over most of the others. The group that had left the precinct was striding towards the perimeter. Behind Fatma, the collective sound of congregational prayer caught her attention. The Mufti was leading a prayer for the Muslims, the Christian Patriarch for his flock, the Rabbi for the Jews and other priests for their own faiths and denominations. Who was saying what was drowned out by the collective voices of the thousands crammed into the Hagia Sophia. They each prayed to God in their own way, without encumbering anyone who chose a different tongue and distinct sequence of words to ask for the same thing. Mercy.

Crash. She was jolted from her contemplative thoughts by the sound of metal crashing onto marble. She looked out of the window to see that part of the fencing around the perimeter had collapsed. The demoniacally possessed now surged through the gap. The defenders who had taken up arms pushed forward, trying to stem the tide, to shore up the space, but bodies were crawling through. A skinny man scuttled through on all fours, seemingly undetected, before one of the Janissaries spotted him and ran a weapon through him.

'No!' said Fatma. She could not bear to see people killed this way. They were brought to this mindless violence by the Jinn that terrorised the city.

More bodies crawled through. Fumu lifted one man clear off the ground and slammed him onto the marble, before crushing his chest under the sole of his boot. The defenders were holding back the horde, for now, but how long could they sustain it? She wanted to do something, *anything*, but what?

The volume of prayers intensified behind her, and she turned to see the Mufti holding up his hands and the congregation following. He prayed for God's mercy to be shown to the city and for its rulers, he prayed for those in the mosque, all of them, he prayed for those afflicted and for those causing the affliction. There was no wrath in his words, only compassion.

Fatma discovered she was repeating his words aloud as tears rolled freely down her cheeks. Before she knew it, she took a step, then some more towards the congregation, the sound of the collective prayers echoing in her heart. She could feel her spirit soar.

Then she was part of the congregation, hands raised to the sky as she uttered the words of the prayer, everything fading into a symphony of harmonic sound. The collective voices grew louder, stronger, bouncing off the ancient stone and marble. She had never felt such elation in her heart, as though she was connecting with a force outside herself, a light from afar, piercing her very essence.

Whatever was going to happen next did not matter: she was for the first time in her life beyond caring about herself. She was only concerned for the souls of all those within the Hagia Sophia.

39

IMMUNE

THE BODY OF THE JINN rippled red like the waves of the ocean with the sun setting upon it. It was a beguiling image, making Awa dizzy if she stared at it too long. Instead, she decided to concentrate on the menacing eyes, which sent a shiver up her spine. Zawaba'a was a foul demon, yet here they were. There was no denying what they had to do, but now at the eleventh hour, what options remained? They had to stall for time, ensure the Jinn did not unleash anything else upon the city, whilst waiting for Gurkan to return with the religious artefacts. Given the fractured relationship the Konyan had with the Englishman, he was the last person she had wanted to send, but they had had no choice. She needed Anver to show her how to get to this place, and it was her responsibility to banish the monster she had released. Then if she saw out the night, she would find her father.

'I tire of this talk. I am a creature of action, I initiate and others do. Begone from here, children, before I smite thee,' Zawaba'a said.

'You know we cannot do that,' Awa said.

'And what would you, child of the Sahara, have me do?'

Awa asked Anver for the brass urn. 'There is only one thing for you to do.' She held up the brass urn.

'Hah!' Zawaba'a's scornful voice boomed around the underground cavern, sending a ripple along the rock and causing some loose stones to crumble.

'I don't think he's too pleased at the idea,' Anver whispered.

'Solomon the Wise imprisoned you, and we were foolish enough to release you. Now we must undo what should never have been done in the first place,' Awa continued, progressing towards the Jinn.

Zawaba'a for his part continued to laugh, his bloodcurdling hilarity echoing around them. This was fine, Awa thought: it was eating into the minutes, giving Gurkan more time to retrieve the religious relics. She could use this approach, keep him distracted long enough, and they might just give themselves a chance.

'I have not laughed so much for ... well an aeon. Thank you, child,' the Jinn snorted.

'I am serious,' Awa pressed on.

'I think you're getting a bit too close,' came Anver's concerned voice behind her.

'Begone, child of the desert, before I decide to take you and your friend seriously,' Zawaba'a said, brushing his hand to one side, as though he were swatting away a fly.

'We are very serious,' Awa moved closer.

'Awa!' Anver implored her to come back.

The Jinn's eyes narrowed and he seemed to take in the brass urn for the first time, examining it in detail. He partially turned his head to one side, surveying the chamber, before staring back at Awa. His hands came to rest on the armrests of the throne and he lifted himself up to his full height, which was at least half as tall again as the tallest man she had ever seen. Muscles rippling in the red mist, the Jinn's laugh turned to a cruel smile as he moved towards her.

Awa responded by taking another step towards his throne. She was only a few feet from the dais, when the Jinn glided down to her level. He towered over her, and she had to tilt her neck back to gaze at his face.

'You,' Awa pointed up at him, 'are going in here,' she motioned to the brass urn.

'Enough!' boomed Zawaba'a, backhanding her.

The blow was powerful enough to cripple a person. It should have sent her flying across the cavern, breaking her jaw and possibly her neck, but it didn't register as anything more than a mere touch upon her face.

'What!' Zawaba'a screeched, examining his hand. Furious, he drove an open palm straight at her face. It should have smashed her nose back into her brain. It did nothing.

'It cannot be,' hissed Zawaba'a.

Now Awa advanced and Zawaba'a backed away, before leaping forward and slamming both his palms against the side of her head, covering her ears entirely and pressing with all his might. Her skull should have collapsed. Nothing happened.

'What magic is this?' Zawaba'a cursed, moving around her, examining Awa with a devilish eye.

'*The one who unlocks a Jinn after it has been cast into captivity, remains sheltered from its dominance,*' Awa responded. 'These were the words of Solomon the Wise, for he knew a day might come when the likes of you would be released, and the one who let you out will be the one who must imprison you once more. So, here I am,' Awa smiled.

'Curse the Master,' Zawaba'a glided away, circling, remaining out of her reach.

The hours spent in the Library of Hidden Sciences had not been wasted. When she had come across these words, she hadn't been sure if they were true, but now she believed in them. Prophet Solomon had cast the spell in such a way that it could be undone, but only by the one who released the Jinn.

Overhead, through the opening in the ground, the commotion of the maddened mob was now interlaced with a rhythmic vibratory hum. Awa thought she was imagining it, but it sounded like thousands of voices intoning, chanting, singing and praying.

Awa turned towards Zawaba'a, stalking him as the Jinn moved to the side, keeping out of her way. She followed the demon with the brass urn in her outstretched hand.

'You will go in here,' she commanded.

The Jinn's eyes became round. Uncertain what was happening, he made to dash back down the tunnel he had led them through to come to this chamber, but he froze in mid-step.

'No!' Zawaba'a growled. 'It cannot be. Humanity is divided. Petty and pathetic.'

Awa whirled to see Will holding aloft the Staff of Moses, Gurkan wearing the Turban of Joseph and the Chinaman who had been with Will holding a number of other items.

'Here, I think you should have this, Anver,' Will said, throwing the Staff of Moses towards Anver, who plucked it from the air. As he placed the tip of the Staff to the ground, it triggered a spark.

'Woah! It's never done that before,' said the Venetian.

'Take this, Awa.' Will came up to stand beside her, bestowing the Seal of Muhammad on her. Will stepped away, next giving the Sword of David to Gurkan and the Pot of Abraham to Li. He himself held aloft the Scrolls of John the Baptist. The Armour of David had been left in the satchel on purpose, as they all knew the adverse effect it had on the wearer. The Rüzgar and Li formed a circle around the Jinn, who grew agitated.

The prayers from above ground grew louder, a vibratory force gripped the cavern around them, drowning out the baying of the frenzied, infected citizens.

'Draw it, Anver,' Awa instructed.

The Venetian, clutching the Staff of Moses, removed a bag of chalk from his sack and purposefully traced a path so that he passed beyond the reach of the Jinn. First one triangle took shape, then the next.

'No!' screeched Zawaba'a, when he realised they had drawn a hexagram around him.

The five companions moved to five corners of the hexagram and Will left the Armour of David beside the sixth point. As they took their positions at the tips of the hexagram, the prophetic objects they held started to sparkle, as though a firecracker had gone off.

'Pray!' Awa implored the others. 'In your own language, whatever you know, pray, and loudly.'

The five companions held the religious relics as they joined their voices to the chorus from above ground, and the prophetic objects glowed white.

'No!' Zawaba'a rasped.

The Jinn, now trapped within the hexagram, lashed out. The cavern around them reverberated as he unleashed his anger. Rocks fell from the ceiling. He pulled objects towards them, trying to knock the companions off their feet.

Awa advanced, the brass urn in one hand and the Seal of Muhammad in the other, as a thin light beam connected all of the prophetic objects together, forming a web of light around them. The Jinn, seeing her advancing, tried to fly away, but the beam of light prevented him from passing through it, inflicting agony as he fell back.

'Close in on him,' Awa instructed as they advanced, restricting the space around the demon. The scream of the Jinn and the howling of the wind he had unleashed made each movement arduous, the air buffeting their faces, pushing them away. Awa gritted her teeth, advancing, as did the others around her.

She was almost within touching distance of the Jinn when she placed the brass urn on the ground. It spun as the wind whipped around them.

The Jinn locked stares with her. 'I will send a plague upon this city before the third Eid, one the like of which has never been seen before,' the demon said through gritted teeth.

'Closer,' she instructed the others, shouting to make her voice heard above the howling of the air. Zawaba'a leapt from one side to the other, even trying to fly up to get away, but the field of white light around him would not let him escape. As the companions blocked all passage out, the Jinn's frenetic movements became restricted to a single spot, the place where the brass urn was placed. The companions could have reached out and touched him, so close were they, the rippling red light of the muscular form of the Jinn glowing upon their faces.

'Aghh!' the Jinn screamed as the objects the companions held drew closer.

'Keep going!' Awa shouted.

The demon before them began to shrink, collapsing in on himself, the ring around him shutting down any room to escape. At first the reduction in size was barely noticeable, then he dwindled to the same size as Will, then Awa.

'Hold firm,' Awa urged the others as gusts of wind threatened to blow them off their feet.

Then, in the blink of an eye, the enormous Jinn was sucked into the brass urn, his ruby form vanishing like water disappearing down a drain. The whistling gusts of air around them ceased, the cyclone dissipated, the howls and screams of the mob above ground halted, and all that they could hear was the melodic sound of prayer, emanating from ground level, in a variety of languages and dialects, though to Awa they all sounded the same. It was the most soothing sound she had ever heard.

40

RECALIBRATION

WHATEVER WAS DEVELOPING OUTSIDE THE Hagia Sophia, Fatma was now lost within the cacophony of majestic voices, soaring in a multitude of languages and dialects, calling for God's mercy. The resplendent vocal expressions echoed around the ancient building, rising in a crescendo of supplication and devotion.

The gathering of humanity in the assembly within called for salvation from the evil lurking outside, asking for light to obliterate darkness. All her doubts melted as Fatma felt herself became part of the flow, a current on a vast river, all gushing in one direction back to the primordial source. Her anxieties and trivial insecurities were gone, as tranquillity filled her breast, soothing her inner being, providing clarity about life and its purpose. The Princess felt tears streaming down her face.

The grizzled old woman beside Fatma reached out and took her hand, clasping it in her own. The human touch of warm, soft skin against her own made her feel that her burden was being shared by another. She regarded the old lady, a street merchant by her attire, and the Princess smiled with a genuine sensation of compassion for this other human being whom she did not know and who would take a lifetime to earn what Fatma spent on a single dress. The Princess bent down and hugged the woman. The aged one whispered into her ear, 'All will be well, child.'

The Princess nodded, wiping away tears with the back of her hand. She remained in the warm embrace of the old woman for some time, and when she eventually let go, the Princess straightened up to see the reinforced doors beside the Ablution Fountain swing open. There was a collective gasp from the faithful congregation before an elated Janissary cried out, 'It's finished, ended, whatever it was.'

'What do you mean?' asked one of the men, who appeared to be a palace official.

'The people outside, they aren't possessed anymore, they're ... normal,' said the soldier.

Cries of joy echoed around the Hagia Sophia as some rushed out to witness the miracle, while others remained inside, and thanked their Lord one more time, before they, too, began to flood through the narrow exits.

The Princess remained where she was, hugging the old woman again before she shuffled away into the crowd. For the first time ever, Fatma felt a quiet serenity in prayer and it settled her soul. It was, she thought to herself, as though she had been asleep, coasting through life, and only when death was imminent had she finally woken up, arisen from a slumber of trivial sycophantic living. She didn't want to go back to the way she had behaved before. She remained where she was, sobbing, lifting her hands up to pray before placing her palms over her face and gently rubbing her cheeks.

The evening air filled the building as it emptied of the faithful. Fumu appeared at the entrance, and she gave him a wave to say she was fine, despite the weeping. The bodyguard nodded, remaining close to the entrance from where he could see her.

'Young lady, are you all right?' said a man's voice.

Fatma turned to see Sheikh Dawood, a man venerated amongst his peers and regarded as a magnificent light amongst the faithful.

'I am better,' replied Fatma.

'Alhumdoulillah, praise be to God,' replied Sheikh Dawood. As he started to move past her, she stopped him.

'Sheikh Dawood,' Fatma said.

'Yes.'

'What just happened?'

The wise old Sheikh smiled. 'Everything is written in the Tablets of Light,' he pointed skywards. 'And what was destined, happened.'

This left Fatma confused. 'So even if we didn't pray together, this madness would have just ended?'

'I didn't say that,' he smiled. 'Everything is penned in the Tablets of Light. Yet when humankind, men and women, upon the face of this earth, make a sincere collective effort, then God recalibrates the Tablets of Light, and a new future awaits. This is easy for Him.'

Fatma felt hopeful once more. 'So the future is written, but ... it can also be rewritten?'

'Yes,' said Sheikh Dawood with a smile. 'So few seem to understand this simple notion, and they become morose and despondent with their lot in this world. God knows your future, but God can change your future, too.'

Fatma nodded.

The Sheikh made to move on once more. 'What can I do?' Fatma asked.

'One of our sages wrote that when a forgetful man rises in the morning, he reflects on what he is going to do, whereas an intelligent man considers what God is going to do with him.'

'I ... don't understand?' Fatma asked.

'Forgetful people's gaze is only on themselves, their attributes, their actions, their egos. Therefore they become trapped. Intelligent people are not overwhelmed by the most difficult task, because their gaze is fixed on God and the journey back to Him. Therefore they live a life of serving others, showing love to all and beautifying the noble traits of character.'

'Thank you,' whispered Fatma as the old man wandered out into the night.

The Princess slowly gazed around the Hagia Sophia one more time, taking in the magnificent location, remembering the evening when assassins came to murder her father and the organist played his haunting melodies. Then she thanked her Creator one more time and made the commitment to be like the intelligent man: to serve others no matter what life threw at her.

***

The streets crawled with people. It was as though the entire city had just emerged from the darkness hanging over it. In many ways it had, thought Will, as he strode through the thousands of people, searching for one face and one face alone. The person Will sought had to be here somewhere, amongst the throngs of individuals, but where? He had said he would remain in the city for a few more days. After leaving the underground cavern the Englishman realised how close they had been to the Hagia Sophia. In fact, it appeared as though the chorus of voices they had heard at prayer had been coming from this very building. So formidable and resonant had it been, that the vibratory sound even penetrated underground as they fought the Jinn. He didn't understand what had happened, but the collective masses offering prayers with humility had somehow ignited a bond between the prophetic objects, and it was this connection that enabled them to surround Zawaba'a and ultimately banish the Jinn into the brass urn.

Will sped up when he saw a large Moroccan delegation by the steps leading into the Hagia Sophia. He knew them by their distinctive attire. Scanning the faces, he couldn't see the one person he was looking for. Then he spotted a man whose back was turned to him, but whose clothing was West African in style. Skipping into a run, Will advanced.

'Mahmoud al-Jameel,' he called out.

The scholar from Timbuktu turned to see the young Englishman striding towards him, but was immediately distracted by the companion just behind Will.

'Awa!' yelled Mahmoud, rushing towards his daughter.

'Father!' Awa leapt into his arms. The two held one another tight, tears rolling down their cheeks.

Will knew exactly what it was like to lose a parent: he had been without his mother for most of his life. A broad smile was on his face as he left father and daughter together, both weeping and laughing in unison.

Strolling away from them, he came back to join Gurkan, Anver and Li. His relationship with the Rüzgar was strained and he owed them an explanation. Will would have died only an hour ago if the man from Cathay had not come to his aid.

Li had turned on his English master, burying his dagger in Sir Reginald's throat. Will vaguely remembered how the Oriental had squeezed his windpipe and how suddenly Li had made his choice and acted, throwing the blade that killed Will's would-be murderer. Will could only imagine the nobleman's look of disbelief at what transpired. He still hadn't had the time to ask Li why the Chinaman had finally turned on his masters, but judging by the derogatory way they had treated him, Will could hazard a decent guess.

'They have my mother,' Will said.

'Mrs Ryde!' Gurkan said.

'It's why I've had to serve the Earl since I returned to England. I had no choice. Commander Berk was in league with the Earl, and it's the only reason he released me from prison and promised to spare your lives.'

'I didn't know,' Gurkan said, placing a hand on the Englishman's shoulder. 'I thought ...'

'It's all right, I would have thought the same,' said Will, holding out his hand. Gurkan gripped it and they embraced. Will knew things would never be quite the same with the Konyan as during the heady days of their first adventures, as a lot had happened since then to cast suspicion and doubt in each of their hearts, but it was good to have cleared the air before he left the city for good.

'Where is that snake Berk?' Gurkan asked.

'In all this commotion,' Will looked around, 'he's probably hidden himself away.'

'And the Earl of Rothminster?' enquired Gurkan.

'Who knows? A man like that is more slippery than an eel,' Will replied.

'I knew you were all right, Will,' said another voice, coming up from behind. Anver, his young Venetian friend, slapped him on the back.

'Really?' asked Gurkan. 'How?'

'He saved my life when he didn't need to, back in Venice. A person like that doesn't become someone else. Deep down he is still the same,' Anver said.

'Thank you,' Will said, embracing the Venetian.

'How does the load on your back feel?' Will asked. He had seen Awa give the brass urn to Anver for safekeeping after they had trapped Zawaba'a inside it.

'Honestly, my sack has never felt so heavy before,' Anver quipped. 'I hope Awa knows what to do with ... you know what ... as I can't be carrying it around forever.'

The three of them, along with Li, remained for some time in companionable silence, each lost in his own thoughts about what had transpired a short time ago. Will felt guilty at having left his friends to deal with this fiend, which he had been partly responsible for releasing and which was the cause of the death of his dear Master Huja, the eccentric jester who sometimes played the role of a scholar. He missed that man and his cryptic comments.

The Englishman's thoughts turned once more to the last remaining member of the Rüzgar, and he gazed at Awa and her father, who were both laughing, embracing. They had so much to catch up on, the lost years apart. Will knew the feeling. Where would they start? Perhaps the Battle of Tondibi would be a good place, thought Will. He wished them well.

His mind returned to the most pressing matter at hand. He had to get out of the city now, when there was still pandemonium, slip away in the night. He motioned to Li.

'Shall we?' he asked the Chinaman.

Li nodded.

'What? You can't be leaving, not now,' said Gurkan.

'I need to get back to England as fast as possible. The Earl of Rothminster is still at large, and if he returns before I do, my mother's life will be in danger. I have to leave this instant.'

He knew it was the only way and any long goodbyes would only place his mother in further danger. He recalled the time when he had delayed returning to see her in England, first going to Chancery Lane, only to find that the giant Stukeley had abducted her. He was not going to make the same mistake again.

'The Chinaman knows how to handle himself,' Gurkan said rubbing the crown of his head. 'You working with him now?'

'Seems like we've both broken free of the shackles of the same master, so it would make sense to look out for one another.'

'He's pretty good with those hands,' Gurkan, made a slicing and chopping motion, imitating Li's fighting style.

'Tell me about it,' Will replied.

'Then may God put wind in your sails, Will Ryde, and if it is in our destiny, we will meet again,' Gurkan said, holding out his arm. When Will took it, he pulled the Englishman into a warm embrace.

When he let go of him, Anver clutched Will even more tightly. Will could see the tears welling up in the corners of his eyes. He let go of Will, and the Englishman asked, 'Where will you go, Anver?'

The Venetian turned to Gurkan. 'For now if Gurkan will have me back, I'll go with him to his village in Konya. I have a workspace there and can help the farmers irrigate their crops with some new watering techniques I'm working on.'

'Always welcome, my brother,' Gurkan said, placing an arm affectionately around the Venetian's shoulder.

There was only one other person Will needed to say goodbye to, but when he turned, Awa was sitting hand-in-hand with her father, wearing a faraway look. He moved in her direction, then hesitated.

'Let her know,' Will said to Gurkan and Anver, 'that I will always cherish my friendship with her, and she will always have a place in my heart.'

The remaining Rüzgar looked at one another and nodded. Will turned one last time to his Konyan and Venetian friends, smiled and left the precinct outside the Hagia Sophia, where the entire city seemed to have come out to celebrate.

41

INTERMENT

Days in her father's company passed like hours. There was so much to catch up on. Awa told him everything – well almost everything – that had transpired. She left out the parts she felt would cause him distress, such as her capture by Odo and Ja, and the blood she was forced to spill in the arena. Instead, she spoke about a time when she felt most alone, leaving out the details of her imprisonment in the metal box, when she dreamt of him in a vision, instilling hope in her heart and a desire to live. In truth she hadn't known whether he had survived the Moroccan invasion of Songhai lands, but every day, in every prayer, five times a day, she had asked God that whatever was the best for her father might happen.

For his part, Mahmoud informed her he was treated with immense respect as one who had been one of the foremost scholars at the renowned university in Timbuktu. The Moroccan ruler, Ahmad al-Mansur, was inviting scholars from all parts of the Muslim world and providing them with patronage. It was, Awa learnt, a way to demonstrate his power to other rulers, showing his commitment to the advice of the Prophet Muhammad, to seek knowledge, even if it meant travelling to distant lands such as China. Her father was in an academic role worthy of his standing in the city of Marrakesh, where he was given a monthly income and a comfortable house with helpers. In contrast to what had befallen her, Mahmoud was honoured and his mind guided to the further pursuit of knowledge.

Observing him now, her heart warmed at the sight of her dear father once more. Mahmoud stood opposite her. Between them lay a deep grave.

To her father's right was the miniaturist Lütfi Abdullah, who was now restored to himself, his possession lifting the moment they had captured Zawaba'a. The miniaturist peered over the edge; the two gravediggers were almost done, it seemed. This particular grave was being dug very deep, for it was going to contain a demon none should ever unearth.

To one side of Awa were the remaining Rüzgar, Gurkan and Anver, and to her right was the former Grand Vizier Sardar Ferhad Pasha who oversaw the proceedings. The presence of Sheikh Dawood had a calming effect on Awa. The gentle old man observed matters from his position at the head of the grave.

'They are ready,' announced Sardar.

The two gravediggers clambered back up the narrow ladder that had taken them a full twelve feet down into the ground. The former Grand Vizier turned to Awa.

She took a deep breath, looking to her father for support. He smiled encouragingly and she turned to Anver who picked up his sack, took out the small brass urn containing the imprisoned Zawaba'a and handed it to Awa.

The Venetian sighed, as though a heavy burden had just been lifted from his shoulders, and immediately Awa felt the dense weight of the tiny object that was only a touch larger than her hand. She slipped it into her satchel, then strapped on the Armour of King David, before placing her foot on the first rung of the ladder and slowly making her way down. As she did, she uttered every protection prayer she could remember. It terrified her, this task, but Sheikh Dawood insisted that she was the only one who could do it, for as Awa had read herself she was immune from being harmed by the Jinn. *The one who unlocks a Jinn after it has been cast into captivity, remains sheltered from its dominance.* Even though Zawaba'a was trapped within the brass urn, no one was willing to take any chances.

As she descended, the soft earth of the walls of the grave started to wriggle; she noticed worms and spiders appear in the soil. Recalling what had happened under the Tower of David in Jerusalem, Awa realised the presence of Zawaba'a even within the brass urn was drawing out these insects and arachnids. She hastened down, arriving at the hardened steel coffin that was built specifically for this grave. It was the length of a normal man's coffin, though it was not going to house a person. The wriggling worms of the earth dripped like rain along the walls, making their way down with her. She considered the fate of Commander Konjic and Master Huja, the mentors she had lost, and Will, the English friend she had loved like a brother, but who had left without saying goodbye to her. At the time it had grieved her, but she forgave him, for there was little point holding a grudge in one's heart: it was only detrimental to the one housing the pain.

She reached the steel coffin and slipped off the Armour of David, placing it neatly in the rectangular steel box. She then removed the brass urn from her satchel, and felt it throbbing in her palms. There was heat emanating from the inside, as though a fire glowed within it. Something akin to it did, but it was not a benign flame, far from it, as they had all learnt. Handling the brass urn with care, she slid it inside the Armour of David and folded the Armour around it. Stepping to one side, so she was to one side of the steel coffin, she was joined by the two gravediggers, who appeared to be in considerable distress as they came to perch beside the coffin, noticing the showering of beetles and other hidden worms crawling out from the soil and making their way towards the coffin.

'Shut it quickly,' the scraggy gravedigger said.

The two of them slammed the lid of the coffin shut and set about hammering in steel nails, so that the coffin remained sealed.

'Let's get out of here,' said the other gravedigger as he ushered Awa back up the ladder. When she turned around, she saw that the men had placed steel panels over the top of the steel coffin before climbing out of the pit.

'Fill it up,' ordered Sardar.

The two gravediggers set to work, shovelling the earth into the grave as fast as they could. It was only as the soil started to fill the enormous grave that Awa was able to breathe normally once more. Her heart slowed and she looked up to see her father, whose face showed concern for her condition. The workmen continued for a further half-hour, till they were sweating and panting like dogs. Gurkan and Anver, taking pity on the fellows, helped them with the final half. Her companions also looked exhausted by the effort.

When it was done, Sheikh Dawood standing at the head of the grave said, 'Say: I seek refuge with the Sustainer of the rising dawn; From the evil of aught that He has created; And from the evil of the darkness wherever it descends; And from the evil of all human beings bent on occult endeavours; And from the evil of the envious when he envies.' Awa recognised the words from the Holy Book, which were used as a prayer of protection. They all stood silently, only the distant chirping of birds audible. The ceremony was complete and Sheikh Dawood withdrew.

Awa noted Sardar placing a heavy bag of coins in the hands of each of the gravediggers. He then whispered something to them, at which their eyes bulged in fright. No doubt, he had threatened their lives and those of their families should they ever reveal the details of what took place here or its location. The men gulped before hurrying off to one side, waiting for the visitors to depart.

The Songhai woman who had travelled so far turned to gaze at the vast open field around her. It was empty in every direction but for a thick woodland with a forest of fine oaks, sycamores and cedar trees behind her. The bustling city of Istanbul was to her east, a distant dot on the horizon. She could not imagine anyone would ever venture so far out to disturb so deep a grave in such an isolated spot. In fact, there was not even a name for the place they were presently in, so removed was it from any human habitation. It had taken them half a day to reach this spot after they left the borders of the city. The former Grand Vizier had been very particular in choosing this venue, and had consulted with Sheikh Dawood, who had come out here a few days earlier. The religious scholar told them he had wanted to seek the permission of the soil before they buried such a malevolent being in it.

'It's finally done,' said Gurkan.

'Praise be to God,' said Awa.

Having paid the gravediggers for their silence, the former Grand Vizier was now deep in conversation with her father and Sheikh Dawood.

'When do you leave for Marrakesh?' Anver asked.

'Tomorrow,' Awa replied. It was not a difficult choice. Her father was a scholar-in-residence at one of the most prestigious teaching colleges in Marrakesh, he had a home, and more than anything she wanted to pursue her childhood passion of becoming a scholar, as many women in her community had done. If she didn't have to lift another sword in her life, then it would be a happy life she had lived.

'I hear there is a new *Mellah* in Marrakesh for the Jews of the city. Perhaps I will visit it one day,' proclaimed Anver.

'And you will always have a home to stay in,' Awa replied, before turning to Gurkan. 'And what of you?'

'Back to the village to farm, and then who knows? I still have some adventures I feel I need to go on before I find a good Turkish wife and settle down.'

'You do that,' Awa said.

There was a time, albeit a very brief moment, when she and Gurkan had shared a moment of something that might have grown into more than friendship, yet it had passed just as fast as it had appeared, and now destiny was going to separate the friends once more.

'And you and your future wife,' she smiled playfully at Gurkan, 'will always be welcome at our home in Marrakesh.'

'As will you to our home,' Gurkan replied.

'What of Will, then?' Anver asked.

It still hurt when she thought about him going without saying goodbye, yet it was less painful now than on the first day, and she knew soon enough it would not inhibit her feelings of friendship towards him.

'Will has a way of turning up at the most unexpected of times and in the strangest of places. If he and that Oriental stick together, then I wouldn't be surprised if he were to end up in the lands of the Tartars beyond the Great Wall of China.'

'To Will, then, wherever you are, we send our glad tidings and peace,' proclaimed Awa.

'Amin,' said Gurkan.

'Amen,' added Anver.

Awa didn't know if she would see Gurkan and Anver again. As for Will, as Gurkan had commented, he had a knack of turning up when you least expected it. She could imagine that one day in the future he might arrive unannounced in

Marrakesh. in Marrakesh with a new venture in full swing. Would she join him in that endeavour, if such a thing came to pass? No, definitely not. Her days of swashbuckling exploits were over. All she wanted to do now was begin writing about her travels since leaving her homeland and train to become a scholar, like her father.

But for now the young Songhai woman stared up at the horizon, took a long deep breath, and for the first time since the Battle of Tondibi, felt at peace.

42

EPILOGUE

TWO YEARS LATER – 17 JANUARY 1595

Her father was dead. Fatma knew he had been a divisive figure; some considered him as having lacked the steel of earlier Sultans, such as Selim and Suleiman. Yet whatever they said of him, he was still her father, Sultan Murad III. Now he was no more. She had received word of his demise moments earlier and now waited outside his official chambers. Inside was her brother Mehmet, the Crown Prince and heir apparent, and her husband, the Grand Vizier Kanijeli Siyavuş Pasha. Together with select officials these were the only people at the bedside of the deceased Sultan, the only ones to record his last testimony, the only ones who would write the history of his parting, as they perceived it.

The wide oak doors swung open, and her brother emerged. He had never been known for his humility, and even now at the moment of their father's death, there was a certain haughtiness to his manner. His head was held high, as he was to be the new Sultan, ruler of the Ottoman Empire, the most powerful man in the world.

Yet only two years ago, Mehmet had been driven mad when the plague of the demon Zawaba'a struck the city. Many perished during those terrible times. Mehmet lived because their father insisted he be restrained within his chambers, where he could do no harm to others, or to himself. When the demon was vanquished by the Rüzgar, Mehmet regained his mental faculties, and though it must have affected him in some way, he behaved as though he were recovering from a fever. Never once did he discuss it with anyone. But Fatma recalled him saying foul things, particularly about his brothers, when he was possessed, and she did not know whether these were odious thoughts he had always harboured or were the result of being possessed.

Fatma's husband emerged from the chamber behind the new Sultan. During the two years of their marriage, her relationship with her husband had been one of mutual toleration. As there was no love in the marriage, so there was little potential for marital bliss.

'Summon my brothers now,' instructed the new Sultan Mehmet.

'Which ones?' asked the Grand Vizier, Fatma's husband.

'All nineteen of them,' ordered Mehmet.

Fatma's husband seemed to hesitate, shifting his sight from the new Sultan to her. Fatma took this as her opportunity.

'Why would my brother and Sultan wish to see all his beloved siblings at this late hour?' Fatma enquired, trying to make her tone soothing.

Mehmet turned on her. 'Do you question your Sultan?' he barked.

'No, my brother. I simply wanted to point out that the youngest are only a few years old, and they will be asleep by the sides of their mothers,' Fatma replied.

The new Sultan advanced towards her. 'I know where they will be and I know what I must do,' Mehmet replied, his voice like steel.

Fatma's heart quickened. He would not do it, surely not. Unfortunately she remembered all too well the words he had uttered through the chamber door when he was possessed. In a voice like thunder he had said, *I will kill my brothers, all of them.* And kept repeating it till she fled in terror.

'Please, brother of mine, do not take this path.'

Mehmet did not even glance at her. Instead, he turned to the Grand Vizier and spoke directly to him. 'Your wife must learn when to speak and when to hold her tongue, for both your sakes and the sake of your son. Or would you prefer your son to join my brothers?'

'No,' the word barely left her throat.

Fatma felt her blood turn cold when her brother mentioned her own son. She wanted to say more, but instead lowered her gaze and refrained from speaking.

'Kanijeli, have my brothers sent to the hunting lodge and make sure there is plenty of bowstring available. I will await them there,' Mehmet ordered, before marching away, striding down the corridor where other advisers waited for him, eager to ask the new Sultan for his opinions on matters of state.

A tear slid down Fatma's cheek as she prayed for her brothers. Murder was in the air, and it would be on a scale never before witnessed in the wretched halls of the Topkapi Palace.

***

The equipment he rigged up was only his latest attempt; he'd lost count of how many times he had tried to make this particular object work. Yet in his heart of hearts, Anver knew that what he was working on was going to be ground-breaking. How to provide unlimited energy to enable the farmers to reap their harvests was the problem he had been working on for two years, since the end of their adventures as the Rüzgar. He remained in the Konyan village, assisting the locals by automating many

287

of their tasks, in return for being given accommodation and anything else he needed to sustain himself.

Anver recognised it was a temporary arrangement and he couldn't stay there forever. But until he cracked this particular problem, he was adamant he was going to remain, till his welcome was exhausted. Maybe tonight he would solve it, but then he had been hoping that for the past two hundred days, since he had been actively working on this particular conundrum.

He studied his sketch pad, remembering his conversation with the late Commander Konjic, who had asked him about his drawing. At the time, Anver disclosed he wanted to build a device that captured the energy of the sun within it and then expelled this energy when it was applied to a task, such as when farmers needed to push water up a gradient to irrigate the land or when they needed to lift a heavy load. Anver dreamt about a mechanical device that could force water to run against its current as well as a pulley that would enable a single farmer to lift the load it would take ten men to cope with normally. The Venetian even made small metal figurines illustrating how these would operate. Yet what was missing was the raw energy to make it happen.

Still, he had witnessed what was possible. Two years ago, below the city of Istanbul, deep in the caverns, he had watched Zawaba'a the demon pour his power into the obsidian rocks, so that these objects activated later on when lit. It had led the Venetian to conclude that it was possible to store energy within a rock or stone.

'Right, one more time,' Anver encouraged himself.

He looked at the piping connecting various tubes together as well as the stove he had built over the hearth. He removed the obsidian stone he had kept from the night of demonic terror in Istanbul and placed it carefully within the metal holster he had built for it. He had already done this hundreds of times, but perhaps tonight was going to be different, as he had radically modified the set-up of his equipment.

'Please, this time, show me what's inside of you. I know it's there,' Anver said.

He lit the flame below the holster and moved away. As before, on the dozens of occasions he tried to do this experiment, nothing happened. The minutes went by, and he was left scratching his head once more. What was it that wasn't quite in the right place this time? As he moved towards the gear to check how it was aligned, a spark of red light caught his attention.

Anver froze, his eyes on the obsidian stone. It glowed! In fact, he could see the red hue coming off it. As the strength of the light increased, so the piping which was connected to the holster rattled and the ball bearing he had placed within it shot off, racing along the pipe and flying out the other end, crossing ten feet in the air and smashing into the pillow he had placed there.

'Woah!' Anver said.

He turned to look in awe at the obsidian stone, the red light illuminating the Venetian's surprised features.

'It works!'

***

The court of the Isa Khan, a Muslim Rajput chieftain leading the Baro Bhuiyans, the twelve landlords of Bengal, was one of the most lavish and opulent places the Englishman had ever visited, and Will Ryde had been to a few. Jewels sparkled, silks shone, drapes adorned the outer wall of the palace. The air hummed with the sound of the exotic animals the Chief maintained, including a Bengal tiger, which looked like a beast Will didn't fancy getting too close to. All manner of retainers had lined up, from the Vizier standing a foot down from the throne, through various ministers, academics and artisans. The last fellow in the line looked to be some sort of entertainer by his flamboyant attire. The fellow reminded Will of his dear friend Master Huja, but he doubted this man was as perceptive.

The previous delegation who had come to petition the Isa Khan, leader of Bengal, were from a central Asian tribe Will had not heard of. They completed their request and were moved on.

'Will Ryde and Li Zong of the Muscovy Trading Company of England,' the crier announced to the court, before signalling to Will and his companion Li to draw closer to the throne.

After their departure from Istanbul, Will had returned to England and whisked his mother away from harm by moving her to a place in the countryside north of London, before taking up employment with one of the new joint stock trading companies looking for young men to travel East. Li stuck with him, for his own reasons, but Will suspected it was partly because he treated the Chinaman as an equal. In fact, in Will's estimation, from the little he knew about the Chinese, Li came from a highly advanced civilisation, and it was the English who were the ones who could learn from them.

Yet the world was turning, and though England was still a plucky nation, punching well above its weight, Will had the sense that the joint-stock companies were going to take them places. With many stakeholders invested in their success, including most of the parliamentarians, there was little chance of these commercial vehicles running out of money or losing steam.

The Vizier turned to Chief Isa Khan, who nodded. The ruler rested on a padded throne, placed under a canopy. He was dressed in a shiny Sherwani coat, his turban glimmered with a diamond in the centre of it, and the ruler's fingers were adorned with rings of ruby and emerald.

'You may address His Excellency,' the Vizier proclaimed.

Will cleared his throat. He had been practising what to say for some weeks now, and had seen others use a similar opening line when addressing a new ruler.

'Oh eminent Chief Isa Khan, ruler of Bengal, supporter of the needy, sovereign to his people. I bring greetings from Her Majesty Queen Elizabeth of England, a nation far to the west of the Ottoman Empire. I also bring glad tidings on behalf of the Muscovy Trading Company. We have journeyed to your blessed land because we wish to establish a licence to trade in your kingdom. In return we would seek to buy from the merchants of Bengal, and with this humble transaction, begin a journey that takes our two peoples towards a blissful trade alliance, mutually beneficial for all parties and sanctified in the sight of God.'

Will stopped, hoping he had remembered to say everything he was planning to. He heard Li grunt beside him, indicating he had spoken well. It pleased Will that his companion agreed with his speech, but would the Chief agree with the tone of his request?

The Chief was a solemn man in appearance, and he leant forward a touch on his throne and announced, 'I welcome the establishment of trade with the officers of the Muscovy Trading Company, and you will be granted a licence to trade in Bengal, but you will need to make one modification to your request.'

Will was elated that his application was accepted, though he had already been told in advance by the Vizier it would be. This part was more ceremonial, for the courtiers and merchants to witness. However, Will had almost missed the bit about making a change, till it struck him and he replied. 'Yes, of course, Chief Isa Khan, state your wish and we will comply.'

'The name of your establishment, the Muscovy Trading Company, is not a befitting one for Bengal. We are not in the land of the Russ nor the Slavonic people. We are in Bengal and you must change the name of your company if you wish to trade here.'

This wasn't a demand Will was expecting, but now that it had been made, his brain worked fast to respond to something that appeared to him a bureaucratic quibble, but a necessary one according to the region's ruler. He had already heard some Venetians were looking to establish an outfit by the name of the Bengal Trading Company and the Chief knew it, too. He had to come up with another name, and agree it now, or he would end up waiting months before being granted another audience with the Chief.

'With your permission, your Excellency, we will call it ... the East India Trading Company,' Will said.

The Chief tilted his head to one side, before smiling. 'It has a nice ring to it.'

Will noticed the Vizier give him the nod of approval and a gesture to move on as the next delegation behind Will, from Portugal, was waiting its turn.

Will thanked the Chief and his court once more, before moving off to the side with Li.

'I have good feeling about the name, Li. The East India Trading Company. You never know, might even make some money along the way.'

***

The moon shone a radiant white, high in the evening sky, above the city of Marrakesh. The cold air of winter bit into the city's residents, who wore warm shawls and thick coats as they scurried about the narrow lanes. Up in the living room of a first-floor building, overlooking the courtyard to the Ben Youssef Madrasa, Awa Maryam al-Jameel completed the final flourishes of her *risala*, her chronicle of her travels with a fine young group of Janissaries and those who commanded them. It had taken almost two years from when she first declared her intention to write about her exploits, covering the period from lining up at the Battle of Tondibi to the day they buried the brass urn containing the demon Zawaba'a.

'Dear, are you almost done?' said the voice she had grown to love these past months. Her husband and fellow young scholar Jibril was the most beautiful man she had ever set eyes on. He was described by all who met him as handsome, but it was his inner beauty, the refinement of his character, which illuminated everything he did. She loved him dearly for it.

'Almost,' Awa replied, smiling as she turned to face him from her desk, which looked out of the window and across the courtyard. They were both studying at the Ben Youssef Madrasa and had been given a slightly larger room than other students after they announced they were to marry. It was kind of the college to do so, but she always suspected it was the presence of her father, who had become one of the most sought-after scholars in the city and the respect the educational establishment had for him, which had really enabled this to happen.

Whether she would ever see the dashing Gurkan, the inventive Anver or the good-natured Englishman Will, she did not know. But she had documented their stories and their characters in her own words, and these were now penned for her descendants to read and perhaps learn from.

The journey had been a difficult one, with dark times and darker people, yet always she retained hope, for this was the one thing she was certain of. God was most just and compassionate and, whether in this world or the next, matters would balance out. She just had to try to leave the rest to fate. The night they captured Zawaba'a had confirmed this. They had had very little with which to combat the Jinn, yet in the end because they had made the effort, they prevailed. Had they refrained from even trying, then, well who knows what the future might have held for her, her father and all the people in the city of Istanbul.

The virtuous Mehmet Konjic had told her as he died, 'My ending is your beginning.' Now taking one last look at her *risala*, as she flicked back to the title page, she realised what he had meant. After much deliberation, she had decided to begin it with the name of the Englishman, for had it not been for the kindness he had shown to her in Alexandria, when he was not obliged to intervene, she had no doubt she would have been dead by now. She decided therefore to call her *risala*, *The Chronicles of Will Ryde and Awa Maryam alJameel*. She hoped one day Will would also have the opportunity to read it.

She would always remember her friends, and the way she would do it was to serve others, helping those who needed it, even the ones she did not know. With that, Awa rose, went over and embraced her husband. The moon was bright tonight, and wherever her friends were, she prayed its tranquil light also shone down on them.

AUTHOR'S NOTE

ONE OF THE MOST IMPORTANT questions everyone addresses at some point in their existence upon this earth is – what is my purpose in life? Is it to cultivate the planet for the betterment of its inhabitants, taking from it only what is needed and retaining the mindset of a steward who is part of a chain linking back to the people who came before as well as those who will come after? If it is, then this is a healthy worldview and one I am sure our fictional characters, Awa and Will, living in the sixteenth century would recognise.

The idea of people plundering the earth's resources would not have been a familiar one when our protagonists were gallivanting around the Ottoman Empire and neighbouring lands. Then, the world seemed simpler, people had greater clarity and human beings were content with their place in the world and ultimately their purpose in it. This, of course, is a decidedly subjective comment from within the distracting prism of the twenty-first century and uses a contemporary lens to peer back into the past. No doubt those in the sixteenth century also stared back through history and perhaps reflected in a similar manner.

The irony is that each generation senses that something has been lost, though over time it becomes increasingly difficult to articulate what has vanished and become absent from our existence, dissipated from the collective memory of the living. For our characters, their stories commenced with a sense of loss – physical and emotional, yet I do hope their individual narrative arcs ended with a clearer sense of purpose. Awa's chronicles began at the Battle of Tondibi when her world was shattered, but we conclude with her working towards becoming a scholar and imparter of knowledge. Will we joined as a galley slave, and we leave him as a merchant adventurer in the lands of the Mughal Empire in India. Others have found their own path. Yet our characters are not real people and so they are eternal, fixed in time and space with their own distinctive endpoint.

However, the world in which they have been cast was real and so it is for this reason I must point out some aspects of the setting that I bent or warped to suit the interests of the novel. These are as follows.

Leeds Castle in Maidstone, Kent, in England gets another rendering in this third novel, after we first encountered it in *A Tudor Turk*. Once more it is home to the twisted Earl of Rothminster and his cunning plans for power. There is no evidence that I have come across to suggest that it was ever a hotbed of rebellion against Elizabeth I nor that it was owned by the Earl.

The great Trade Fair of Istanbul in September 1593 is entirely fictional. It does sound rather modern for the time but was a useful plot point to bring much of the world to one of the great capitals and then unleash upon them the might of Zawaba'a the Jinn. There are obvious parallels between the cosmopolitan setting of the Ottoman Empire and people being possessed or infected and the plight of so many in 2020–1 as the plague-of-our-times ravages nations and cities across the earth.

The notion of possession by demonic creatures is for some a reality and for others mere fantasy. Wherever you stand on this spectrum, the use of Zawaba'a to create mayhem in Istanbul is fictional, and there is no record of the Crown Prince Mehmet becoming possessed by a demonic force – though it is telling that a great plague was visited upon the city a few years after the events of this novel, during his reign, and you can make of that what you will. Elsewhere, I have portrayed the English Consulate in Istanbul as being more established than it arguably was at the time.

The mix and interplay of cultures, ideas and religions during the 1590s made it a rich period about which to write and in which to set an adventure novel. I thank you for staying the course, and I am sure, like me, you will be pleased to see that our main protagonists, Awa and Will, made it safely through to the end of the trilogy.

Rehan Khan
www.rehankhan.com
twitter.com/rehankhanauthor

ACKNOWLEDGEMENTS

A NUMBER OF READERS ASKED me not to end the final novel in the trilogy on a cliffhanger. I did not, but I think I left a few open threads from which a fresh patchwork of a narrative can be spun in the future. For now, I must acknowledge a number of people who have assisted me in numerous ways during the designing and writing of *A Demon's Touch*.

I have been very fortunate to have once more an excellent first reader and reviewer in Lorna Fergusson whose steer on the sixteenth century is always welcome, as I am forever inserting modern language into a not-so-modern period. Charles Phillips, my editor, has brought his magical touch to the manuscript and helped amplify the human story. As before, Rosemarie Hudson, my publisher, is helping writers such as myself punch above our weight and make an impact in a market that is biased towards the same-old, same-old stories. Thanks, again, to James Nunn for the cover of this and all the books in the series, and to all the others at HopeRoad who have contributed to bringing this story to readers.

A special thanks to Isobel Abulhoul and Ahlam Bolooki at the Emirates Literature Foundation and Festival as well as Flora Rees, Annabelle Corton, Tamreez Inam and others for presenting me with many opportunities to reach a wide array of readers and writers.

A few friends deserve a special mention as follows: Layla El-Wafi for her impassioned support of the material and advocacy of it to others; Peter and Hafsa Sanders for opening doors to pathways, which before then were invisible; Mohammed Paracha for encouraging me to get the next novel out; Ashar and Farah Khan as well as Harris and Sadia Irfan, for their continued support; Muhammed and Noor Mekki, as well as Neil and Hadeel King, for their love of the written word and inspiring stories of their own.

In addition there are a couple of family members whom I would like to thank. My niece Ayesha Khan and nephews Abdullah and Ali Khan, for their unquenchable interest in the *Chronicles*. My mother, always a promoter of all things Ottoman. My two children, Yusuf and Imaan, for their curiosity and enthusiasm, and finally my wife Faiza, fellow traveller and soulmate on the path.

BOOK GROUP / TEACHERS' GUIDE

Character analysis

1. Will and Awa are both from very different backgrounds. Will is a poor destitute young man from England, a country few have heard of in the 1590s. Awa is an intelligent, sophisticated young woman from an affluent and vibrant Songhai Empire in West Africa.

   a. What draws them together? What do they have in common?

   b. Who are some of the other characters they interact with? What life lessons do they draw from them?

2. The Rüzgar unit, a fictional outfit of the Janissaries, are composed of a diverse set of individuals. What are the strengths of diversity and what can be some of its limitations?

3. How diverse is your own friends and family circle? How do you think your life could be further enriched by meeting people who are very different to you?

4. What does it mean to accept diverse viewpoints, whilst maintaining your own identity and not losing a sense of who you are?

5. Will and Awa have their lives turned upside down when they are both enslaved at different points. Will is kidnapped as a young boy, and Awa falls into slavery after the Battle of Tondibi.

   a. How do you think they both felt after becoming enslaved and shorn from their families?

b. What would have been some of the challenges they encountered after becoming slaves? How did they respond?

c. War has a direct impact on the lives of many people. During these moments, there is often an absence of government and authority, during which time vulnerable individuals can be enslaved. Think about a recent conflict and research the impact on individuals who became refugees or stateless – sources such as the UNHCR will be a useful place to take a look.

6. The slave traders Odo and Ja were using Awa in a gladiatorial ring so they could make money from her martial skills. Today, modern-day slavery and human trafficking still exist. What are some of the ways slave traders use slaves today? What can we do to highlight this issue and try to stop modern-day slavery?

7. Commander Konjic is in many ways like a father figure for both Will and Awa. How would you describe his character? Why didn't he strap on the Armour of David when fighting with Azi Dahäg? What does that say about him?

8. Huja is a jester of sorts, and in *A King's Armour*, we learn he is also a scholar. How would you characterise Huja's appearance? What is his true character; who is he really inside? Select one of his cryptic sayings and discuss what you think the meaning might be.

9. Anver is a brilliant maker/craftsman and inventor of things, yet he sees the world very differently from those around him. What makes him different? How does he use this difference as a strength?

10. Fatma is an Ottoman Princess, who we get to know as the *Chronicles* progress. How would you describe her character arc from when we meet her to the climactic ending of the story in the Hagia Sophia?

Historical discussion

1. Why was Tudor England, a Christian nation, trying to form alliances with Muslim empires, such as the Ottoman Turks and the Moroccans in the sixteenth century? What role did the Spanish Armada of 1588 have in shaping this decision?

2. Throughout the *Chronicles*, trade and commerce is often referred to. Peter Frankopan, author of *The Silk Roads* (2015), suggests that the history of the world is a history of trade. For European nations, trading internationally in the sixteenth century with Africa and the East was a new experience, whereas Africans had been trading with the Middle East and the Far East for hundreds of years before Europeans arrived on the west coast of Africa. What were the types of products and commodities that the English began trading, and what else did they trade over the course of the century? Useful historical analysis can be found in books such as *This Orient Isle* (2016) by Jerry Brotton; *A Fistful of Shells* (2019) by Toby Green; *The Year 1000* (2021) by Valerie Hansen; *God's Shadow* (2021) by Alan Mikhail.

3. After English trade with the Ottoman Empire and the Moroccans became established in the 1590s, what were some of the exotic foods, spices and beverages that began to appear in England?

4. After the forging of political and commercial alliances between England the Eastern powers such as the Ottomans and Moroccans in 1590s, characters from the East began appearing in the works of William Shakespeare. Name some of the characters who we encounter in Shakespeare's plays who originate from the East and take a note of when those particular plays were written in the context of the time period of the *Chronicles*.

5. The Ottoman Empire, at the height of its powers, ruled over a vast portion of the Mediterranean and the Middle

East. Name some of the countries today which were part of the Ottoman Empire. What evidence can we still find of Ottoman rule in some of these countries. For example, the bridge of Mostar in Bosnia. Useful historical analysis can be found in books such as *The Fall of the Ottomans* (2016) by Eugene Rogan.

6. There were a number of joint-stock trading companies established in England during the sixteenth and seventeenth centuries, such as the East India Trading Company. Over the course of the next two hundred years, these became extremely profitable for their shareholders. What were the main things they traded? What was the human impact of their trade, particularly on Africa, India and the Far East?

Creative writing

1. Pick up the story thread at the end of the Epilogue and write what you think happens next to one or more of the characters. You may want to compose the very next moment in their life, or you might want to think ahead and imagine what they might be doing after one day, one week, one month or longer.

2. Choose up to three locations in the *Chronicles* and write a brief history of the place you have selected. Locations can be a city which the characters were in or even a building or monument. When composing your thoughts, consider the cultural connections between the location you have chosen and the wider world. For example, if you selected London Bridge, then explain its history and significance, or if you selected the Basilica of St Mark's in Venice, or the Umayyad Mosque in Damascus or the Hagia Sophia in Istanbul, once more explain why it was built and what has been the cultural significance of the location.

3. Select one of the overseas locations in the *Chronicles*, and write a scene from the sixteenth century in which either Will or Awa or both are present along with some members of the Rüzgar. Try and imagine a scene, before or between one in the *Chronicles*, and think about what they might be doing. For example, in *A King's Armour*, the unit travels from Aleppo to Damascus, but what happened in between? Or in *A Demon's Touch*, Will leaves Istanbul and arrives in Maidstone, but what adventures happened to him on the way?

4. Imagine the following scene. It's 1605, and we are in the city of Marrakesh, where Awa is teaching a class full of students. The door to her classroom is pushed open, and three figures enter – they are Will, Gurkan and Anver. What happens next?

If you would like Rehan Khan to speak at your school, university, book club or library, then please feel free to get in touch with him through his website www.rehankhan.com.

Rehan Khan has always been intrigued by the way in which legends and chronicles from all over the world have the power to cross time and space to delight and unite us centuries later – whoever and wherever we may be. A lover of history, he has read extensively about past civilisations and the struggle between the forces of good and evil. His exciting descriptions of swordplay, weaponry and close combat in battle are the result of these studies, although in real life Rehan himself prefers to wield a tennis; racket rather than a scimitar.

When not writing, Rehan is a telecoms and technology consultant and teaches management. Born and educated in London, he now lives in Dubai with his family.

You can follow Rehan on:

f www.facebook.com/rehankhanauthor
◯ Twitter: @rehankhanauthor
◯ Instagram: @rehankhanauthor
www.rehankhan.com